Bitter Edge

BITTER EDGE

RACHEL
LYNCH

CANELO

First published in the United Kingdom in 2019 by Canelo

This edition published in the United Kingdom in 2019 by

Canelo Digital Publishing Limited
57 Shepherds Lane
Beaconsfield, Bucks HP9 2DU
United Kingdom

Print ISBN 978 1 78863 551 6
Ebook ISBN 978 1 78863 267 6

Look for more great books at www.canelo.co

Printed and bound in Great Britain by Clays Ltd, Elcograf S.p.A.

Chapter 1

Across the expanse of Derwent Water, from the top of Walla Crag, Jenna Fraser could easily make out the muffin-like dome of Crag Hill on the left and the pyramid summit of Grisedale Pike to the right. A steamer chugged gracefully in to Hawes End Pier and dropped off a bunch of hardy visitors to the west of the lake. No doubt they'd be off up Cat Bells to take a photograph to post on Facebook, and then back down in time for a pint near some open fire. The steamer barely seemed to move; only the V-shaped wake behind it gave away its progress. Winter was quiet in the Lakes, and daylight hours short.

Jenna had hiked Cat Bells when she was three years old.

Fell racing was in her blood. Her father was a Bob Graham Round champion. Jenna herself held the junior record for the fastest time to Dale Head, taking in six peaks, a record she'd set two years ago, when she was only fourteen. She'd brought her medals with her today. They clinked around in her bag when she moved, but now they were silent. Only the sound of her panting breath could be heard above the stillness of the fells. At this time of year, close to Christmas, few people ventured along the pretty walks so rammed in the summer, and she knew she'd be alone.

She wasn't dressed for a winter run, but it didn't matter. She'd slipped on what was at hand, and that happened to be a pair of comfortable shorts, which she'd slept in, and a vest top. She'd pulled on trainers and pushed a cap onto her head, then filled her bag with the medals. The other stuff she'd packed last night. When she'd left the house, she'd attracted a few stares of disbelief, given the cold, but as she ran out of town towards the Keswick Launch, steam puffing out of her mouth in clouds, she'd seen fewer people, and found the solitude she sought. She'd run past perhaps three cars, but her concentration had been focused on pounding the pavement rather than looking about.

The tears hadn't started until she'd left the Launch behind and entered Great Wood, curving away towards Derwent Water's east shore. Now they came in waves and stung her eyes. She didn't bother rubbing them away as she began the steep climb to the top, and they mingled with the snot running from her nose. The only thing that concerned her was ridding herself of the noise in her head that wouldn't go away. Her legs should have ached, her heart should have been beating out of her chest, and she should be freezing, hypothermic even, but the obsession with the noise had kept her driving forward until she'd come across this place of isolation, above the lake. Alone and exhausted, she'd stopped and looked out from Walla Crag, beyond the lake and towards the west, where, underneath the cloud, the sea came close to freezing. She'd dropped her bag and scratched her forearms where her veins burned.

Jenna was no longer a champion, but she had one more run to perform. A broken leg last year had seen her racing career crash to a painful end; landing badly on a loose rock had resulted in a broken tibia and fibula and a fractured talus bone. It had taken three weeks for the swelling to subside enough for an operation to be performed, then she'd needed two metal plates to bolt her bones together. Healing was quick, but rehabilitation was excruciating. She'd been prescribed OxyContin for the pain.

Until it ran out.

The steamer drifted out of sight and the sky rapidly changed colour, as it was wont to do at this time of year, when flat light made everything more dramatic. Clouds circled the peaks in the distance, and the fells in front her were like two piles of sand pushed together at the beach. The valley in between looked uneven and changeable.

She closed her eyes, but the drumming in her head kept pummelling her temples. Words formed, but then dissolved into sharp, offensive blasts of sound: drums exploding, percussion clattering and pipes screaming. All had begun as comments made by text or WhatsApp. There were a hundred different ways that one could invite language into one's life without ever having to speak to someone face to face, and they were all electronic. Now the phrases took on life, as different tones and pitches came together to torment her. She sat down and hugged her legs to her chest, holding her temples and banging her fists against them. But still the noise wouldn't stop. It was as if there were thousands of unusually heavy tennis balls bashing the inside of her head, thrashing against the sides of her brain, each one making a larger dent than before, until surely they would break out of her skull, sending battered brains, steaming clots of blood, and splinters of bone flying into the air and down onto the wet ground.

Her chest screamed as the physical exertion of the run caught up with her: her heart rate was that of an unfit twenty-year-old smoker compared to the fell-running legend of two years ago. She rummaged in her bag and brought out a small package containing powder, a steel dessert spoon and a lighter. She opened the packet and sprinkled the powder on the spoon, wetting it with a little water from a bottle then heating it from underneath. The greyish powder turned brown and she mixed it with the top of a syringe. Happy with the consistency, she drew the liquid up into the syringe, then rummaged about in her bag once more. She found an elastic strap, which she wrapped around her arm, biting the other end tight.

She looked at her arm. Many of the veins were hard and unfit for purpose, having been destroyed by months of abuse. She tapped one in her wrist and it came alive. Her hand shook slightly as she tried to focus, and she grasped the loaded syringe from which she'd gain peace and quiet. The tiny needle made contact and went in easily: she was an expert. The brown fluid entered her bloodstream and she loosened the strap, dropping the syringe on the ground.

Instantly, her eyes flickered and her head nodded forward. She began crawling away from the edge, turning her back on the stunning view for the last time, leaving the bag containing her medals on the ground. She managed to stand and, with the aid of the surrounding bushes, staggered fifteen paces towards the trees. Then she turned around so that she was facing the edge of the crag, and the lake, once more.

She felt an overwhelming calm. At last the racket inside her skull had quietened. With her eyes tight shut, she pulled back her right arm, flexed her right knee and stretched her left foot forward into the running stance that had put her name in the history books. She bounced three times, albeit unsteadily, stunned into action by the absurdity, though there was something about it that made sense to her. Then she bent her head and slowed her breathing to that of her race pace. The birds, the breeze and the distant rumble of thunder disappeared into a void. She held her breath.

A force seemingly outside of her body pummelled a mighty release of adrenalin into her and she shot forward, arms pumping, and legs powering. After less than fifteen paces, she ran out of rock and entered the sky. For a lingering moment, her legs still projected her forwards and her arms still thrust back and forth, but then she began to fall, not making a sound, to the treeline below.

She hit the first branch with a loud crack, snapping her neck and breaking both arms and one leg. When at last she came to rest, lodged in between several branches, her body resembled a twisted bauble suspended in the large pine like a Christmas decoration. Blood splatter charted her path, and gouts of the stuff pulsed out of her, until her heart eventually stopped beating. The red-brown liquid travelled downwards across knots and twigs, coating them like melted chocolate and finally dripping onto the hard ground below in perfect round splashes.

Drip. Drip.

Jenna Fraser was finally at peace.

Chapter 2

He watches.

Swarms of hysterical children of all ages run wild, flailing their arms and screaming. They bump into others who are also here for only one thing. The thrill of losing control, the primitive addiction to fantasy, the terror and danger and the risk from extremity: all drive the crowds on.

The air is hot with anticipation and the heady aroma of burnt sugar. Night falls quickly, and soon the heaving mass of bodies is shrouded in darkness, but this only heightens the delight. Shrieks compete with ear-splitting thumps of bass, accompanied by the latest beats, pounding out of huge black speakers set up along the high street. The waft of greasy burger vans sits atop the hordes, and neon lights challenge spatial calculation.

The fun of the fair.

He puffs on a hand-rolled cigarette and cradles his pint of honey-coloured locally brewed beer, surveying the frivolity before him. Girls. Hundreds of them, from three to twenty-three in age, all just as beautiful to gaze upon. But he is fixated by one in particular, who has become separated from her mother. He calculates, in his vast experience, that she is around nine years of age, and, as is common now for the younger ones, she wears provocative clothing that invites attention, at the same time remaining blissfully unaware that it makes her look so enticing.

No one in the crowd knows him. His colleagues on the forty-foot trailers heaving the gigantic rides around the country only know his name. In three days, the fair will be gone, on to another town. Keswick is the next stop after this one.

He watches.

The ancient castle at the top of the hill stands proudly over the townsfolk, revelling in their yearly indulgence, as it has done for eight hundred years. Its mighty walls glow green, then orange, then neon pink, and the girl is immersed in the magic. He notices that her mother has now moved at least twenty feet away, and she still hasn't noticed that her daughter is not beside her. He sees the girl watching older, taller children being whizzed around high up above her head on the Hurricane, where they experience almost three G of force. It's one of the most popular rides; they can charge five pounds a pop. Parents haemorrhage an eye-watering amount of cash, grateful that the fair only comes once a year. But for him, it's a nightly affair.

Transience, like vagrancy, can hide a multitude of misbehaviours.

The life suits him. He's paid in cash, he sleeps in a decent trailer, he gets a steady stream of women – some more keen than others – and he exists invisibly in a twilight on the fringe of electronic identity. He has his motorbike; though technically it is borrowed, it might as well be his. The machine is his pride and joy, and he can still feel the thrust between his legs after two hours driving around, trying to still the noise in his head. All that as well as a fledgling lucrative business that is doing very well indeed. Only tonight a new contact from Manchester drove all the way to this shitty little backwater known as Dalton-in-Furness to meet him.

The mother looks around her nonchalantly. Nine-year-olds are apt to wander off; he's seen it many times before. This girl is on the cusp of independence, and her mother, her attention elsewhere, trusts her quasi-grown-up judgement. The woman lazily checks out the immediate area, but when she can't track the girl at first glance, her face shows only a flicker of concern. She says something to her friend, who stops filling her greedy face with chips, and looks around, shrugging. It will take long minutes more before they become truly anxious.

He knows that the girl has gone round the back of the Hurricane to pet a dog that is tied up there. It's Old Joe's dog, Molly May, and he heads over there now. The noise fades to a thudding hum behind the trailer, away from the lights and the crowds. The girl is talking to the mutt sweetly, and Molly May wags her tail.

'Ah, she's a good dog, she is,' he says.

The girl is startled, but she has trusting eyes. He sees a sadness behind them too, and figures there's some vulnerability there. That's good.

'She's called Molly May.'

He bends down next to the girl and strokes the dog. Their hands almost touch. The trailer next to them shudders as gangs of youngsters are thrown around in the ride's cages. The girl stands up, as if she has suddenly become aware of her isolation.

'What's your name?' he asks.

She doesn't answer. He watches as she blushes.

'I need to go now,' she says.

'Don't you want a sweetie?' He holds a little tablet in between his thumb and forefinger and smiles slyly, watching her terror. Toying with her innocence is almost as satisfying as taking it would be, but it's too busy tonight. He stands up and blocks her way back to the safety of the fair. He sees that her heart has begun to pound in her chest, which heaves up and down. He smiles at her, and his eyes wander down to where he can make out the shape of her pre-adolescent breasts.

'No thank you,' she says.

He holds the small bright blue pill up and offers it to her again.

'It'll make you want to fly,' he cackles, and the sound turns to a racking cough.

The girl freezes and stares at him with wide eyes. Close up, she might even be younger than nine.

'You look so grown up! This is what grown-up girls do.' He nods to the pill. 'I bet the boys are queuing up for you, eh? Are you a tease?'

The girl's eyes grow wider, and she closes her coat, covering her naked midriff. His brow creases as his view is denied. Her hands shake and he imagines little beads of sweat forming along the soft skin on the crease of her back.

The game is over; he needs another pill.

He steps aside and allows her room to get past him, should she wish to do so. He can tell that she's unsure at first, thinking it might be a trap, but she tiptoes forward and he doesn't move. He imagines he can hear the rapid beat of her heart threatening to jump out of her small chest. She is almost past him, and he takes a deep breath,

9

his eyes never leaving hers. Then her instinct kicks in, and she darts past and away to safety, beyond the darkness behind the trailer.

—

The girl sprints away at such a speed that she can't stop in time when she crashes into somebody. It's a boy from her class, and his mates gather round and laugh as he rubs his arm. But the girl continues to run.

Finally she spots her mother and races towards her, only now stopping to gain her breath and fling her arms around her. The mother is at first angry that her child has caused a scene, but then she notices her distress. The girl babbles about a man behind the trailer, and her mother looks at her friend in panic. A small, concerned crowd has gathered around the mother and daughter, and a burly man asks if everything is OK. The mother repeats breathlessly what her daughter has just told her, and the man's face darkens. He rolls up his sleeves and puffs out his chest and marches towards the Hurricane. But when he storms around the back of the massive structure, there is no one there, just a small, scruffy dog who is very pleased to see him.

Chapter 3

Kelly Porter heaved the freshly felled Norwegian pine into the boot of her Audi Q6. It smelled like Christmas. Johnny shoved it from behind. He'd carried the thing on his shoulder as Kelly watched out for obstacles on the way to the car park. There were others doing the same thing. Families with shrieking children, couples gazing at one another lovingly, and men on their own, ticking off a last-minute job before heading home to surprise their families.

They pushed it in, trunk first, and slid it all the way to the front window. They had to bend the top around in a semicircle to fit it in, and as they slammed the boot down, they both crossed their fingers that they hadn't chopped it off. The tree seemed secure, and Kelly got into the driving seat, with Johnny having to manoeuvre himself into the back, ducking underneath branches that were contained for the moment by mesh. The journey back to Pooley Bridge was unique, surrounded by the smell and tickle of pine.

Getting the thing into Kelly's living room was another task altogether. Her house in Pooley Bridge was a small stone cottage, overlooking the River Eamont. The wooden terrace, suspended over the river to the rear of the property, had been its selling point, and Kelly spent most of the year out there, any time of the day, in any weather, contemplating what had gone, what was, and what was to come. Sometimes she found answers and sometimes she did not.

Inside, the house was modest but spacious. Even after almost a year, she still hadn't filled all the rooms, and the small third bedroom remained a dumping ground. The spare room wasn't much tidier, but the rooms that were lived in and cherished were tidy and bright. She'd had a new bathroom fitted, getting rid of the dated avocado suite and replacing it with a modern wet room; and she'd bought a huge, luxurious corner sofa for the living room, along with a vast TV. She hardly watched the TV, but Johnny did, and he paid for the Sky Sports subscription. He watched extreme fell races and sailing mostly. He still hadn't bought the boat he'd promised himself.

Johnny kicked the door shut and they propped the tree up across the hallway. It filled the space. Kelly went to take off the mesh.

'Wait a minute.' Johnny held up his hand, panting. 'If you do that, we won't get it into the living room.'

Kelly's hat had slipped over her eyes, she was sweating under her padded walking jacket, and the woollen scarf at her neck tickled. She was quickly losing her sense of humour and wanted a glass of warm red wine. She left the tree and went to open the double doors that led to the living room, then snatched off her hat and quickly undid her jacket.

'Any time tonight,' Johnny said. It had taken them two hours to choose and transport the tree, and Kelly knew that he'd be off to do it all again tomorrow with his daughter, Josie, for his own house.

She smiled at him and deliberately took her time walking back to her end of the tree. She picked it up, and they manoeuvred it to where they'd agreed it should go, propping it up against the sofa next to the stand. It was one of the growing list of things they had in common: neither of them was precious about stuff; things were just things, and they were both more interested in the outdoors.

'Should we have a glass of wine before we get it up and decorate it?' Kelly asked.

Johnny nodded, and they left the tree and unpeeled themselves from their heavy coats. The fire was ready to be lit, and Johnny set about doing that while Kelly fetched two glasses from the kitchen to the side of the hall. The two rooms were all that comprised the entire downstairs, and it made the little house comforting and cosy. They both took off their shoes, and once the fire was lit and roaring, Johnny placed the guard in front of it and they sat on the sofa. Kelly put her feet up.

'Good job,' he said.

'Thanks for helping me. I feel as though I just want to leave it there now. No wonder Mum and Dad never bothered with a real one.' Kelly checked herself. *Dad* was such a natural and common expression that not to use it would have been weird. But she hadn't yet decided how she felt about finding out that John Porter was not in fact her biological father, and the phrase slipped out as it always had. She fiddled with her ponytail and Johnny put his hand on her knee.

'He's still your dad, like he always was,' he said. Johnny had never met John Porter, but Kelly had described him many times.

She laid her head on his shoulder and mused on how it might feel if they lived together like this. They rarely disagreed, they didn't get in each other's way, and they liked the same kind of things, whether it be what snack to eat on a hike, or which song to play on a Friday after a long, exhausting week.

The fire began to throw out its heat and the first sips of wine made her insides warm. Johnny wasn't on call for the mountain rescue tonight. There was no doubt that he could still navigate Striding Edge after a glass or two, but that wasn't the point. It was a rare night off. They'd been busy lately, with accidents on Broad Stand, on Scafell Pike, at a record. The series of steps and slabs of sheer rock linking Scafell to Mickledore on Scafell Pike is described as a scramble, but anyone who has negotiated it knows that it is anything but, and falls are usually fatal. For her part, Kelly had been dealing with the awful case of Jenna Fraser. Due to the horrific nature of the girl's injuries, they'd assumed murder – any violent death in such circumstances was suspicious – but they'd found nothing to support the theory.

'Shall we?' Johnny said. 'Come on, it'll distract you.'

She looked at the boxes of decorations. She'd dragged Johnny around countless shops, antique and otherwise, searching for baubles and hanging bits to adorn her dream tree, and now the moment was here. The task would take all night, but Johnny was committed; he couldn't back out now. It was his turn to cook, and they had enough wine to keep them going for hours. He would stay here tonight, knowing Josie was all right on her own until their trip back to the forest tomorrow for their own tree. Josie was fifteen years old and perfectly capable of looking after herself. She enjoyed a great deal of freedom for her age, but Johnny trusted her. She'd turned up earlier in the year, fed up of living with her mother. It had been a shock for Kelly, but they'd both had to get used to it. A few years ago, she might have run a mile rather than even think of becoming a stepmother figure, but Josie wasn't needy.

'Let's crack on. You can unpack all your shiny things and I'll get the curry on,' he said.

'Is that your final standard operating procedure?' She poked fun at his army jargon, but he didn't mind. Johnny had been out of the army for six years now, but he still used its peculiar terminology. His ex-wife had hated it, as she had hated anything to do with the army, but it brought about the opposite response in Kelly. Language in the police force was similarly old school, and they understood one another.

She waited and watched him, smiling. She'd softened him. He was no longer hard, the fighting man he'd described to her after his return from Afghanistan. She couldn't imagine anything other than the peaceful strength she'd grown used to, but he'd told her that for a while, he'd carried his anger round with him like a great weight. She saw the odd flash of it – when he heard that a former colleague had committed suicide due to PTSD, for instance – but Lakeland life had generally calmed him and absorbed his brutality. The demons had all but gone.

She touched his hand and he put down his glass of wine, pulling her towards him, kissing her. The fire crackled and kept them warm as he peeled layers off her. They threw their clothes onto the floor and Kelly lay down underneath him. The sofa was large enough to double as a bed, and only the sound of the cushions moving and their bodies pushing against one another punctuated the sizzle of logs and the puffs of hot air. Johnny buried his head in Kelly's neck as they both tensed, and she wrapped her legs around his back, holding onto the moment. Stepdaughters and dead teenagers were all forgotten in the time it took for their motion to quietly subside.

They were suddenly cool from the night air and aware of the fact that they had a job to do. They both looked at the tree and reluctantly got up from the sofa to search for hastily discarded garments. Kelly hopped into her jeans and took a swig of wine before crawling under the tree. Johnny took the top and began to heave it into the stand, with Kelly calling directions from underneath. At last it was straight, and they stood back to admire their work. Kelly nodded, and Johnny cut away the mesh. The tree sprang into life and spread out, sending bits of the forest everywhere. Kelly knew exactly where she wanted it, and they pushed it into place together before she went to get a jug of water to pour into the base.

'Sorted?' he asked.

'In the bag,' she replied.

He nodded and went to the kitchen to start his culinary masterpiece, leaving Kelly to unwrap the delicate pieces of glass, metal and jewels and place them gently on the sofa. Her plan was to lay them out and design the look of the whole tree, rather than fling them on randomly. She might be some time.

She flicked Sonos on via her phone and chose Jamiro-quai.

By the time Johnny came back through to ask her if she wanted naan, she'd unpacked all the precious items and was kneeling by the tree trying to wrap the lights around the back. He poked life into the fire and left her to it, filling his glass as he went.

Chapter 4

The grim task of performing the post mortem operation on Jenna Fraser was left to the senior coroner for the north-west, Ted Wallis. He was in the process of training a new recruit, who would hopefully take over from him in the coming months, but for now, this job was one that had to be carried out by someone of Ted's calibre. A fell runner had discovered the poor girl hanging in the gargantuan regal pine, and Ted shook his head at what on earth the poor fellow might have dreamt about since.

Ted had seen fall victims before. Without a trained eye, it would appear impossible to accept that the jumble of limbs and organs in front of him once had a human form. He'd performed the autopsies on two students who'd committed suicide by jumping off the top off Bowland Tower, in the middle of Lancaster University, within three years of one another. The damage inflicted on their bodies was classically consistent with vertical deceleration injuries. These differed extensively from, say, car crashes, where the deceleration forces were horizontal. In other words, when the body crashed into something ahead of it, it suffered different injuries from those that occurred if it slammed into something from above.

Jenna had vertical deceleration injuries, and Ted could tell from a preliminary once-over – though it was tricky to identify parts of the body that had ended up where they shouldn't – that she'd fallen feet first. In his mind, this meant that she'd jumped rather than being pushed. Somebody fighting for their life at the edge of a cliff wouldn't remain upright in a fall; they'd be thrashing and twisting until the final impact, and would have massive lacerations from where they'd tried to grasp for safety in the canopy. Jenna had none. He knew Kelly Porter wouldn't be happy.

The students who'd jumped off Bowland Tower had both sustained major foot, leg, hip and vertebral trauma. The bones in the feet and legs had literally shot up through the body and ripped the soft tissue apart from below. Jenna was different in that she'd landed in trees, but Ted could still tell that she'd come down feet first.

It would be a long operation because he'd have to locate every skeletal structure first and compare where it should be with where it actually was, removing countless foreign bodies thrust into her as she passed through the trees, like a chef trimming thyme to sprinkle on a slab of lamb. Only then would he be able to eviscerate, and this posed its own set of problems, because most of her major organs south of her sternum had been impaled and torn apart by branches. He guessed that the only thing he'd find intact was the girl's heart. Protected by the chest cavity and the sternum, the organ most associated with vitality had probably survived the forces of collision, though he wouldn't know for another few hours.

He'd studied the photographs from the scene very carefully before turning to the body, because he wanted to know what her path of downward descent had been: it would determine his calculations when he worked out her initial velocity as she left the cliff. This would prove critical to the final report, because standing jumps were very different to run-up jumps, and this girl had landed quite a way from the face of the cliff, indicating that she'd left the edge at considerable speed. So she was either chased, or possessed with an immense desire to die.

The case had brought him into contact with Kelly again, and it had been awkward. After numerous investigations together, their relationship had cooled, and Ted couldn't help but conclude that Kelly wasn't happy that he was seeing her mother. He'd known Wendy for forty years, and meeting her again had brought all the memories back: the painful ones as well as the wonderful ones. Years ago they'd had an illicit fling that had started at a grand party thrown by the Earl of Lowesdale. Those were the days, he reflected. He wished now that he'd had the courage to pursue her, to ask that she leave her husband for him, but propriety had won the day and they'd both stayed in pedestrian marriages.

It was only when John had died that Ted had thought about getting back in touch, but even then, it had taken him a few years to pluck up the courage. Working with Kelly had given him the push he'd needed, and he'd finally visited her. She'd been as pleased to see him again as he was her, and he'd felt like a teenager again. There was only one problem: Wendy was seriously poorly. He kicked himself daily for leaving it too late, but they were making the most of their time together, and his thoughts turned to the surprise he'd booked for her for Christmas Eve. It was only two weeks away.

He turned away from the body and looked at the photographs. Forensic officers had reconstructed the scene and drawn black pen lines on possible trajectory and impact sites, based on the damage to surrounding foliage and Jenna's final resting place. There were photos of blood pooling and spatter, and Ted formed a picture in his mind of her final few moments. To him, or anyone sane, they would have been moments of horror, but to someone bent so irrefutably on destruction, they could have been welcome.

That was what had led to his argument with Kelly only this morning.

'Assumption is the mother of all fuck-ups, Ted,' Kelly had said when they'd first discussed the death. Ted wasn't offended by her coarse language, though he'd prefer her not to use it. But she had spoken to him like a child, and not the senior coroner that he was, and he couldn't help deduce that she was tetchy. At some point he'd have to have a serious conversation with her about his relationship with her mother. He was adamant that he wasn't going to lose Wendy again, so Kelly would just have to accept it. They could still work together. They had to work together.

'I'm not assuming, Kelly, I'm using science to give you my informed opinion.'

'You haven't even seen her body yet,' she said.

'But I will this afternoon, and I will report straight back to you.'

'But your mind is already made up,' she challenged him.

He'd sighed. It was a blatant insult to accuse a pathologist of circumnavigating science to reach a conclusion. It was the very opposite of what he stood for, but it was Kelly, and so he let it go. For now.

'I'll call you when I'm done,' he'd said.

Ted didn't want the girl to have committed suicide either; no one did, least of all her family. But the facts were conclusive. By the time he'd finished sorting out the jigsaw puzzle that was Jenna Fraser's body, he had worked out her initial velocity as over five metres per second. Yes, she could have been running away from something, but if that was the case then she would have sustained massive hand and arm injuries as she clutched at branches to break her fall, and those simply weren't present.

More telling were the track marks up her arms and in her groin. The toxicology result confirmed it: the girl was a heroin addict. It was well known that a bad trip could encourage hallucinations, and although heroin was a painkiller rather than a hallucinogen, a rogue batch could lead to unexpected results. He was seeing more and more drug deaths – they all were, pathologists up and down the country – and it was a worrying trend.

Jenna's addiction made some sense when they learned from her parents that she had been prescribed opioids after a bad injury and had become hooked on cheaper street drugs after the prescriptions stopped. Ted remembered reading articles about the athletic achievements of the girl now on his slab, and her death suddenly seemed even more tragic.

Chapter 5

Kelly slammed the front door, threw her coat over the banister, and sat heavily on the couch. She stared at the Christmas tree. It was a symbol of pure joy and celebration, but in Jenna Fraser's house, it would forever become the hallmark of despair. An overwhelming sensation of defeat assaulted her, and she wiped away tears. Jenna had been sixteen years old. It wasn't often that Kelly Porter faced the awful realisation that nothing more could be done; she was used to seeing a case through to the end, whether it be a triumph or a disaster. The result of this enquiry was neither, and she felt simply flat. Deflated, dejected, and despondent.

People committed suicide all the time; it wasn't a crime, but Kelly wanted this to be a crime. A sixteen-year-old with so much to look forward to driven to despair and madness was quite incomprehensible. Kelly needed the final jigsaw puzzle piece to slot in to finish the composition. She demanded a cause, a perpetrator, a guilty party; anything to take away the damning conclusion that a child could be driven to this. She was desperate to understand, in a way she couldn't remember for a very long time. If only they'd been able to find out who'd sold Jenna the drugs, they might get a conviction. She'd even looked into indirect murder of a minor with oblique intent, but their inquiries led to one conclusion alone: Jenna had thrown herself off the cliff. In fact, she'd run off it.

Acceptance was the last thing Kelly thought she'd signed up for. Policing often required a strong stomach and time spent in the company of scum, but submission wasn't in the job description: at no point had anyone asked her if she was willing to approach death as a docile, passive spectator. She'd never sat in an interview and agreed to surrender, or shrugged her shoulders and said, 'Ah, well.'

But that was how she felt now.

A search of Jenna's bedroom had yielded various empty packets containing traces of the drug that had altered her mind to the state where jumping off a cliff edge wouldn't have seemed so bad. But that wasn't all; they'd also found Adderall, a stimulant popular among students, and in large enough quantities to conclude that the girl was a regular user. In a shoebox they'd discovered spoons, sterile syringes – presumably stolen – and elastic straps. The puzzle pieces that Kelly so desperately wanted to find were the wrong ones. Nothing about the girl's original profile had prepared them for the final conclusions.

Jenna's bank account had been emptied of prize money, her school performance had dwindled to virtually remedial, her remedial training had dropped off and her behaviour had become erratic: all signs of a drug-addled brain. The girl had so much to live for, but she had nothing to keep her alive. Her developing addiction had fried her future and ended up with her impaled on a tree. Kelly wanted to kick something. What had started out as the hunt for a bewildering cause of a tragic suicide had become a predictable demise. It made her sick to her stomach. There was no call for a lengthy investigation.

The case was closed; the true cause of the girl's obliteration was kept out of the press, at the behest of her parents, who didn't want the shame to stain their daughter's memory, but gossip fluttered around the Lakes with impunity.

Kelly got up and went to the kitchen. Johnny had left her a note: he'd gone off for a training run, but she should call him if she wanted. *If she wanted*. It didn't matter what she wanted. She wanted Jenna Fraser to still be alive, so she could talk to her and explain that no matter what it was she no longer cared about, it was worth fighting for. But she'd spoken to drug addicts before, hundreds of them, and each time she was left in no doubt that a drug-altered mind was a mere shell. She had to let it go.

She opened the fridge and took out a beer. She opened it and took it outside onto the wooden terrace overlooking the river, grabbing a blanket on her way. The night was cold and the weather forecasters said they should expect a white Christmas. She curled up on a lounger, wrapping herself in the blanket. The water was still and the sky was clear, enabling her to gaze at a canopy of bright stars.

Johnny knew the guy who'd found Jenna. Kurt Fletcher was an experienced fell runner and he'd seen some injuries in his time; in fact, at Johnny's suggestion, he was applying to join the mountain rescue. Kelly had visited the crime scene herself, and she'd studied the photographs for hours. She'd thought hard about who else in her team should see them. Kate Umshaw had three daughters around the same age as Jenna. She remembered a senior officer saying once that the police were just people, and it was true. Jenna Fraser's body was something that no one should ever have to witness. But at the same time, it was their job.

In London, Kelly had seen gunshot wounds, knife wounds, beheadings and beatings. It was the fact that she was being told that Jenna had done this to herself that she couldn't stomach. Her deep respect for Ted as a professional fought with her visceral need to seek justice. Ruling a suicide and leaving the family to throw away unopened Christmas presents wasn't justice; it was criminal. The problem was that suicide wasn't a crime. The Murder Investigation Manual, used by every detective in the country, said that all death was to be treated as criminal until proven otherwise. But she'd looked at it from every angle, and still couldn't get away from the fact that Jenna's death was self-inflicted. She knew that she'd behaved like a child towards Ted, and she also knew that they would have to have a grown-up conversation sometime soon.

She was aware of the front door opening, and craned her neck to beyond the living room, knowing it would be Johnny and smiling in relief. If anyone could understand, it was him. It wasn't only the fact that during his time in the army he had witnessed the mangling of human bodies, whether it be from execution or war; it was more that he knew what she was thinking. It was the pessimism that accompanied a waste of life that he understood.

He came out to the terrace and kissed her.

'Case closed today,' she said.

'I'm sorry.' He sat down. He looked tired and dirty.

'Where d'you go?'

'Just up Fairfield.'

'Just up Fairfield' was actually a vertical scramble of almost nine hundred feet. Johnny had his sights on the

Lakeland 100, a hundred-mile race through the fells beginning at Ullswater that took even elite runners over twenty-four hours to complete. Ninety per cent of entrants dropped out at the halfway point, gaining Lakeland 50 status instead. Kelly thought him crazy, but she knew he'd do it. She looked at his muddy legs.

'You follow the beck?' she asked.

He nodded. He moved over to her lounger and placed his hand on her hip.

'I need a shower,' he said.

They'd stopped inviting one another over to stay the night. Instead, they'd fallen into a rough pattern of seeing where the day ended up. They led similar lives, in that their rhythms were irregular, a mixture of intensity and complete quiet, and of course Johnny now had Josie to think of. Neither could have existed in jobs that brought a nine-to-five tempo to their days. Each understood the other's absence and equally appreciated the time they had together between the chaos. As a result, they'd yet to book a proper holiday, preferring instead to hike together and come home to a fire and a bottle of red, or in summer to find a hidden pool or tarn and eat a picnic.

'I've got soup and cheese in the fridge,' Kelly said.

'Perfect, I won't be long.'

She could have told him what Ted had said; it would be normal for her to go into the details of his findings. Sharing her cases with Johnny had become part of unwinding at the end of a long week. Likewise, he shared his experiences of the fells with her; the ways in which people got themselves lost or harmed on the mountainside without preparation or supplies. He knew that she'd talk to him about Jenna when she was ready. She'd already told him that the girl was considered a classic suicide profile. In other words, her mental state had been proven to be such that she'd provided her own motive. In any death, the detective looked for weapons, wounds and whys. Jenna Fraser ticked all the boxes. That was why Kelly had to let it go. Her weapon was forest and crag. Her wounds were consistent with running and jumping. And her why was crippling lack of self-esteem, compounded by learning difficulties and a lack of mental health intervention, along with isolation that had started at the age of eleven.

The girl was bullied for her success.

When Kelly had suggested that she'd been chased off the cliff by a pursuer, Ted had reminded her that she'd had time to remove her bag of medals and place it by a rock, intact. And she'd got high. The symbols of her extraordinary success in life had been left intentionally as the only thing to accompany her to her death. Kelly couldn't begin to understand the mind behind an obsessive suicide, and that was just what it was: it was carried out with such vigour that it was as if Jenna had been going for another gold.

It was true that where there was a death, there was always blame, but in this case, the perpetrator was already dead.

Chapter 6

Eden House was stifling in the summer and freezing in the winter. As soon as the clocks went back in October, the heating system usually packed up, and it took three weeks to get engineers to come and have a look. The grand old radiators, struggling under countless coats of gloss paint, caused much sucking of teeth, and every year, HQ would refuse funding to get the whole system replaced.

And so they wore coats and scarves.

This was intended to be the last full team briefing before Christmas, and they sat around a large table in the incident room, cradling mugs of coffee. The latest news was the promotion of Detective Constable Will Phillips to detective sergeant. It was, everyone agreed, thoroughly deserved. Phillips was a popular member of the team, and his eye for written detail never failed to prove critical to a case. DS Kate Umshaw, with the help of her three daughters, had made cake.

The promotion had given Will a positive push. At thirty-two, he was doing well, and pay rises were few and far between these days. It had been a toss-up between him and Kate, but HQ believed she hadn't been a DS for long enough to make the leap to DI. Kelly felt her junior's disillusionment: they were the same age. But then Kelly had no kids. It wasn't an excuse, but three girls between the ages of thirteen and sixteen was no picnic, and many times Kate had turned in looking as though she'd locked herself in a wardrobe and started a fight. She had dark circles under her eyes, and she smoked heavily. Kate wasn't a poor operator; Kelly had just been lucky. Her promotion in London had been quick, and she was handling three murder cases a week there while a DS in the Lakes might handle one in a lifetime.

Their attention turned to what they might expect over the Christmas period. They fully anticipated plenty of GBH and disturbances of the peace, but the bulk of those would fall to the uniforms. Detective work usually dropped off, except for domestics and suicides. Kelly fully expected it to be quiet.

She then announced the desperately sad conclusion of the Jenna Fraser case to the team.

'It's not the outcome we were hoping for, but the pathology report is watertight. Rob, any news on Blackman's computer?' She couldn't help but move on quickly. They'd put so many resources into investigating Jenna's death that, as was always the case with a minor, they'd exhausted themselves emotionally and mentally. Now they had to focus on other things, and it wouldn't be easy. She had to distract them.

Their most active case right now was the arrest of Keswick teacher Tony Blackman. He'd been reported by a pupil at his school for luring her to his apartment, where he'd allegedly groped her. Upon further investigation, police had found indecent images of children on his computer, alongside the addresses and ages of others. Unfortunately, the case was a constant reminder of Jenna, because she'd attended the same school: the

Derwent Academy. Kate's girls went there too. It was difficult sometimes when cases overlapped and there was personal involvement, but it happened. Cumbria was a sparsely populated county and people knew one another. The school was going through a tough time, that was for sure.

'Seventy-nine indecent images, fifteen of them of the highest category. CPS says they're interested, and I've got the green light to put the case together.'

'And we have his confirmed DNA all over the keyboard? What about the hard drive?' Kelly sounded as though she knew what she was talking about, but in fact she knew little about the workings of a computer, which was why she'd selected Rob to take the case with Will. Things were going to get technical, and they were her geeks.

'It'll take time. There are several unusual firewalls installed and some serious threats of multi-systemic contamination,' Rob said.

They looked at him. He smiled. 'Sorry, I'll let you know as soon as the computer people get back to me. Let's just say that the brain of the computer is protected and doesn't like being picked apart. It needs to be done methodically – which means slowly – or we might lose everything.'

'Great,' Kelly said. Proving ownership in an indecent image case was fundamental. 'Will, what do you make of the stored details? Potential targets or what?' She was referring to the files on the teacher's computer detailing every aspect of the lives of several children who were all in foster care.

'As a teacher, he has access to secure files at the local education authority that Joe Bloggs on the street couldn't read, so he could sell on the information, or plan to use it himself. The youngest child is only two years old.'

'Christ.' Kelly vocalised everybody's thoughts. No matter how much one studied human psychology, paedophilia just wasn't rational. 'Let's see,' she said. Will passed her the file. The others munched cake and waited.

'What's up, guv?' Will asked.

'We know this boy.'

They all stopped eating and looked at her.

'Remember the baby left outside the White Lion pub in Patterdale two years ago? The nurses at the Penrith and Lakes called him Baby Dale. His mother was found close to death in the Greenside lead mine behind Glenridding. She disappeared from hospital.'

'Bloody hell, you think this is him?' Kate asked.

'I know it's him. He was granted asylum and put into foster care. The surname he was given was Prentice, after the judge presiding over his case. It touched a few heart strings. I got a friend at the Old Bailey to let me know how he was getting on. He was placed with a family back here in Cumbria.'

'We need to find out if he's OK,' Kate said.

'Agreed. Check that out, will you?'

Kate nodded. The room was more subdued after the news and the flashback to one of the nastiest cases they'd cracked. It had turned out that the mother was a refugee from Sarajevo who'd paid somebody in good faith to get her to Britain. As of today, she still hadn't been traced. Her husband, Nedzad Galic, was also said to have travelled to the UK at the same time, but he hadn't been traced either.

'We'll need to check all the names on that list to see if their guardians have noticed or reported anything suspicious.'

So far, Blackman's defence was that the pornographic images had been planted by the pupil, whom he'd innocently invited to his flat to borrow a poetry book. Their profile of the girl was a fairly negative one, but that didn't mean she was lying. It wasn't a clear-cut case, and that bothered Kelly. When she'd first met Blackman, he'd come across as a decent man: hard-working, committed and polite. Sometimes you just couldn't work people out, but the CPS saying they were interested meant that that was exactly what they'd have to do. They'd already established that Tony Blackman had taught Jenna Fraser, but they had to try to put that to the back of their minds and separate the cases in their heads. It wasn't easy.

Tony Blackman had been suspended indefinitely from the Derwent Academy, where he worked in the English department, while the case against him progressed. It was big news in the local press and the guy had been hounded.

'What's the school like, Kate?' Kelly asked.

'It struggles with discipline issues and drug use is rife, according to the girls. I'm not sure that the teachers have a handle on things. The girls also told me that rumour has it that suicide is now the new cool. There were two other kids a few years ago,' Kate said.

Members of the team shook their heads. Kelly's insides stirred and she wondered if the gossip would be the same if she showed pictures of Jenna Fraser's broken body in assembly.

'Suicide cool? Jesus,' she said.

'The girls can be overdramatic, but they said that another girl and a boy died before they were there. I haven't looked into it. It could easily be urban myth.'

'Well let's find out, for God's sake!' Kelly said.

There was an awkward pause, and Kate said she'd go and make the phone call to find out about Dale Prentice. Doubtless she'd squeeze in a fag break too. Kelly looked around the table.

'Why are you all staring at me? Don't you think it weird that the school is haemorrhaging kids? I want to know why, and whether we can launch an investigation.'

Her usual cool had deserted her. Everybody had a bee in their bonnet about Jenna Fraser, but Kelly was taking it personally. Maybe it was because parenthood was a sensitive subject at the moment; maybe it was because Ted had described the girl's injuries in such detail. Maybe it was because she gave a shit.

'Emma, find out if there's any truth to the other deaths. I want to know. And I want to know if Blackman taught those pupils too.'

She got up and walked towards the window. The rooms were all airless and dim at this time of year. Only an artificial yellow hue gave them any semblance of light. They were like vampires, arriving in the dark and leaving in the dark. Kelly took a few deep breaths. Kate came back into the room stinking of cigarettes.

'As far as the authorities know, Dale Prentice is fine and at home. He attends the Little Fellwalkers Nursery in St Bees.'

'Good.' Kelly breathed a little easier. 'OK, I'm on duty over Christmas. Will, it's your turn for New Year. What are we all doing for Christmas?' She was trying to recapture the spirit of goodwill that had been in the room before she'd brought up Jenna Fraser and the subject of death.

'I've got the family this year.' Kate spoke first.

'What was it at last count? Fifteen?' asked Will.

Kate rolled her eyes.

'Christ, good luck with that. The girls will help, right?'

'Kind of, in between fighting over phone chargers and showers.' The atmosphere relaxed again and Kelly listened to everyone talking about their families. She felt a pang of guilt that she hadn't provided her own mother with the pleasure of grandchildren, but her sister Nikki more than made up for it with three of her own. And when Kate got started on one of her tales about A&E and chest infections, or long journeys, or clothes shopping, Kelly didn't feel as though she was missing out one bit. Josie was handful enough; Kelly couldn't imagine three of them.

'Rob? What are you up to?'

'I'm taking Mia to a lodge in Buttermere.' He smiled, and the team spotted the fleeting glaze of pure love. They smiled back at him and he snapped out of his haze. Kelly laughed.

'You bloody romantic!'

Rob shook his head, mortified that he'd let his guard down. He blushed a little and reached for more cake.

'Don't go making any babies. They'll ruin your life.' Kate did this now and again. Her black humour was used in particularly stressful times when she was struggling with the girls. By all accounts, her husband was useless and spent most of his time at the pub watching Sky Sports. They'd been childhood sweethearts. Nobody at Eden House had met him, but then they all kept their private lives very much out of the office.

'No, he's just going to practise.' Will said what everyone else was thinking. It worked, and the air was cleared.

'Will?'

'Just me and the missus this year – pure bliss. I'm locking the doors on Christmas Eve and not coming out again until I'm back on shift.'

'Same advice, pal.' Kate chipped in again.

'What about you, guv?'

'I'm hosting. Just my mum and… a few friends.'

They all knew Johnny. He'd become quite a local celebrity, as well as helping out Eden House several times, albeit unofficially. But their boss was fiercely private. They knew that her father was no longer alive, and that her mother had a few health issues, but apart from that, the most they knew about Kelly Porter was that she was the first one in the office, and the last one to leave. And she had no kids.

Chapter 7

Michael Shaw sat at the dining table doing his homework, listening to his mum argue with his sister. After twelve years, it was a regular feature of his daily rhythm and nothing to be concerned about. His mum and dad had different approaches to parenting, and he figured that was normal. His mum was soft, but that was how he supposed mums were designed to be, but his dad didn't like it, and that was what they argued most about. Michael just got on with his homework, or played the Xbox in his room.

Earlier, when his mum had gone upstairs to take a bowl of fruit to Faith, his sister, Dad had registered his annoyance by rolling his eyes.

'She can come and get her own bloody bowl of food,' he'd said. Now, after Faith had finally come back downstairs to look for a shoe, the argument was about what time Faith should be allowed out till. They were both heading to the fair, and Michael knew that his own curfew was nine o'clock. Next year it would be later, but to be honest, he'd usually run out of money by nine anyway.

The house was a small terrace and there were few places to find privacy. Faith was on the phone to Sadie and they squealed together, making Dad wince. Michael rolled his eyes. He just didn't get girls. To him they were giggly and dramatic. He'd had two girlfriends this year already, but they'd both dumped him live on Snapchat, so he'd made a promise to himself that he was off them for now.

'How are you doing, Michael?' his mum asked. He was completing maths homework and so he needed little help, if any.

'Good,' he said.

'The difference between girls and boys!' She often said this, but it was true. Faith caused so much drama.

His dad tutted and agreed. 'Boys are so easy.'

Michael thought the phrase unfair and felt a pang of guilt. Faith was always getting it in the neck from both parents, but they mostly left him alone. It was true that she was stroppy and often annoying, but he still felt like she wasn't that bad, for a sister. Faith ignored them all and continued to look under chairs and piles of ironing.

'In my day, she'd be down here making her own tea, not having it delivered,' said his dad, as if she weren't in the room.

'Was that the sixteenth century, Dad?' Michael quipped. Both parents laughed and looked at one another, resigned to the fact that they would soon have two teenagers to handle.

'Clever dick,' his dad said to him.

'You said dick.' Michael giggled and blushed. Faith disappeared upstairs again.

'Can't say anything these days!' His dad shook his head and went back to watching the news.

When Faith came downstairs ready to go out, her eyes were firmly attached to her phone, and so she didn't notice her father's face. Michael saw his dad glare at his sister and hoped there wouldn't be trouble. Faith got on Dad's nerves, or that was how he put it, and Michael felt sorry for her, because he himself didn't seem to get on anyone's nerves. But Faith was brave and so clever, while he didn't really speak up for himself unless he was asked. She had an opinion on everything and he watched and took it all in, fascinated by where she learned all this stuff about human rights, famine, poverty and the government. But it drove his dad insane. Once, she'd called him a bigot and a Tory, and Michael had had to look them up. It had led to her being grounded and sent to her room.

'Faith, put your phone down. We need to talk about tonight.' Their father looked stern and Michael knew what was coming. 'Faith!' he shouted. She jumped and dropped her phone.

'What? For God's sake!'

'Don't you for God's sake me!' Their father was now on his feet and Michael thought about going upstairs.

'Colin.' It was their mum's role to intervene and pacify the situation. This was how it usually went: Faith pissed their dad off, he lost his temper, their mum calmed everyone down and they all carried on as normal. Until the next time.

'She's only looking at her phone.' Their mum turned to Faith. 'No talking to strangers.'

'Mum, I'm not seven years old!'

'It doesn't matter. These predators have all the tricks: pretending to be into whatever you're into, luring you away from friends...'

'At Keswick fair?' Faith said sarcastically.

'You are this close to being grounded! Listen to your mother!' Dad's voice was becoming louder, and Michael put his head in his hands.

Faith tutted and rolled her eyes.

'She's not that stupid!' Michael couldn't help himself, and they all looked at him as though, previous to his interjection, he'd been invisible. 'I'm just saying she knows what a paedo is.'

'Same goes for you, Michael,' his dad said.

The situation defused, Faith went to get her jacket. Michael thought his parents underestimated both of them, but also that Faith didn't handle it well. If only she'd keep her mouth shut, she'd get away with a lot more.

'How do you know what a paedo is?' his dad asked him.

Michael sighed. 'Everyone knows, Dad! It's called the internet.' Sometimes his parents behaved like dinosaurs, but then given their childhoods, which they had described in laborious detail over the years – no mobile phones, no internet, no bloggers, no reality TV – that was what they were.

Faith and Michael soon lost interest in these conversations, although they did find it fascinating that there was once a time when no one had a mobile phone. The concept of not being reached: that was interesting.

'You'll catch your death in that.' Mum was now focused on Faith's choice of top. It was rather short. She'd only started wearing stuff like that because of Sadie. Michael knew that Sadie was called a slut at school, but she didn't seem to mind. He had a pretty good idea what a slut was, and they usually looked like Sadie Rawlinson. He'd heard their mum quizzing Faith about her best friend, and it never sounded positive. Everybody knew that Sadie took drugs regularly, but this never came up in the house. Michael reckoned that half the stuff kids got up to now would floor his parents. Apparently when they were younger, people only did drugs at raves.

'Mum! Who uses expressions like that?' Faith was laughing. 'What does catch your death even mean?'

Even their dad was smirking.

'I'm going,' Faith said.

'You can't go without something to eat!' their mum protested.

'I'll get a burger at the fair. And candyfloss. We agreed I wouldn't have tea tonight.' Faith gazed pleadingly at her mother. Colin gave his wife the 'you're so weak' look and went to check on Michael's homework. Maths was his strong point too.

'Who are you going with tonight?' he asked.

'Ethan and Adam.'

'Adam Pearson? I'm not keen on that kid.'

'I know you're not, Dad. He's all right.'

'God, you're worse than the thought police! Chill out.' It was Faith's departing shot before she put on her coat and checked her phone again, ready to leave.

'I'll pick you both up dead on nine thirty, outside the Royal Oak.'

'Nine thirty!' Faith was outraged. Her curfew had been nine thirty last year too. But arguing about it was futile and she knew it. Michael watched as her shoulders dropped. She was defeated.

Their father wasn't finished. 'And change your top.'

Michael watched Faith glance at Mum, trying to put her in the middle. It almost worked, but on this occasion, Mum agreed with Dad. Faith rolled her eyes, ripped her jacket off and stomped upstairs, returning wearing a long green jumper instead. She grabbed her jacket and was gone.

'Nine thirty!' his dad shouted as the door slammed behind her.

Chapter 8

'The fair? Really? Why on earth would you want to go there?' Johnny was studying a Lakeland map that was spread across Kelly's dining room table. It had been there for two days and he'd made notes on it in different-coloured pens. He didn't look up as he answered, and she was irritated. She needed something to take her mind off work. She looked at the map and contemplated hiding it.

'Oh come on! It'll be different. You've been poring over that map for days; we need to get out. *I* need to get out. I don't mean to go on the rides; I just think it would be fun to have a look at the Christmas market, maybe pick up some presents, something for Josie? We could get a pint at the Dog and Duck. Please?'

Kelly widened her hazel eyes and feigned sadness, making herself difficult to resist. She went to him and put her arms around his chest from behind, resting her face on the crease between his neck and shoulder. He stopped looking at the map and softened, and she moved closer.

'You smell good,' he said. She was wearing the Lancôme perfume he'd bought her for her birthday, and her auburn hair fell on his shoulder. It was still faintly kissed at the edges from the summer sunshine, but had darkened elsewhere since the end of that glorious season. She had grown it longer only recently, and the golden

43

streaks looked more pronounced when it was down about her face. She knew when she had him cornered.

'What are you doing anyway? You know these hills like I know the Penrith and Lakes NHS goddamn Trust.' She nodded to the table. 'You hardly need a map,' she added.

He gripped her arms, enjoying her strength; she, in return, refused to let go.

'I'm mapping the route for the race.'

'I know you are, I'm just saying that it's months away and you really don't need to.'

Johnny had planned to do the race last year, but the surprise visit from Josie had scuppered his plans. The Lakeland 100 was the type of race that needed to be prepared for like the D-Day landings: nothing could be left to chance, and in the end he'd decided he wasn't fit enough. And Josie was too important to lose again.

'You're losing too much weight. I don't like it.' Kelly squeezed her hands together across his chest and pressed against him, feeling the hardness of his body. He'd been training for months. He was conditioned anyway, from the fells and ridges over which he scrambled daily to reach casualties, but lately he'd become what her mother would have called fitter than a butcher's dog.

'You're disappearing. It makes your face look gaunt; you look older.'

'Thanks.'

'No problem.'

'Tell me what you really think.'

'I will.'

Johnny ran his hands through his dark hair, silvery round the temples. Next year he'd be fifty, but he didn't look a day over forty-five. The mountain air halted the ageing process in the Lakes like it did for Peruvian goat herders.

'Do the race with me,' he said.

'No way! Not a hope in hell. Why would I put myself through that when I can drink a bottle of cheap wine and eat a curry?'

He smiled. 'You don't mean that; come on, you need a challenge.'

'No I do not!' Her indignation was an act and Johnny saw straight through it: he could tell that she was tempted.

'What do I get if I agree to take you to the fair?' he asked.

'Ah, it's blackmail now, is it? I might let you keep your map on my table for another day.'

He squeezed her. 'It's freezing out there,' he said.

'You think it's cold now? Wait until you're on your fortieth mile of the Lakeland 100, freezing your nuts off with just your torch and a whistle to keep you warm.' She said 'Lakeland 100' with dripping resentment, as if the race had become his bed partner in preference to her, and in a way, it had. Where once, on a Sunday morning, they'd eaten bacon and eggs and contemplated an afternoon run to recover from a hangover, now he was up at 8 a.m. preparing for the week's mileage test. This morning had been a twenty-miler, and he'd been out for three hours. Kelly wouldn't admit to it, but she'd needed him. She'd wanted him in bed, not out on the fells setting records.

'Are you having a mid-life crisis?' she threw at him.

'It'll happen to you one day.'

Kelly understood the attraction of self-flagellation; she appreciated the need to commit, and to sacrifice, but that didn't mean she approved of his chosen method. He'd earned his stripes five times over and didn't need to keep proving his own resilience and limits. But she knew why he did it. It was only when he pushed himself that he could be at peace. She was the same, but her quests usually took on a different form. Catching a lowlife wasn't quite the same as a hundred-mile race ascending some nine thousand feet, but it felt like it sometimes.

She softened, and he saw it.

'Did you never go to the fair when you were a kid? The rides, the lights, the smell of fags and burnt cooking oil?' she asked.

Johnny laughed. 'Glamorous.'

'I know.'

She had to admit it was warm inside her lovely cottage, and it would be easy to not venture out. But she spotted a chink in his armour and wrapped a cashmere scarf around her neck on top of the knitted sweater, adding to her cosiness.

'Come on, they pack up tomorrow, and then I'll sulk for a whole year. I haven't been in ages. I think the last time was when I was fifteen. Nikki and I hung around the waltzers eating chips and candyfloss, waiting for this dodgy-looking guy that she fancied. I think he took her behind the Ferris wheel and showed her his greasy pole.' She giggled.

'You have such a dirty laugh, Kelly Porter. All right! Bloody hell. I'll come for an hour. Then we come back and relight the fire, agreed?' He turned towards her and smiled.

'Agreed,' she said.

She pulled herself away from him and went to find her hat and gloves. It was minus three outside, but it felt colder. Still, she had no doubt there'd be plenty of girls in short skirts and strappy dresses hanging about the fair, waiting for attention. The fairground workers had never appealed to her, though she saw the allure: the risk, the temporary high, the unknown and the dark lured the girls in a steady queue. All Kelly saw was the ingrained dirt, the stink of lorry fumes, the bleary eyes and the lack of anything tangible. Always the copper, she didn't trust any of them.

Johnny pulled on his North Face coat and tied a scarf tightly around his neck. He stomped his feet and clasped his hands, like a toddler affirming its annoyance at being asked to wrap up warm for a bracing walk. Kelly smiled.

'You won't feel the benefit of all that if you put it on now,' she said. He rolled his eyes and undid his jacket, opening his hands for her approval. Kelly grabbed her bag and keys.

The night air assaulted their exposed faces and their breath escaped in vast clouds around their heads. They jumped into her car and Kelly started the engine quickly, turning up all the heating dials. The windscreen was misty, and she wiped the space in front of her to see better.

'Is there still time to talk you out of it?' Johnny asked.

She smiled at him and switched on the headlights.

'Not a chance.'

Chapter 9

As they drove away from the small house in Pooley Bridge, snow began to fall, as predicted. It was a week before Christmas, and it looked as though the fells would be covered for the festive season. It was a double-edged sword: while it made the peaks a picture of pure awe and wonder, it also filled the mountain rescue with dread because of the predictability of casualties, and the increased difficulty in finding them.

Johnny shivered dramatically. 'I can't believe I'm leaving the house on a night like this when I could be lying in front of the fire with you, drinking moderately expensive red wine.'

Kelly smiled at him. The holiday season had begun to work its magic, and there was the luxurious feeling of everything stopping, even if for only one day: no shopping, no work, no traffic; just being. It was like travelling back in time to a more peaceful era when families sat and played games, and cooking smells wafted on the air; relatives visited and Christmas carols told of peace on earth and all things virtuous. Of course, the reality was nothing like that. Christmas was in effect one long battle to buy food, booze and stocking fillers that lay discarded after the big day. It was like a hotly anticipated date with a hunk who'd wowed with his profile picture, only for it to turn out that he had bad breath and a small penis.

For Kelly, there was no holiday really; not if the past was anything to go by. Some drunk always ended up in A&E having been glassed, or worse, and figures were on the up. By and large, the poor coppers unfortunate enough to be on duty over the break dealt with the pissheads admirably, but occasionally an incident went further and the detective on call would be hauled in. This year, it was Kelly's turn. She didn't much mind; after all, it was just another day.

'How's Nikki?' Johnny broke into her reverie, and Kelly bristled, as she always did. She also knew that the subject couldn't be avoided.

'You'd know more about that than me. Are you still helping her to get counselling?'

Nikki's PTSD came and went. Kelly thought it more bipolar, but all the experts agreed that she'd had a tough time recovering from her abduction over eighteen months ago by one of the Lake District's most famous residents: a serial killer nicknamed 'the Teacher'. Even Wordsworth had become insignificant during the search for the crazy fuck who left poetry on his poor victims. Nikki had had a lucky escape, but not so her mind.

'I haven't spoken to her in ages,' Johnny said. 'I put her in touch with a mate of mine who works for an army charity specialising in PTSD, but he said she went cold on him.'

'I'm not surprised. She likes the attention initially, then gets bored. I'm sure she's OK, or Mum would have said something.' Kelly hadn't spoken to her sister for some time either. Finding out that they were only half-sisters instead of full ones had removed some of the angst and guilt surrounding their tempestuous relationship. It seemed less important now; getting to know her real father was Kelly's priority, and the last thing she needed was Nikki ruining it.

'Nikki doesn't know about your dad, does she?' It was as though Johnny could read her mind. 'Are you going to tell her?'

Kelly gripped the wheel. 'I'm torn. Half of me wants to scream it out so she leaves me alone for good. The other half wants to keep it to myself because I know she'll try to make life very difficult for Ted.'

'Assumption is the mother—'

'Oh, please! Don't preach to me. She really doesn't deserve to know. You keep seeing this chink of humanity in her that I don't – that I've never seen. I let her in last year after her horrendous experience. But come on, she loves the attention! Did you know she said that you're too hot for me?'

Johnny raised his eyebrows.

'You have no idea how vicious she is when no one's looking.'

'What's hot?' he joked. It made Kelly laugh and defused the tension. He changed the subject.

'Is your mum set for Christmas?'

'Yes, she's looking forward to coming.'

Josie was coming too. At fifteen, Johnny's daughter was turning into a madam; an even bigger one than she already was. It was pretty much the only source of tension between Kelly and Johnny. There was nothing especially wrong with the girl, but it was the way she manipulated her father that bothered Kelly. She'd caught her several times grinning after she'd got her own way, as if to say to Kelly, 'I have way more power than you do.' Kelly supposed that like any doting father, all Johnny needed was a flicker of cow eyes to make him melt, and Josie knew it.

Christmas dinner had the potential to be fraught, but they all knew that Kelly might have to leave them to fend for themselves should she get a call on Christmas Day. She half suspected it might be a welcome diversion. Wendy had met Josie several times and had a knack of disarming her, which was partly why she'd been invited. Besides, last year, Wendy was at Nikki's, so it was Kelly's turn.

The subject of inviting Nikki and her family had been skirted round several times, with Kelly finding a way out each time. She swung wildly between caving in for the sake of her three nieces, and a stubborn refusal to entertain her sibling no matter how they struggled. No one pushed the idea, not even Wendy. It had been a tough year for Nikki, of that there was no doubt, but Kelly wasn't a charity, and even the blood they shared ran thin. Kelly believed that the olive branches she'd held out on many occasions had been too often thrust back into her face, causing long-lasting scars. Nikki still wasn't back to her normal self, and she wasn't good in groups. Even Johnny agreed that she wasn't ready; she was unpredictable and in the very early days of rehabilitation.

Kelly drove out of Pooley Bridge and up to the A66. The snow began to fall more heavily and she needed to use her wipers. She looked at her temperature gauge: minus two degrees. It would freeze tonight.

'It's so beautiful,' she said. It was true: the snow blanketed anything ugly and discoloured and kissed the whole landscape with a clinical white blessing.

She took it slowly, but others whizzed past them.

'Wankers,' she said. She'd seen enough RTAs to know the importance of respecting the weather. Last year a woman had swerved on black ice at over sixty miles an hour on this very road and killed her three kids sitting in the back. That kind of thing slowed Kelly down. Not like these idiots.

It wasn't long before the lights of Keswick came into view ahead and the great silhouettes of Blencathra and Skiddaw towered over them on their right-hand side.

Parking was always a nightmare in Keswick, but Kelly found a space at the police station. She'd got to know many of the local coppers over the last few years, and she knew that Stan MacIntyre was on shift. From there it was a short walk into town. They fastened their thick walking coats and pulled on hats, and headed towards the fair.

They heard it before they saw it. Screams carried on the freezing air, and they heard the juddering of powerful machinery and the chugging of the lorries powering it. Petrol lay heavy in the air, as well as caramel and burger fat. It was the Christmas market that Kelly was interested in, but she also loved walking through the fair and watching. She linked Johnny's arm and they spotted the first crowds.

'Why am I doing this?' Johnny asked.

'Oh come on, you old fart! Where's your sense of adventure?'

'I get enough of that in my day job, and this weather isn't going to help. I dread to think about the halfwits who'll get stuck up there this year. Remember that guy who tried to ski down Helvellyn last year, pissed out of his brains?'

'Christ, yes. He was shit-faced. He's lucky to be alive,' Kelly said. The snow always brought out way more walkers because it made the fells look so pretty. But the weather changed so quickly in winter and the days were brutally short, trapping even experienced walkers. Johnny wasn't on call over Christmas, but knowing him, if they were particularly busy, he'd turn up anyway. One misjudged slip up on the higher peaks could be fatal.

Their pace slowed as they hit the bulk of the thrill-seekers. The attractions were overflowing, and people of all ages waited in long lines for their turn. It was still quite early, and so young children milled about with their parents, eating candyfloss and pointing to the bright lights. Older children showed off and paraded in front of the opposite sex. Kelly's eyes were drawn to one group, and she stared at their attire. The girls all looked the same: skinny jeans, midriff tops, bulky biker-style coats, chunky sneakers and tons of dark make-up. She couldn't tell if they were pretty or not, they were hidden behind so many layers of cosmetics. Oh shut up, Kelly, she thought. It's called youth.

She suffered an acute moment of melancholy as a vision of Jenna Fraser entered her mind. She tried to push it away. At the funeral, Jenna's father had said she was finally at peace. It was as if her death had been inevitable, and she'd somehow been born with an innate sense of fatality.

'Come on, I'll win you a teddy,' said Johnny.

'Really? So you do like the fair! You tease!'

He smirked. He couldn't walk past guns without having a pop. He paid the shifty-looking guy a crisp fiver and was handed a rifle. Kelly had never seen him cock a weapon; he looked like a pro.

'Best shot in Basra,' he boasted, and squinted through the sight. The pellet pinged and hit the first-prize target. The stallholder looked utterly pissed off and eyed Johnny suspiciously.

'Professional?'

'No, mountain rescue, mate.'

'You need to do that three times.'

'No problem.' He cocked the weapon again and pinged another one off. The guy shook his head as Johnny hit the same target, and reluctantly set it up again. Johnny hit the mark for the third time and handed the rifle back.

'Sight's a bit off, mate,' he said. They all did it, those stalls – put the sight off a touch so no one ever won – but Johnny knew how to spot it and make the necessary adjustments. 'Beginner's luck,' he added.

'You can choose anything from the top row,' the guy told Kelly, knowing the gift was for her; what man won himself a teddy? Kelly chose a huge unicorn and Johnny rolled his eyes.

'Will you carry it for me?'

'Of course I will,' he said.

They walked away, and the stallholder watched them until they disappeared round the corner. Kelly held on to Johnny's arm, both of them on high alert. She had noticed this about him after only knowing him a short time: he never stopped searching out the enemy, even if it was only a bartender short-changing him. His eyes were never still.

'I don't trust any of these guys; they're dodgy as hell,' he said, glancing around. They all looked as though they only emerged from the underbelly of society at night. Some were old and some were young; all looked unclean and criminal.

'I know. They give me the creeps. My sister used to go out with one of them; they'd meet every year and I'd lie to my parents. He stank,' she added.

'You lied to your parents?'

'Believe me, Wendy had hawk eyes. If we wanted any fun, we had to cover for each other.'

'And what about your dad?'

'Which one?'

'I mean John,' he said.

'Sorry, it was rhetorical. I was being petulant.'

'I know.'

'He always favoured me. I guess he didn't know I wasn't his.'

'Does *he* know?' He meant Ted Wallis, the senior pathologist and Kelly's biological father.

'I don't know.'

'Will you tell him?' he asked.

'I really fancy some glühwein.' She changed the subject.

'Do you want me to drive?' he asked.

'If you don't mind. This snow looks like it's getting thicker. We shouldn't stay out long anyway.'

They walked towards the stall and ordered a cup of the warm spicy red wine, and a coffee for Johnny. It was as if the fair was divided into two ghettos: the rides, and the stalls. The former frequented by kids and predators, the latter by shoppers and lovers.

There was no room to sit, and so they took their cups and wandered through the little wooden stalls that popped up every year selling trinkets, woollen goods, food and drink. They chose some local artisan cheese, some Cartmel sticky pudding, and a couple of bottles of red wine, as well as a hand-carved wooden trinket box for Josie, then made their way back to the car.

Kelly's cheeks were flushed from the alcohol, and she felt warm. She held onto Johnny's arm as they navigated around clumps of people. The demographic of the multitude had changed somewhat, the younger children and their parents conspicuously absent. The atmosphere was different too. Now huddles of girls followed gangs of lads swaggering and smoking.

Kelly shivered. It was time to go.

Chapter 10

Away from the main street, two men chatted in a doorway. They wore dark baggy clothes and a guess at their age would have been unproductive. A car pulled up and one of the men walked to it and handed something over, receiving a small package in return. The car carried on and the men walked down the street and into a terraced house.

The house was dark and quiet, though voices could be heard coming from several of the rooms. The men split up and entered separate rooms, where they were greeted like old friends. All over the house, lights were dimmed and windows shut, creating an ethereal atmosphere, reminiscent of a brothel where secrets were swapped and innocence traded. But none of the occupants of the house wanted sex. They were there for something far more powerful.

They'd scored, and managed to cobble enough together to pay for it. Soon they were huddled around, each waiting for a tiny bagful of powder to be handed to them. Their addiction took over, and nothing else mattered. The boy, horse, mud, thunder... whatever the name for it, the effects were the same, and the risks just as high as the trip they anticipated. No one was ever quite sure what was in the small packages; it could have been rat poison for all they knew. But they didn't care.

A girl whose parents lived in a million-pound house on the shores of Windermere held out her hand, as did a guy who used to own five car dealerships; a woman who'd been a primary school teacher shuffled forward, next to a man who taught the trombone. All scratched and rubbed sores and imaginary itches as they waited, barely able to contain their anticipation.

They sat on unkempt, stinking mattresses and began their rituals. Some helped others coil straps around their arms, and a few injected into necks, if veins elsewhere wouldn't perform. The only sound was of rubber ties being released, and groans as individuals gradually collapsed one by one into pools of satisfaction, fists unclenching. As they sank into oblivion, pain receptors, designed to ward off danger, both physical and emotional, stopped working, and minds floated off to a world of nothingness, if only for an hour or so.

The house fell quiet once more and the radiators belted out oppressive heat, floating over bodies that looked like corpses. The line between overdose and recovery became more blurred every time they used, but they continued to do so because it was scarier not to. High, they couldn't dwell on family disappointments, debt, abuse, neglect or depression. High, they couldn't feel a thing, and that was the point.

The shit coursing through their bloodstreams had travelled thousands of miles from the fields of Afghanistan and made certain people very rich, including the man who had overseen the evening's delivery to Keswick charter fair. He cared nothing for the dark deals in quiet streets, or for the losers burning their brains on the stuff. All he was interested in was profit, and the business was developing nicely. It was a natural progression out of the cities, where coppers heated everything up and spoiled lucrative trade. Moving to the country was the obvious answer, and there were still as many takers. Of course, supply in the city never dwindled, but more connections were being made in the provinces, and the Lake District was as attractive as any.

The man who supplied ninety per cent of the drugs to the Lake District was clean; he'd never been an addict. But he didn't mind those who were, and if he could facilitate his customers in any way, he was happy to oblige. Yet the profit from his business, which had quadrupled in one year, wasn't his only reason for being in the Lake District. He really didn't have to make the journey from Manchester to Keswick to deal with these lowlifes who threw their futures away on heroin. He had other interests in the area, and one of them was his son.

The last time he'd seen the boy, he'd been in the custody of the local authorities, and one woman stood between getting him back and losing him forever.

Her name was DI Kelly Porter.

Chapter 11

Michael Shaw stopped in front of the Pendulum. His heart thumped. He knew that he could no longer use his size as an excuse to avoid it; this year, he was tall enough. He looked up and swallowed. The thing must be a hundred feet tall, the cages hurtling round at ridiculous speeds. Screams echoed on the night air as the riders whizzed past, open-mouthed and wide-eyed. As the arm descended to earth, he realised that Faith was on the next cage to belt past the awe-struck crowds below. Loud, pulsating music throbbed in Michael's ears, and he felt nauseous. Faith was with Sadie, and they howled as they hung on tight.

As he followed their cage with his eyes, his friend tapped him on the shoulder.

'Well fit, your sister,' he said.

'Fuck off, Adam,' Michael replied.

The trio had hooked up at football training in Year 5 and had been inseparable since. Recently, though, Adam had begun to attract trouble, and the others had started to walk a different way home. Problem was, Adam had noticed and had begun to pick on Michael, the smallest of the three. Adam himself wasn't particularly tall, but what he lacked in inches, he made up for in volume.

'Look at her tits jumping up and down on that thing!'

Michael's face turned purple and he scowled. Adam spread his hands in mock apology, then placed them on his chest and began to pretend to fondle himself.

'Ah, yeah. She's asking for it,' he jibed.

Something shifted on the caramel-laden air; the music dipped, someone screamed and the ride slowed. Michael charged at his tormentor and felled him in one hit. Adam, taken by surprise, never saw what was coming. A small crowd noticed the commotion and gathered round the bodies writhing on the floor. They began to cheer. Ethan could only watch, frozen and unsure what to do. Michael was sitting astride his tormentor now, and the pair grappled for dominance.

The crowd parted and Faith fought her way through the gap. She screamed at Michael and dragged him off.

'What the hell are you doing?' she yelled.

Adam lay panting on the floor. His eye was cut and had begun to swell. Faith looked from her brother to his victim and back again. Michael glared down at Adam, then threw up his hood and left the scene. He didn't know where he was going, but anywhere that put distance between himself and humiliation would be good right now.

–

'Ethan, what happened?' Faith asked breathlessly. Ethan looked past her to where Adam was being helped up.

'Adam was dissing you. Michael stuck up for you,' he said.

'Oh shit.' Faith looked about for her brother, but he'd vanished. 'Where do you think he's gone?' she asked.

Ethan shrugged. Faith looked at her watch: it was ten past eight. She had plenty of time to find him. Sadie asked what was going on, then rolled her eyes. It was obvious that there was only one thing on her mind tonight, and that was hooking up with Luke Miles, who owned a car and had offered to take them to get spiced. Luke was a sixth-former, and his parents were rich and lived in a massive pad on the outskirts of Keswick, so attention from him was flattery indeed, and Sadie wasn't about to miss the opportunity.

Faith was nervous. She'd never been that into drugs, but she knew that Sadie was. She wanted to be like her friend, to be cool and interesting, but she didn't like what it did to her brain and her stomach, making her feel sick and out of control. She always knew when her friends were close to making a deal, as they spoke in coded riddles to outwit people who might disapprove, like parents, teachers and coppers. 'Spice' and 'joker' were nicknames for chemical marijuana, and they sometimes smoked it dipped in ozone to make a wet joint. When Faith had tried one it had nearly blown her head off. If they were planning on doing that tonight, she should really make her excuses and leave. But first she had to find Michael.

'What's going on?'

Luke had arrived. He looked at Faith and his eyes wandered to her unzipped coat. She'd changed back into the short top as soon as she'd found the first pub toilet. She followed his gaze and he smiled. Her pulse quickened and she felt as though she was on a precipice. He'd told her that he had some new stuff for them to try, and she was torn between her sober brain telling her the right thing to do, and her teenage brain that wanted to experiment and not let her friends down. She also couldn't deny that she was hopelessly in love with Luke Miles. Out of the corner of her eye she saw Sadie fiddling with her hair and rubbing her nose: she'd already been at it.

'Are you OK? What happened?' Luke asked.

'Nothing, just my brother, he got into a fight, I don't know where he is.'

Faith felt dumb. She fully expected Luke to tease her about her concern, or perhaps make a joke. But he didn't. He was so close, she could smell him; it was a mixture of skunk, tobacco and cologne, and it thrilled her.

'Can I help?' he asked. Sadie's mouth fell open and Faith saw that she was jealous. She saw Luke as her own. The problem was that Sadie was always smashed off her tits, and Faith knew that it bored him.

'Please,' she said.

'Let's spread out. It's Michael, isn't it? Call him,' Luke said.

Faith called her brother's number but it went to voice-mail. She shook her head.

'My dad's meeting us at the Royal Oak at nine thirty. He might have gone straight there to wait.' It was out before she could take it back, and Sadie giggled. Luke ignored her.

'Let's check there first, then.'

Luke spoke into his phone, presumably to his mates, and the girls followed, with Sadie applying make-up and taking selfies in front of neon signs and flashing lights. Away from the chaos and din of the main fair, they made their way towards the pub, hoping to find Michael and put an end to the escapade. Luke and Faith checked down alleyways and behind vans as they went; occasionally Faith tried Michael's number again, without success.

Suddenly her phone rang; the caller ID said it was her brother.

'Michael!'

The small group stopped walking. They were halfway down a residential street and the odd car sped past. Away from the heat of the burger vans and the huge industrial light bulbs, it was freezing, and the girls pulled their coats tightly round them. They'd noticed the snow as they left the fair, and now it fell in great clumps. Already the cars parked along the road were covered.

'Where are you?' Faith shouted into her phone. She nodded and rolled her eyes as she spoke to Michael for barely a minute before hanging up.

'I'm sorry, everyone, he's fine. He's back at the fair, eating chips outside the Cuckoo with Justin.' Luke smiled. Justin was one of his friends. 'Sorry,' Faith said again.

'Hey, it's just a good job he's OK,' Luke said. 'Come on, let's get back to the vibe.'

Faith could feel Sadie's eyes burning into her as Luke chatted to her all the way back to the fair. As they neared the lights, he took her hand.

'Have you got to meet your dad at nine thirty as well?' he asked.

Faith smiled, dying inside. 'No, just Michael.'

'I could give you a lift home. I promised to go and get Justin, come on. You can check on your brother first.' He looked at Sadie and waited. They made a perfect foursome.

Chapter 12

Kurt Fletcher knew that he had to descend quickly. Grisedale Pike wasn't a challenging Wainwright, but it was bleak at the top and he could tell that the snow was heading his way. He saw great swathes of the stuff to the east over Derwent Water. The familiar shape of Cat Bells sat steady and lazy on the distant shore and he knew that she'd be covered in cloud soon.

He'd started out to bag the peak late, but he knew it well; he'd worked in Whinlatter Forest for the last four winter seasons. Besides, this was his second time completing Wainwright's 214, and he'd climbed Grisedale Pike at least ten times; it was one of his favourites. He'd come prepared. He wore several layers of under-armour, waterproof leggings over thermals, and a thin windproof jacket, as well as carrying a backpack inside which were a whistle, a GPS, sweet treats, water, a map, a phone, and a torch.

He liked to walk alone. It was the same when he was competing. There was something approaching divinity when he sat on a peak, sipping ice-cold water, breathing quickly to still his heartbeat, unwrapping a Kendal Mint Cake to replenish reserves. The wind was punishing today, but he still sat and stared down and around the Coledale Horseshoe, taking in the breathless scenery of the Derwent Fells beyond. He missed Tarn, his spaniel, who'd bagged over two hundred peaks with him. He'd spread her ashes in Wastwater: the cradle of the storms.

He packed away his water bottle and replaced his gloves over his numbing hands, then took in the scenery for the last time and stood up. Cloud rose over him, bringing with it heavy snow. He put up his hood and made his way back to the ridge. As long as he could feel the ground beneath him and put one foot in front of the other, he'd be down to the frozen bogs of the forest soon enough.

The snow came down in buckets, and he was soaking by the time he reached the fence at the treeline. The forest was deserted, and he ploughed on down a steep patch of frozen moss and fern that led him to the first gate. He had an overwhelming urge to look up at the pines; to see if he could stare at one long enough without seeing the body of the dead girl. He shivered. The image was embedded so deep in his brain that he had contemplated seeking therapy. Johnny Frietze had experience in PTSD and said there was no shame in it, but each time he thought about it, he came to the same conclusion: he wasn't the victim, the girl was, and he would come to terms with what he'd seen eventually.

A few hundred yards further on was the Revelin Moss car park. It had been deserted when he began his ascent, but now he heard a car.

Another hiker, he assumed. Good for them. A lot of Lakes visitors were fair-weather friends who only attempted to explore during the warmer months. There was a certain privileged exchange of respect between those who braved the peaks in winter. Of course, there was the usual collection of idiots who underestimated the conditions and became trapped on the fells. He'd assisted in more than a few rescues himself, and was considering volunteering for the mountain rescue team here in Keswick, Johnny said he should do just that and was eager to recommend him. But after finding the girl, Kurt had questioned his resolve.

As he neared the car park, he saw not just one car, but two. One of them revved its engine, and he heard music playing. Perhaps they weren't hikers after all, just kids having a good time. He'd left his own car back in Braithwaite, another twenty minutes' walk away at least. The beat of the music cut rudely through the serenity of the forest, and he kept his head down as he got closer, minding his own business and looking forward to his pint and a paper, in front of a roaring fire. That was one of the things that had convinced him to settle near Keswick: the number of pubs with open fires and open hearts. The Cock was his favourite, and he'd head there tonight, after a hot shower.

The snow was less of a problem under the canopy of the forest, but the dark was all-consuming, and he stopped to get his head torch out. Something about the eerie shadows cast by the enormous trees made him remember the dead girl. Since he'd found her, she'd haunted him, and now he found himself getting angry with the youngsters in the car, wasting their lives on smoking and drinking. He was tempted to go back and lecture them on how lucky they were to be alive. He didn't.

He saw no other vehicle or walkers on the way back to Braithwaite, but that didn't bother him. When he reached his car, he divested himself of several layers of wet kit, steam pouring off his sweating body. He shivered, then pulled on a warm dry jumper and jumped behind the wheel. Reaching over the dash, he opened the glove compartment and took out a dual silver hip flask. One side contained his own home-made liquorice vodka; the other, Baileys. He swigged the Baileys. It warmed him instantly.

He was home within ten minutes. By the time he walked into the Cock and ordered a pint, it was gone ten o'clock. It had been a good day, and images of the girl had subsided. When he left the pub, four pints later, the snow had drifted three feet up the sides of cars and doorways, and his way home was distinctly precarious. It was slippery underfoot, and the four pints didn't help his balance. He'd sleep like a baby tonight. Tomorrow he had three Wainwrights planned, but looking at the weather, he wasn't sure that would happen. Like anything in the Lakes, any time of year, he'd wait to see what morning brought.

Thoughts of the dead girl had gone, for now.

Chapter 13

Tony Blackman peered out of the window.

Unless he could prove he'd been set up, he was facing trial on charges of being a child molester. His flat in Keswick had become a prison; if he ventured out, he was either egged or verbally abused by waiting yobs desperate to get their hands on a paedophile. The police had provided a presence outside the house, but the damage had already been done to his reputation. Parents of pupils at the Academy weren't interested in detail. They wanted blood. It was a scandal, and his life was ruined. He knew that much. Even if he was found not guilty – which he was convinced would happen when a jury heard the truth – if he was allowed to prove it, he'd still be remembered as the teacher who was sacked for being a paedo.

He'd worked out in his head what must have happened. And he had Sarah backing him up.

Sarah Peaks was his English deputy, and they'd hit it off from the day of her interview. She'd never believed what they were saying about him and was doing all she could to prove his innocence. It must be tough for her in the staff room, he thought. The pack mentality was difficult to break, and there was no denying that indecent images had indeed been found on his computer. However, what the police didn't know, and what he would soon prove, was that they had been put there on purpose to frame him. It sounded ludicrous, but all he needed to do was wait until the defence was given access to his hard drive and could get a specialist to look at the download history. He knew the day, the hour and almost the minute it had been done, because that was when the bitch had been at his flat.

He regretted the day he'd involved sixth-formers. It had seemed a good idea at the time: they were open to suggested rebellion, they embraced risk, and most important of all, they trusted him. They'd done well out of it. It was a more than satisfactory arrangement.

But now they'd outsmarted him and he faced complete destruction. Unless he could prove what they'd done. They must have been planning it for weeks, if not months, and he'd never seen it coming.

He heard Sarah in the kitchen. She was helping him put a few things together to take to her cottage. It was private there, and he couldn't stand the siege outside his own property. Interest had died away recently as other news stories overtook his in the press, but he was recognised wherever he went, and it choked him. His career was over, but he still had funds. All he had to do was hold his nerve and he'd survive, if he didn't go to prison.

He and Sarah had talked about leaving the area permanently, but they couldn't do that until he was either tried and given a prison sentence or acquitted. The best-case scenario would be for the CPS to find out the truth before trial and kick out the case, but at the moment that didn't seem likely. He'd still leave the area once it was all over, whether Sarah came with him or not. He wouldn't teach again, but he had plenty of other options and he knew a man who could help him make a new life, maybe even under a new name. It was ironic that the state could fund a change of identity for someone found guilty, but not if they were found innocent.

Looking on the bright side, this could be the break he needed to get out of the empty shell his life had become. He was sick of small-town mediocrity anyway. Keswick was the size of a postage stamp, and even though people raved about the hills around the town, he didn't know what all the fuss was about. They were mere fucking humps compared to other national parks around the world. New Zealand, Africa, South America: each held an allure for him, and it was about time he went travelling and lived a little.

The insects who had set him up would get their come-uppance, if not now, then sometime, and he'd laugh his arse off when they did. They had no idea what they'd done. His anger bubbled just under the surface and it had begun to change him. Sarah tried to soothe him with her support, but his sense of injustice sat heavily in his heart and threatened to explode at any moment.

He'd grown a beard, and it was itchy. He stood scratching it and gazing into boxes, wondering what to pack. Sarah's car was parked in the back alleyway, and he checked out of the window to make sure no one was loitering about there. The snow was thick on the ground and it kept people indoors. Good.

Sarah came out of the kitchen with two beers.

'Here, get this down you,' she said. She was a keeper.

'Will you come around the world with me?' he asked.

She smiled. 'Of course I will! When do we go?'

Chapter 14

At Keswick police station, Sergeant Stan MacIntyre got a call from an initial responder in Kendal about a phone call they'd had from the worried sister of a man they suspected might be lost on the fells. The brother's name was Danny Stanton; he was twenty-two years of age, and he'd taken it upon himself, after watching a short clip on Facebook, to take a tent and a map and camp in the fells for a few nights on his own. His sister was frantic, as the young man was suffering from depression and had been acting strangely recently, dropping out of college and becoming more secretive about what he was up to.

Apparently he had set off from his home in Manchester on Friday, hoping to tackle the Coledale Horseshoe. He'd done it before, visiting the Lakes regularly, but he'd never gone so long without contact, and the sister couldn't reach him on his phone. His last post on Facebook was from the summit of Grisedale Pike on Sunday morning: one of the worst days they'd had on the fells in a long time. The weather had been evil that afternoon, and mountain rescue had received fifteen calls for help.

Stan dialled their number now. As he was doing so, he studied a map. The sister had said he was camping, so they had no address for a hostel. But they did have the registration number and description of Stanton's car, and his next job would be to get someone up there to check. He might even take a drive up there himself. The closest car parks to the Horseshoe were either in Braithwaite, or on the Whinlatter Pass.

'Why would anyone do the Horseshoe on their own, in winter, with no experience?' asked Helen at the Keswick mountain rescue office, incredulous. But that was the essence of their job: they dealt with people who were either incredibly unlucky or incredibly unprepared.

'The sister says he knows the area a little. He bought a few things off eBay and he had a guidebook.'

'All right, I'll get someone up there now. Where was that last Facebook post?'

'Grisedale Pike summit, 1153 hours. I'm looking at it now; it says, "A few wild days ahead." At least we have a picture of him; it's a selfie.'

'Oh Christ. Right, we're on it. I'll get back to you as soon as I hear anything. The weather is terrible today; it'll be tough for the boys. If we don't have any luck, I'll try and get the helicopter out.'

'Thanks, Helen.'

They hung up.

Protocol said Stan needed to let HQ know, so he sat down at his computer to write a report. When he'd completed that, and emailed it, he went to find a colleague to let them know of his plans. He suspected he wouldn't be long. The car either would or wouldn't be there. The lad could have given up after the Pike, cold and shocked by reality, and headed home to Manchester without telling anyone. But he hadn't been answering his phone.

Stan's feet crunched in the snow outside and he looked up to Skiddaw. The summit was covered in freezing fog, and he hoped the lad was inside his tent, sitting it out. He thought about good places to pitch a tent in the Horseshoe. Anywhere in the forest would be good and sheltered, but he couldn't guarantee the lad would be that savvy. He hoped he was underestimating him.

People thought they could map-read. But when actually handed a map, most didn't have a clue, and when the weather came in, and the landscape changed, blurring any points of reference, it was a challenge for even the most seasoned fell walker to get it just right. He knew, though, that if this lad was out there lost, mountain rescue would find him.

The gritters had been out twice, even three times a day, but the roads were still treacherous. Through the town was all right, but Stan hoped he wouldn't have to venture too far up Whinlatter Pass. He tried the two most frequently used car parks in Braithwaite, but no vehicle meeting the description was there. He checked the streets closest to the start of the common paths: again, no luck. He'd have to take the Whinlatter Pass.

He went slowly, and eventually came to the first car park, Revelin Moss, hidden behind trees and deep in snow. The pass had been well looked after by the gritters, but the car park hadn't been touched. He had to stop short of the gate and go on foot. The forest was silent. The day was darkening already, and he took a torch. The main car park was deserted, but he carried on to the overflow to take a look there. As if they hadn't had enough snowfall already, the air became leaden once again and flakes as big as ten-pence pieces began falling around him. His feet sank into the snow and he wished he'd worn boots.

As he came around a tree, he saw that there was one vehicle in the overflow car park. He could tell it had been there a while, because the snow on and around it was about four inches thick. Drifts two feet high clung to its flanks.

He retrieved the registration number from his pocket.

The car was the right colour – black – and it was pretty small, matching the description of a Ford Ka. Patches of bodywork were visible where snow had fallen off or been disturbed by birds. He reached the vehicle and bent down to scrape snow away from the registration plate.

He congratulated himself as he read the number: he'd just found Danny Stanton's car.

Chapter 15

The atmosphere in the staff room at the Derwent Academy was gloomy. The school stood on the site of a nineteenth-century boys' school in the heart of Keswick, near Fitz Park. It was built from Westmorland green slate shipped from Honister on horse-drawn carriages over one hundred and fifty years ago.

The sullen teenagers gracing the school's prefabricated corridors and add-on buildings of formed concrete were not thinking of its illustrious past, however; there were other things on the minds of the eight hundred pupils and thirty staff. The suicide of Jenna Fraser was still recent and raw. But it wasn't the only gossip to grip the academy: the suspension of Mr Blackman was also big news, and many children thought it funny to post paedophilia memes on Facebook. The school was struggling to keep up with the sick and twisted jokes doing the rounds on social media, and a doctored picture of Tony Blackman had emerged, dressed as the Grim Reaper and surrounded by terrified kids, his tiny pink penis dangling out of his robes.

Sarah was unsure how many people truly supported Tony. It was a tricky topic and she didn't know whether to raise it or not. One thing was for sure: people were avoiding her. The staff dotted around the room pretended to look busy, heads sunk into exercise books and newspapers. She went to her pigeonhole to check it for notices, and then to the kettle to make a coffee. She sat alone. It was difficult to keep a relationship quiet in school, and most people suspected that she and Tony were lovers.

From the perspective of the staff, Sarah reckoned a lot of them didn't believe the charges but didn't want to get involved. She didn't know what the children thought, because it wasn't openly discussed, for good reason, but if she had to place a bet, she reckoned that the parents believed the accusations. It was the natural reaction of most people: throw enough shit and some would stick. It provided something to gossip about apart from the awful GCSE results. All their woes were suddenly the fault of Mr Blackman and his perverted mind, whether it be their child's autism, increased drug abuse, or a cold snap in the weather.

Since his suspension, and Jenna Fraser's death, the school had been thrown into a dark mood. It was now common knowledge that Jenna had committed suicide, though most people didn't know exactly how. Sarah knew, and it was shocking. Drugs. They ruined everything. There was a pervasive feeling that the school had hit rock bottom, and the head was under growing pressure to rescue it, the year quickly turning into her *annus horribilis*. Sarah was on good terms with one of the office managers who had a loose jaw; that was how she'd found out the details of Jenna's death. The woman had also told her that the head was thinking of quitting.

Now the police were asking about two other pupils who'd taken their own lives, one of them two years ago and the other a couple of years before that. It happened.

Suicide was the biggest killer of ten- to twenty-five-year-olds now, and they had to go to school somewhere. The problem was the drugs angle. They just couldn't keep it out of the schools. The staff regularly attended conferences on it and implemented policies recommended by Manchester and Kendal drug squads. But the dealers always found a way.

Sarah was a believer in the old saying that the devil made work for idle hands. Kids these days had nothing to do apart from sit like zombies in front of screens. That was what drove them to try other stuff. It made them so overstimulated that it bored them to death: the dopamine paradox, it was called. Of course, drug use was nothing new; it was one of the oldest and most lucrative trades on the planet and no one could change the demand. What they could do was tackle the supply, though it was only when the drug squads had tip-offs that they could set up surveillance and catch the sick bastards who were killing their kids. The school worked very closely with specialists who trained staff to look out for the warning signs of drug abuse. But it was so hard to prove that a child was using, and they weren't allowed to search them. It was crazy.

The head came into the staff room. She had spoken to everybody who worked closely with Tony, and made it clear that she would support him for now. So that was the party line. They were saving their skins and waiting to see what a trial said.

What didn't look good was that Tony had admitted to taking the student in question home with him, insisting that his intentions were honourable: she'd asked to borrow one of his limited-edition Lakeland poem collections, and he'd fallen for it. She must have planted the obscene images on his hard drive when he was fetching her a drink, and then found it amusing to inform the police, who had no choice but to act. But he couldn't say what had motivated the girl to do it, or why she'd accused him of indecent assault. His case sounded fairly lame and he couldn't prove his lack of guilt then he stood to get torn apart in court. The injustice of knowing his innocence but not being believed was a shocking reality. Sarah had contemplated confronting the complainant herself, but they'd all been told categorically not to by the head because of the fact that she was a minor, and a legal witness, and any interference could be construed as tampering. The girl was off limits. The injustice of it all stank. And they still had to teach her.

Sadie Rawlinson laughed with her friends, sniggered behind her art folder, swaggered in front of boys and fluttered her eyelashes at both sexes. The girl didn't seem to have a moral bone in her body, inside her skimpy white shirt, tied above her skirt to show as much skin as possible and unbuttoned low to expose her cleavage. Flagrant distortions of uniform rules were considered the fault of the head, but it was an unwinnable war. It wasn't rocket science that discipline was more likely to be successful when minor rules were followed, but imposing them was another story entirely. The pupils of the Derwent Academy had a reputation for flouting certain expectations when it came to behaviour outside the classroom, and to those in the know, it pretty much reflected what went on inside the classroom too. Only a few teachers commanded the respect of the students, whether it be due to their own indiscretions, such as smoking with the sixth formers by the lake, or through sheer skill; the others went to each lesson as if going into battle, prepared to barely make it out alive. Of the former, Sarah Peaks and Tony Blackman were certainly amongst the most popular – or had once been.

The head approached her and Sarah groaned inwardly. Her Google search sat open on her iPad: *Innocent until proven guilty – law – UK*. She glanced at her boss.

'I've got to keep going. Look at this,' she said, showing the head the screen.

'I agree, but I'm not sure it'll get you anywhere. I think it's proving a real distraction for you, Sarah.'

'I can't just do nothing. It's so unfair that Tony's name can be published but Sadie's isn't. One newspaper has even printed a photograph of him, alongside his address.' A few teachers looked over at them.

'I know what you're thinking, Sarah. Don't even consider leaking her name. The fact remains that he invited her to his flat.' Their voices had dropped to whispers, but it was quite clear to the others what they were talking about.

'As if Sadie Rawlinson reads poetry! It makes my blood boil. She went there with the sole intention of framing him.'

'Why would she do that? What's her motive?'

The head had her on that one. Not even Tony had answered this question. Sadie's story was that he had groomed her for weeks into finally accompanying him to his flat, where he'd tried to kiss her and grope her breasts.

'For kicks, I guess. Just to be a first-class bitch and show that she can.'

'Sarah, do you need some time off?'

'No! That would look like I'm guilty too. I need to be here, fighting his corner. Some of the things being said about him are disgusting.'

'I know, but that's kids and gossip. The two don't go together well. We've got to ride this out, otherwise things will quickly spiral out of control. Burden of proof is on the prosecution, don't forget,' the head continued. It was a comforting reminder. 'They'll have to prove her testimony correct, and I believe that will take some doing.'

There was no doubt that Sadie Rawlinson was a troublemaker, and fairly probably a pathological liar, but to toy with someone's life, to get some sort of sick pleasure out of creating misery for others, was a step beyond mere delinquency.

'Why don't you take the rest of the term off? No one will think any less of you. We break up on Thursday anyway.'

'And let her win?'

The bell rang and they all got up to leave the room. Sarah's next lesson was with Sadie's class, and she felt like throwing in the towel and going home, but she couldn't. She had to face it head on.

She found teaching the girl almost impossible. Every time Sadie walked into her room, Sarah wanted to shake her and ask her why she was ruining someone's life. She thought of Tony, funny, gentle, trusting, kind and generous, and then she looked into the over-made-up face of that lying, self-seeking little bitch, and she had to clench her fists. She swore that she'd seen the girl try to stare her out, and she wondered if she had any idea about her closeness to Tony. She was becoming paranoid.

But the feeling was quickly overtaken by something else when she walked into the classroom. The other students were huddled around Sadie, whose eyes were puffy and red. Sarah sighed and was about to call BAFTA to nominate the girl for her performance. But then she overheard what the pupils were gossiping about, and it wasn't Tony; it was Faith Shaw. Faith always sat next to Sadie, but today she wasn't there.

'She went missing at the fair last night, miss,' one child said.

'What? Sadie, is that true?'

The girl began to nod, and Sarah couldn't help feeling sorry for her.

'Are the police involved?'

'Yes, miss, she was reported missing last night.'

'Christ, that's awful. Sit down, all of you, and take a book out. I'm going to check with the office.'

For once the students did as they were told. A sinking feeling gripped Sarah's stomach and she felt sick. This was a disaster for the school. Another disaster.

The kids looked lost. She opened her mouth to speak, but couldn't think of what to say. Instead she left the room and went straight to the head's office. When she got there, the woman's face said it all. Faith Shaw had last been seen at the fair, and was now officially a missing person.

Chapter 16

Kelly drove to Keswick on the A66. The 999 call had come through last night, and had been passed to her office first thing this morning. Statements had already been taken by the night shift, and family liaison officers were with the Shaws. Kelly's involvement was because the girl was a minor. People went missing all the time in the UK, and most of them turned up safe and well within forty-eight hours. But when it was a child, things were slightly different. Especially when she'd gone missing from such a busy event, with thousands of strangers visiting the town.

Kelly was on her way to introduce herself to the family. An investigation would start immediately, but she needed to get a feel for the missing teenager. Was she a runaway? Was she under the influence of drugs or alcohol? Were there problems at home? Had she done it before? Did she have a boyfriend? She was also extremely concerned that this was yet another incident concerning the Derwent Academy.

Preliminaries had painted a picture of a girl not given to rash decisions, with no history of troublemaking and no apparent desire to leave the area. There had been vociferous denials of drug use, but all parents would say that. Last sightings had been at the fair on the same night

Kelly had been there sipping glühwein with Johnny. Statements had already been taken from immediate family, neighbours and friends, and work was being started on rounding up as many people as possible at the Derwent Academy. It was a daunting task. There were some eight hundred kids at the school, and then the staff on top of that.

Rob accompanied her. He brought up the Tony Blackman case. Faith Shaw was one of Blackman's students, and she was also the best friend of Sadie Rawlinson, who'd reported her missing. Rob was asking to be moved from the Blackman case to concentrate on the missing girl instead.

'Emma could take my place, guv.'

'So when you say "uncomfortable", Rob, what exactly do you mean?' Kelly drove carefully. Piles of snow had been pushed to the edge of the road, and looking at the clouds above, it seemed there was more on the way. Skiddaw sat moodily above them, covered in cloud. Kelly had been up there in rain and shine, and at the top, the chance of freezing fog was legendary. It was like being on the moon in this weather, but people still did it, as well they might: hiking wasn't something that had a season.

She thought of Johnny. The disappearance of Danny Stanton was still a mountain rescue case, and they were working round the clock to find signs of the guy. Johnny had come in soaked and freezing last night, unable to feel his fingers. They'd been searching Whinlatter Forest and had been out for almost ten hours, finding nothing.

'She's very flirtatious.'

Kelly concentrated on the road. He was talking about Sadie Rawlinson, whom she had yet to meet.

'Towards you?'

He nodded.

'She's a tricky one. What did Blackman say about her?'

'He said she planted the material, and he categorically denies assault or attempted assault. Says she was there to collect poetry.'

'Likely story. Jesus! What an idiot. What guy in 2018 invites a student to his flat for any reason at all and thinks he won't get caught out? So do you think she's playing a game? A witness should know better than to schmooze up to a police detective. It takes a lot to make you squeamish, Rob.'

'Between me and you, guv...'

'Of course it's between me and you.'

'She seems to be enjoying herself. She smiles at me a lot, and winks. You know the type. But there's something else about her. She's dangerous. I just don't think she'd act the same way with a female.'

'Really? It's that bad? What about Will?'

'He said she doesn't do it to him. I wouldn't make a fuss normally, guv. But there are times when I could be alone with her.'

'Not really; she's a minor, so she would always need a chaperone, but I guess it could happen. I'll move you,' Kelly said. 'Now tell me, what do you think of Blackman?'

'Regular guy. There's no supporting evidence that might explain finding disturbing porn on his computer.'

'There often isn't. Sometimes it's the quiet ones who surprise you. I take it he's respected at school?'

'Yes. A very popular member of staff.'

'And have you gauged the kids' reactions? Apart from the hilarious Facebook crap, I mean.'

'Mr Popular, across the board. There's one member of staff who was especially keen to support him and has given a statement about his character.'

'Who's that?'

'An English teaching colleague called Sarah Peaks.'

'Let's catch up with her at some point then,' Kelly said.

She turned off the A66 and dropped down into the town. Entering Keswick always gave her a sense of calm, despite it being for depressing reasons this time. With snow covering all the roofs, it looked like an advert for log cabin retreats in Canada. Walkers clogged the roads, as they always did, but at this time of year they were the serious kind: older, wiser, better kitted out, and ruddy-looking. They wore sturdy boots and expensive climbing jackets, carried poles and generally meant business. There was an absence of what might be considered the summer trade: families with dogs and kids, clamouring for ice cream and boat trips. The winter visitors were the real deal.

The Shaw family lived on a quiet road on the outskirts of town. Kelly parked outside, turned off the engine and sighed.

Rob looked at her.

'I hate this bit,' she said.

'But you're amazing at it.'

Kelly was embarrassed; he really didn't need to dump praise upon her. She did her best in these emotionally charged moments. Most of the time, missing persons in the Lakes were found, and her department never got involved, but she had every right to direct sensitive cases from the inside. It wasn't London, where a dedicated missing persons team was assigned cases like this.

It was northern Cumbria, where there was one team for burglaries, domestics and murders alike, and that was what Kelly loved so much about the job. In London, she'd been a tiny cog, working with thousands of other tiny cogs to make a huge wheel turn, never really knowing if the mechanism was working properly. Here, she *was* the wheel. She oversaw everything. HQ thought it was time she sat behind a desk, but she fully intended to remain in the middle of things.

The house was pretty standard for the area: a stone and slate terrace, with pretty windows and stunning views of the surrounding northern fells. The air was freezing but fresh and escaped in cloudy geysers from their mouths. They retrieved coats from the boot and put them on. Kelly rubbed her hands. The snow showed no sign of ending; even though it was clear today, more was forecast for tonight.

They walked to the door and Rob rang the doorbell.

An elderly woman answered. 'Can I help you?' she said. 'You look like the police.'

Kelly didn't react; she was a professional in the art of the poker face. Liar dice was the one game that Johnny couldn't beat her at.

'You're right,' she said. 'We're here to see Mr and Mrs Shaw. May we come in?'

The woman stood back and nodded. She wore an old-fashioned pinny, and the house smelled of cooking. Kelly assumed that she was a relative or friend performing the tasks that the anxious parents weren't up to.

'And you are?' Kelly asked.

'I'm Faith's nan.' The woman's face didn't move as she talked.

Kelly felt her stomach tighten. At least the family had some support; some of them never did, and it was somehow harder to leave them after the statements were written and signed and the door closed. Close-knit families seemed to fare better.

She introduced herself and Rob. The woman nodded and wiped her hands on her pinny, holding one out in greeting. 'Call me Nanna P.' She had a solid handshake that smacked of matriarchy.

'And where do you live, Nanna P?' Kelly asked.

'Down the road. Number forty.'

They followed her into the hallway. The house was quiet and Kelly felt the burden of bad news bearing down on her. Rob always seemed to know when to make himself smaller or bigger, depending on the occasion. He looked smaller now, and Nanna P had decided to trust them.

'In here,' she said.

Nanna P went in first, and Kelly heard weeping. Inside the room were two members of the liaison team, as well as Mr and Mrs Shaw and a young boy she assumed was Michael, Faith's brother.

'More police,' Nanna P announced.

'Mr Shaw.' Kelly held out her hand. 'Mrs Shaw. May we sit down?'

She surveyed the situation and analysed the parents. If Faith Shaw didn't turn up soon, and foul play was suspected, then these two would be suspects and she had to get to know them. Both had suffered a tortured night, not knowing where their daughter was, and it had taken its toll. The young boy looked terribly lost.

'I guess you're Michael?' she said. He nodded. He had a gorgeous face, innocent and alive, but the eyes were pleading; they said, 'I'm scared and I don't know what to do.' Adults had enough experience to draw on when faced with shock, but kids hadn't a clue; they floundered around and sank quickly unless someone stepped in and showed them how to cope. Kelly made a note to talk to the team about him. He should be with relatives or friends. He really shouldn't be subjected to the parents' emotional roller coaster.

She turned back to Maggie and Colin Shaw.

'I know you were expecting me. I wanted to come and introduce myself, and Rob here. It's important you have faces to put to names. I need to find out everything you can tell me about your daughter: her routine, her friends, her hobbies. I need to figure out a way of piecing together where she's gone.'

'I know she's not coming back. I know it!' Mrs Shaw broke down and sobbed. 'We were talking about strangers last night.' Her head went into her hands and she buried it in her lap. Mr Shaw looked panicked and went to help his wife, but clearly he had no idea what to do. This was the bit that got out of hand very quickly if not handled properly.

'I'll give you a moment,' Kelly said. She nodded to the liaison officer in charge and indicated that she wanted to talk. They went into the hallway and closed the door behind them.

'Why's the boy still here?'

'He insisted. He seems a savvy lad. Blames himself partly, because Faith was so stressed out about him causing a fuss and going off on his own. He reckons she'd be all right if he hadn't upset her.'

'Is this standard for the mother?' Kelly referred to Maggie Shaw's mini breakdown. In under five minutes, she had sussed out Faith's immediate family, and she was quickly realising that Michael might be the one to rely on. Youth still held onto a sense of hope in the direst of moments, she thought. Only moments ago, she'd assumed Michael to be cocooned in fear, but underneath Michael's self-imposed duty to stand by his parents, she could see that he had a core of steel, which could come in very handy indeed.

'Yes. She's handling it very badly; pretty standard stuff for a mum, really.'

'What about Dad?'

'He blames himself, and her mates.'

'Interesting. Why?'

'They're lowlifes, allegedly.'

'In his opinion?'

'Michael agrees.'

'Really? Tell me more.'

As they stood in the corridor whispering, they could still hear Mrs Shaw sobbing and the low tones of the other liaison officer trying to soothe her.

'The family only moved here five years ago, and Faith's life was hell for a while. She was bullied by the gang that she now calls friends. Supposed to be water under the bridge, but neither Mum nor brother trusts them.'

'Bullied?'

'That's what the parents said.'

Kelly's brow knitted. 'Sadie Rawlinson included?'

The officer nodded.

'The brother's a smart cookie. Can I talk to him?' Kelly asked.

'Sure, I'll go and get him.'

They went back in. The officer told Michael that the detective would like a word, and suggested going upstairs for some peace and quiet. 'Maybe you could show her Faith's bedroom?'

Kelly shot Rob a look: he understood that he was expected to stay and smooth the edges, as well as taking notes.

Michael looked up and nodded. 'Sure.' He headed for the stairs; Kelly followed, accompanied by the liaison officer.

'You're being very brave, Michael. You seem older than twelve. I gather you're off school at the moment.' She eased in.

'I'm going in tomorrow,' he said.

'Really?'

Michael nodded. 'I can't stand all the crying. No one's going to find Faith by sitting around.'

Kelly nodded. 'You're right.'

He led her to Faith's room, with the other officer as a chaperone; it was standard procedure when dealing with a minor. The room was what she envisaged for any teenage girl, and she thought of Johnny's daughter, who was the same age. Josie demanded twinkly lights and accessories worthy of Pinterest, and changed her mind monthly. Faith's room was a mixture of greys and creams, with fluffy cushions, the obligatory fairy lights, and framed photos of friends and family. Kelly asked Michael to tell her about the photos and the people in them. He named them all, adding a little background each time, a detail that touched Kelly immensely.

'Did you fall out, Michael?' She smiled warmly, indicating that it was all right to admit negative things about somebody who was missing. He nodded.

'Not really, I got into a fight and she was angry with me until I told her it wasn't my fault. I hate being treated like a baby. She was with Luke Miles when they found me; he's friends with Justin, who looked after me.'

'How did he look after you?'

'He stayed with me until Luke and Faith came, with Sadie, and the four of them went off together.'

'Can you remember the time?'

'I guess it was nearly time for Dad to collect us, so about 9 o'clock.'

'Do you mind if I write these names down? My memory isn't that great.' Kelly found a pad and pencil and Michael nodded.

'But you're a detective. You have to have a good memory, don't you?'

'You're absolutely right, Michael, and my memory is spot on for faces and what happens when, but when it comes to loads and loads of names, I need to write them down.'

'Hmm, I would too. I'm good at history dates. I think it's like being a detective because we had to work out if Guy Fawkes was guilty or not. Test me.'

'OK… What year was the Gunpowder Plot?'

'Sixteen oh five.'

'Impressive. I have no idea if you're right, but I'll take your word for it. And do you think Guy Fawkes was fairly treated?'

Michael thought. 'He shouldn't have tried to kill the politicians, but I can understand why he did it. The Catholics were tortured and executed, so it's no wonder really, is it?'

'Well that's admirable, but detectives don't work out if a crime is moral; just if one has occurred and who did it. To decide what's right and what's wrong, you'd need to be a judge.'

'But I don't like their wigs.'

'That's a dilemma.'

'Doesn't it mean anything, then, if you understand why someone has done something, even if it's illegal?' he asked.

'Do you know someone who has?'

'No.' It was said quickly.

Kelly sat on Faith's bed. Michael continued to tell her about his sister and the fact that she didn't like being told what to do; about how their dad had told her not to wear the short top, but when he saw her at the fair, she had it on. She reckoned he would make a good detective indeed.

'That's tricky,' she said. 'Do you think Faith had had enough and ran away?'

'No. She hates being cold, and she didn't take much make-up. She's also got a thing for Luke Miles.'

Chapter 17

Johnny led the third large-scale search for Danny Stanton in two days. The Coledale Horseshoe had been mapped and separated into grids. The route was popular with hikers all year round, and took in the stunning peak of Grisedale Pike, one of Johnny's favourites. It was something to do with the severe ascent, along the spine, through the forest and up and up, as if on a stairway of heather and rock, until finally the view was revealed at the top, over Derwent Water and beyond.

The route could take in as few as four Wainwrights, but some people did eight, or even ten; it was all dependent upon the climber. Facebook hadn't hinted at which option Danny was attempting; his sister had just said that he'd mentioned a horseshoe, and that was what he'd been searching on his computer. His car had been found by a copper from Kendal, and his tent was missing, along with basic supplies and personal items, so it looked likely that he'd gone out and failed to return. There was a possibility that he was taking his time, perhaps bagging one peak per day, but there had been no Facebook posts since the one on Sunday, and that didn't sound right for a guy who loved social media. Johnny and his colleagues had racked their brains for possible remote areas where he could have got into difficulty, or simply be camping on his merry own without phone signal.

The other nightmare was that half the fells were covered in snow. Given the amount of white stuff that had been dumped since Sunday, anyone falling down a gully or crag could be completely covered and undiscovered until a thaw. The chopper had heat-seeking equipment, but it had to be low to the ground, and they didn't really have a starting point; it would be like trying to find a shell at the bottom of Wastwater. Infrared thermal cameras had been used in the Alps to detect avalanche victims, but the kit was bloody expensive, and they were all volunteers working for a charity. The ultimate would be a drone fitted with a thermal-imaging camera, but that was a long way off. Besides, they'd need a part of the body to be poking out of the snow for it to work. For now, good old-fashioned shouting, blowing whistles and banging metal objects would have to do.

Should Danny Stanton have visited the mountain rescue website, he might have read the section where they advised not to climb alone, and also the part that suggested that if you ignored such advice, you should buy and use a transceiver – and remember to bring spare batteries. It didn't take long to work out that the young man was too busy on Facebook to check any safety concerns. Just because the Cumbrian peaks were thousands of feet lower than the likes of Mont Blanc and the Matterhorn, people thought them benign. Johnny had seen proof otherwise.

They settled on the area around Crag Hill and Grasmoor, two peaks both bigger than Grisedale Pike. Though not taxing for a beginner – and a young, healthy one at that – they were still buggers if the weather came in.

Johnny knew of several places where the path went off in different directions and could confuse a visitor. It was the type of hike he and Kelly would do in spring or autumn. He didn't mind the snow, but there were other places he preferred when facing icy patches and drifts. Crag Hill, especially, had three sections of scrambling, with drop-offs.

They wrapped up warm and checked their supplies. There was no point calling in a chopper; the best way was to drive through Whinlatter Forest over the pass then turn south onto the road to Crummock Water, parking on the road. They were all used to speedy climbs; that was their bread and butter. They weren't sightseeing today. Whinlatter Pass was open, but the gritters couldn't get that high, so the searchers relied on the four-wheel power of their two Land Rovers. Voices carried slowly on heavy, snow-laden air, and the mood was low. They'd agreed a grid pattern, and they were to spread out and meet back at the vehicles in the next hour and a half. They checked their radios, as well as mobile phones, as signal was intermittent, and set off in pairs.

Johnny concentrated on the patch of snow before him, looking for anything out of the ordinary: drag marks, kit, clothing or tracks. People who were severely dehydrated had been known to strip even in extreme cold because their brains told them they were hot. An injured person, alone and scared, might also make rash decisions and stupid mistakes, getting lost and wandering off a sharp edge. Enquiries had turned up no answer as to whether Danny had ice attachments on his boots, or an axe.

There was no one about and the sky was dark, despite it being just past midday. Johnny heard a dog bark and squinted in the direction the noise came from. He made out a lone walker and raised his hand. They were about six hundred metres up; only a local would be up here walking the dog in weather like this. The canine bounded towards him and he bent to stroke it. Its owner beamed broadly, and Johnny recognised him as one of the local farmers, a regular at certain watering holes in Pooley Bridge. These old-timers could sink six pints and be up on the fells for dawn without batting an eyelid, and they all lived till gone ninety.

They shook hands. 'What you doing up here?' the farmer asked.

'Young guy got himself lost,' Johnny said.

The man shook his head and scratched his beard.

'Bloody bad do is that. Hope you find him, lad.'

Johnny thanked the farmer and ploughed on, shouting at intervals with his partner. They heard nothing.

They walked for the full hour and a half, taking in two more fells, but turned up nothing: no equipment, no tracks, no noises and no clues. They hoped their colleagues might have fared better, but by the time they all returned to the vehicles, nobody had heard or seen any signs of life, though they'd all seen the farmer strolling around as if he was on a shopping trip in the Arndale Centre.

Another search was over. If Danny Stanton was in the confines of the Lake District National Park, his time was running out.

Chapter 18

'Morning, all. We're splitting into two today. I want half on Tony Blackman and half on Faith Shaw. Two days is too long for a fifteen-year-old to be missing, and HQ is breathing down my neck. By the way, for reasons that will become clear, I'm giving the Blackman case to the girls: Kate and Emma, it's yours. I'm sure you'll figure it out.'

Kelly had a habit of being cryptic when it merited it, and today was one such occasion. Kate and Emma shrugged. Everybody knew that Rob hadn't done a bad job; there must be more to it, and they'd find out soon enough.

'First, though, before we discuss Mr Blackman, Kate has some information I think you should all hear.'

'Morning, everyone. You all know that my girls go to the Derwent Academy. I've made some inquiries and have had it confirmed that in the last four years there have been two suicides of students at the school, both drug-related, and one of them was a missing person for three days before she was found.'

Glances were exchanged. The suicide of Jenna Fraser was still palpably fresh in their minds. Kids killing themselves was not something that should pop up week on week.

'Neither came to the attention of the serious crime unit; they were ruled straightforward suicides and investigations weren't necessary,' Kate continued.

'I know what you're thinking. I'm thinking it too,' Kelly said.

'*Were* they suicides?' Rob asked.

'Exactly. Physically and legally, yes, there's no dispute; the coroner ruled suicide on both. However, I think I want to know more about why healthy teenagers are killing themselves and it's not considered criminal.' The details popped up on a screen behind Kelly, and she swung round to point at the photos of the two children: Laura Briggs and Jake Trent. Seeing them alive made them real, and the room was silent.

'What about those hideous games that are sweeping the internet now? The ones where a kid gets involved in a game of dare, and the activities become more and more dangerous until finally the last one is suicide?' Will looked at Kate, who nodded.

'I've heard of games like that; they involve a highly encrypted Snapchat or Instagram account, which can close and reopen. They're more prevalent in places like Canada and Australia than here.'

'Jesus.' Kelly folded her arms. 'Would your kids fall for that shit, Kate?'

'It's not a case of stupidity; the software is manipulative and clever. We're talking raised stakes set against self-esteem and face-saving. Adolescents classically lack the natural fear that would put them off, and at the same time need to prove something more than at any other time in their lives. The accounts are also so well encrypted that agencies find them almost impossible to crack.'

'It sounds like we'll be spending some time at the school. I want all this looked into, but subtly. There's been no crime here; it's all background on a culture that could have impacted Faith Shaw's mental state. I spoke to the head; she's been there for sixteen years, an old sweat. Her take on it is that kids commit suicide and they go to school, and it's pure coincidence. Both cases were to do with issues outside of the school gates.'

'But the school is the common denominator.'

'Exactly. She's happy for us to dig around. Right, on to the Blackman case. Rob?'

'It seemed like an open-and-shut case: girl reports teacher for attempted sexual assault, and upon further investigation we find disturbing child porn on his hard drive. He's been charged and the wheels are in motion with the CPS.'

'But?' Kelly interrupted.

'It's a big but. They're serious charges – indecent images of children along with the attempted assault – and the CPS did think it was good to go. However, now there are question marks over the main witness, who's frankly a liability. I certainly don't feel comfortable, given the charges, being potentially left alone with her.'

'Hence why Emma and I are taking over?' Kate asked.

Rob nodded. 'I've no doubt whatsoever that if the images hadn't been found on his computer, the CPS wouldn't touch the assault case.'

'So what have we got so far? The images were graded by the Child Abuse Image Database?'

'Yep, that saves a potential jury from having to look at them.'

'OK. So forensically, it's his computer? Has he admitted to owning it?'

'Yes, but he'll plead innocent to possession of the images.'

'Can we somehow find out when they were downloaded?'

'It's still with the expert in Manchester.'

'The one who sits in a dark room like a mole and examines hard drives for a living?'

'Yes. As I mentioned, there are certain firewalls in place that he's never come across before. I'm on his case daily, sometimes twice a day, and he very patiently updates me if he's found anything, which so far has been little help. These things can't be rushed.'

'What about the technical savviness of Mr Blackman?'

'He swears he's computer illiterate, but it's a difficult one to prove. It all depends on what a potential jury makes of him. He comes across as a nice guy.'

'Jack the Ripper was probably spoken of in much the same way,' Kelly said. 'Can your Manchester mole tell us the origin of the photos?'

'Yes, though again it will take time. It's a lengthy process, but the CPS is inundated with cases like this all the time.'

'How did he explain having Dale Prentice's details?'

'He said he'd followed the case closely since writing a poem about mines in the area and coming across it as part of his research.'

'So purely humanitarian, then?'

Rob spread his hands.

'What about the details of the other children?' Kelly referred to her iPad.

'He gave plausible reasons for all the information, but they need to be checked out. For example, he said that he was worried about safeguarding issues and he's the coordinator in school for liaising with outside agencies.'

'Interesting. Has that been verified?'

'Yes.'

Kelly made a mental note to check up with social services about Dale Prentice. It niggled her that his history could be easily accessed. Meanwhile Rob said he'd do the same for the others.

'So let's talk about Sadie Rawlinson. Was she photographed after she made the complaint?'

'Yes, guv. There were no discernible marks, no sign of a struggle, and her statement has changed a couple of times.'

'Christ, that's all we need. Kate and Emma, get her in again. This might be a waste of everyone's time, not to mention CPS money. I've got one more bomb for you: it turns out that Sadie Rawlinson is Faith Shaw's best friend. I have that on good authority from another teacher, who wants to make a second statement about her good friend Tony Blackman. She requires anonymity, so I invited her here.'

Eyebrows were raised.

'Who is it? Why would she want anonymity?'

'She's called Sarah Peaks.'

Chapter 19

Nedzad Galic stared at his son. The information had been relatively easy to come by and he'd happily have paid more for it. St Bees was a grotty little seaside town on the west coast of Cumbria, and it was fucking cold. The beach looked white and barren and the sand whipped up with the wind. He'd seen snow in Sarajevo, but there it was accompanied by blue sky, not this dreary grey blanket that he'd got used to in Britain. But he wasn't here for the weather. He was here for his son.

The nursery sat back from the beach, on a quiet street next to a housing estate. He had not intended to be here for the actual job, but he couldn't help himself. He'd seen scores of photographs taken of the little boy as he was dropped off. On Tuesdays, they visited a local burger joint after pick-up time, and he'd watched from across the road in a van as his son was fed crap from a box. He wanted to hold him, to kiss him, to take him home where he belonged. The very thought of being apart from him twisted his insides and delivered such pain that his heart raced and he thought he might not be able to breathe.

The journey to where he was now had been long and arduous. He thought back to the night he'd lost Jovana. He'd trusted the lorry driver with their safety, paying ten thousand pounds to make the journey. The plan was that they would be taken to a safe house in London, but the lorry had carried on for another five hours after passing through the Channel Tunnel. By the time he'd figured out his mistake, it was too late, and all he could do was beg the driver to take Jovana somewhere safe.

He'd been forced to fight for his life, naked, with no weapons, as a circle of men betting and drinking beer laughed and threw things at him. He only made his escape because the man charged with watching him overnight was a weakling with no brain. It hadn't taken him long to find Jovana, but they'd had to leave their son at the hospital. Nedzad had always vowed he'd return for him, and now he'd found him.

The woman who called herself his foster mother carried him out of the nursery and Nedzad started his car. The man he'd entrusted to carry out the job was a local. He was a shadow who lived on the edge of society, and a regular courier for Nedzad's goods. So far he had proved himself loyal and, more importantly, ruthless.

Nedzad watched as the woman's car pulled out and headed for the burger restaurant. It would only take five seconds to kidnap the boy. His man had brought a gypsy woman with him to do the talking. When the foster mother's attention was distracted, the boy would be grabbed and he would have his son back. He'd seen it done many times before in Sarajevo, when kidnappings were commonplace during the war. The most important element was holding your nerve.

A light rain began to fall, and Nedzad switched on his windscreen wipers. He stayed close to the vehicle in front, which in turn stayed close to the foster mother as she pulled into the car park. Nedzad had already checked for

CCTV. There was a camera on the corner of the building, and his man had come here in the early hours and smashed it.

The gypsy couple parked near her and got out of their vehicle, chatting about something unimportant. The foster mother got a pushchair out of the boot and fiddled with it. This was their cue. She'd left the child's door open, and the gypsy woman went to her and asked her a question. The foster mother had her back to the car, having turned around to reply to the woman. Surprise was everything: she'd never expected to be asked a question at that moment, she wasn't expecting danger, and she was sure that her son was still in his car seat.

–

Dale's foster mother turned back to the pushchair and got it set up, then went to fetch the boy. His seat was empty. She paused for a second, thinking he must have somehow wriggled out of it. She called his name and searched under the seats and in the boot.

'Dale?' she repeated over and over again. She walked around the car several times before panic began to set in. She ran now, and looked under the vehicle and around her in the car park. The woman she'd been speaking to was gone, so she couldn't ask her for help.

Then she remembered the phone call from the police asking if everything was normal and if Dale was all right. A fire hit her gut and she felt like throwing up. She couldn't remember if the woman had got out of a car. She'd been gently humming to herself and so hadn't heard any vehicles arrive. She screamed to a man who walked out of the restaurant with a box.

'Help me! Help me! My son! He's gone!'

'All right, love. All right.' He asked her to calm down and got out his phone to call the police. Then he looked around the car park and offered to search for her baby son.

'How old is he?'

'Two.' She began to sob.

'He'll be all right, you'll see. He'll have toddled off somewhere. Wait here, I'll ask in the restaurant.'

He left her and she ran to the edge of the car park. The road ran along one side of it, but it was deserted. There was traffic on the main road in the distance, but she had no idea what she was looking for. Tears blurred her vision.

'Dale!' she screamed at the top of her voice.

People came out of the restaurant and comforted her until the police arrived, by which time twenty minutes had passed and the woman was hysterical and hyperventilating.

Chapter 20

'Craig? Good to hear from you. How's Barrow?'

Kelly had worked with DCI Craig Lockwood on a case a couple of years back. It had ended in the conviction of an old flame of hers, and her sister for one wouldn't let her forget it. He was calling from Barrow-in-Furness.

'It's still here, Kelly. This side of Black Coomb is closer to God, you know that.'

'I don't believe in God, Craig, you know *that*.'

He laughed. 'I've got some information that you might find interesting. I saw the appeal for your missing girl on TV last night.'

'Faith Shaw?'

'Yes. It said she was last seen at the charter fair in Keswick, is that correct?'

'As far as we know. She was supposed to meet her dad at nine thirty, but she never showed. Her mates said she went to the loo and never came back.'

'Last week, one of my team interviewed an eight-year-old girl from Dalton who had a nasty experience with a man at the fair there.'

'What sort of nasty experience?'

'She was cornered by him behind a trailer. She was unhurt, but pretty shaken up. He offered her a pill; she said he used the word "sweetie". The officers looking into it made an identification, and they reckon they got the guy: he was sheepish and apologetic, like they always are, and they let him off with a warning. He works for one of the rides, no fixed address. His name is Bobby Bailey.'

'But travellers rarely have previous…'

'That's what I was thinking, but we got his prints and he's pinged up for doing time for various sexual misdemeanours. He's on the sex register, Kelly.'

'What's his record?'

'Indecent exposure, possession of indecent images, and his last one was attempted rape, but that one wasn't prosecuted; the parents dropped the charges.'

'Christ. Can you send the girl's statement to me, as well as Bailey's record?'

'He's clean at the moment, and I spoke to a previous parole officer who said, and I quote, "He's a missing kid waiting to happen." I know the woman who organises the fair every year, from way back. She takes in waifs and strays from all over the place, including Bobby Bailey. She gave me bullshit about his background, but I've got nothing to trade and she's a good source.'

'What about the sweeties? She could be closed down.'

'Exactly, I'm working on her and I've got eyes on him.'

'I'll action a further interview from here, I might be mistaken, but I don't think he's on our list for the Keswick interviews.'

'Makes sense. These guys sleep all day and prowl all night. You probably know this, but the fair's moved on to St Bees now; they'll be there for three days.'

'Thanks, Craig, I owe you one.'

'So what have you got? Any sightings?'

'Nothing. There's been a few suicides up here recently – well, over the last four years; I call that recent – and I'm looking at the drug angle.' She told him about Jenna Fraser, and Craig audibly winced down the phone.

They chatted for a little longer, about what they'd been up to and their plans for Christmas, and swapped theories about where a fifteen-year-old could go, alone and in the snow. It was good to catch up, and Kelly wished she had time to do it more often. She'd had a soft spot for Craig when they worked together.

After she hung up, she sat and thought about Maggie and Colin Shaw, and how awful their Christmas would be if they hadn't found Faith by then. She wondered if Michael had already bought her a Christmas present, and what it was.

St Bees was over an hour away, but inside her patch. The nearest station would be Egremont, and she thought they could perhaps liaise with Whitehaven and send some uniforms to look up Bobby Bailey, who she was now staring at on her computer. He gave her the creeps, but that was only her subjective first impression, which was judgemental and unfair. He was forty years old but looked sixty; he had missing teeth and greasy hair, and all the telltale signs of alcohol and substance abuse: dark circles under the eyes, puffy and yellowing skin, deep wrinkles from dehydration. She zoomed in on his eyes: they were vacant, hollow and… sad. He had the eyes of someone who had given up a long time ago.

She prepared an email and looked up who to send it to in Whitehaven and Egremont. Then she searched the file for the statements taken by Keswick police. The appeal to the public had brought in hundreds of statements from people who were at the fair, but none had any information regarding where Faith had gone after her reported visit to the Portaloo at the fair; if indeed she had ever gone there at all.

Kelly scrolled through the reports. Only three people remembered seeing Faith, and she realised that all girls that age looked the same: tight jeans, tight top, baggy coat and loads of make-up. No wonder Faith didn't exactly stand out. She made a note of the three fair workers who'd given statements, and also confirmed that Bobby Bailey had not been questioned; he'd slipped through the net like so many of these fairground hands. No one could give them a current employee list; it just didn't work like that. The workers were like ghosts in the night.

Next she read the statement given by Sadie Rawlinson on the night itself. Sadie had apparently sat in the Shaws' lounge, sipping tea and crying noisily. Much like she had sobbed her way through her initial interview accusing Tony Blackman. Her statement was followed by those of Luke Miles and Justin Cain. All three said the same thing: Faith had gone to the toilet.

Kelly thought about this.

She cast her mind back to many nights out she'd had with mates, drunken or not, and tried to remember whether she'd ever announced her intention to visit the lavatory. She might tell one friend and another could overhear, but to tell the whole group? She needed to find out the relationship between these kids: were they friends, or more? If Luke Miles was a potential love interest, like Michael said, there was no way Faith would let him in on her bladder requirements.

So her next problem was: if the kids were lying, why?

Chapter 21

Kelly stopped at an off-licence to pick up a bottle of wine. As she parked, she spotted a group of teenagers hanging about with sod all to do but show off and harass passers-by. She wondered why they were standing here in the freezing cold instead of watching a movie indoors. Maybe it wasn't cool to watch movies any more. It was depressing, and reminded her of London, where teenagers gathered in pods, waiting for trouble, because they had nothing else to do.

She kept her head down as she walked past them. But she still caught their attention, and one of the boys made a crude comment involving the C-word. Kelly swung round. Something in her eyes and her body language made the boy's shoulders drop just a little and his swagger deflate. She squared up to him and the gang parted. One by one, they walked away and across the street, looking back occasionally to see if she was watching them.

Kelly went into the shop, her heart racing. She grabbed a bottle of red and examined the label. She'd never under-stood how it was legal to whack on an extra fiver per bottle if your shop straddled a corner, but they somehow got away with it. She took another one and put them on the counter. She paid by card and left. The boys had gone.

Johnny was out tonight, meeting a mate in the pub. Kelly fancied doing the same, but couldn't think of anyone to call. She wasn't in the mood for male company, and that surprised her. She'd always had plenty of male friends, but recently she'd begun to think about her girlfriends she'd left behind in London. Her only female companions here were her mother, her sister and her colleagues. The fact brought her downward spiralling mood even lower. The two most prominent women in her life were growing ever distant: her mother because of the awkwardness that had developed between them since Kelly had found out the truth about her father; and her sister because they'd never got on. The uncomfortable feeling of being a misfit that plagued her from time to time hung about her shoulders and she wished she could swat it away like a pesky fly in summer.

She had once believed that at some point, the childhood squabbles with Nikki would stop. She'd been wrong. The news that John Porter wasn't her father after all made her even less keen to see her half-sister. She also didn't trust herself not to let the secret out. The smug satisfaction she would gain from it was petty but potentially delicious, and she had to stop herself thinking about it. She remained convinced that Nikki should never know, partly out of respect for her mother and Ted, but also because it was none of her sister's goddamn business.

Wendy Porter had crumbled when pushed by her daughter, and confirmed Kelly's suspicions about her paternity. Kelly couldn't decide which was worse: the fact that her mother had had a torrid affair, the fact that she'd tricked her husband into thinking that Kelly was his, or the fact that Kelly now had a new dad. Ted didn't know that he was her biological father, and Kelly had been close to calling him several times recently to tell him. But she still didn't know how to broach the topic.

And she was still full of anger.

It had taken her months to identify the emotion, and the root of her recent angst. Johnny told her that it was a process, like grief. The thought that she was going through some kind of mental healing irritated her: it implied that she wasn't in control, and it made her sound weak, like her sister. It was as if she was looking for something that was missing, but she didn't know what it was. She wasn't generally in the habit of analysing her own feelings, but recently she'd found herself hanging around Kate's desk, asking her about her kids, and asking Emma what she was doing at the weekend. She'd become emotional and it didn't feel comfortable. She'd even taken Emma for a drink and introduced her to her childhood friend, Andy. As it turned out, her not-so-reliable pool partner had fallen for Emma and they were now inseparable; another friend down.

Her life had changed, and for once, she didn't know what to do about it. Johnny told her she needed to look after herself better and be more selfish. Kelly thought this concept ludicrous, and told him so.

'You're missing the point,' he'd said.

'What?'

'You always act in other people's best interests, not your own. The time will come when you'll run out of steam. You need to put yourself first. If you don't, there'll be nothing left when you need it.'

Kelly had laughed loudly. 'Imagine if Nikki heard you say that!'

'Instead of thinking about Nikki's reaction all the time, how about ignoring it and moving on, for your own sanity?'

Kelly was stunned, not only by Johnny's very grown-up lecture, but also by the paradox that seemed to encapsulate her relationship with her sister and mother. It would appear that she'd got it wrong, and that was a hard pill to swallow. The problem was that trying to follow Johnny's advice had left her chunks of time to fill with philosophising, and she didn't like it. She hadn't seen Nikki for at least three weeks, but no one seemed to mind. Her mother never mentioned it, and Matt, Nikki's husband, had stopped calling her every time his wife had a mini breakdown. She was finally beginning to understand that it was all right to avoid those people in life who caused discord. She was getting old, she thought.

When she considered the way Johnny lived his life, she saw that he did stuff his own way and she never judged him for it. Refusing to give up his dream of the Lakeland 100 was a good example. He was also still planning to buy a boat to moor on Ullswater. Kelly tried to follow his advice and started by distancing herself occasionally from her mother's hospital treatment. She had a tendency to take over and treat everything like a project to be managed, a case, something that was helpful in her job but not in her personal life. Wendy was a case. Nikki had become a case. Josie was a case. It was an unhealthy pursuit. She had to drop it. Buying two bottles of red wine with no one to drink them with was not a good start, but Kelly didn't know what else to do. She could go for a run, but it was bloody freezing. It was too dark to do the stuff that kept her sane in summer, such as kayaking, hiking and swimming. She looked at the bottles; she didn't even really want them.

She knew what she did want, and she sighed heavily. She'd been avoiding it for too long. She wanted to go and see her mother.

As she drove, she went over and over in her head what she might ask. They hadn't discussed her lineage at length since Wendy had dropped the bombshell; or rather, since Kelly had worked it out. For days, she'd sat with piles of old photographs of her family, trawling through them, spotting differences in her jawline, in her hair, in her eyes, in the slope of her shoulders. It was a strange feeling. Her memories of John Porter hadn't been diminished, but she felt a deep sorrow that he'd been a victim of such duplicity. She questioned what Wendy had told her about him never knowing, and how plausible it was. She searched her bank of stored data – images, stories and memories in full Technicolor – and couldn't find any clue that John Porter had not truly believed her to be his own. Poor bloke.

She'd asked Johnny how he thought it might feel. He'd said he wanted to be as honest as he could, and it had sounded like a warning. He couldn't speak for all men, but to him, it would be a pretty fundamental betrayal. They'd had a discussion about infidelity. Johnny admitted to cheating on Carrie, his ex-wife, a few times. Suddenly it didn't seem so unusual. But she needed to ask Wendy if it had been a fling or something more serious. If it was the latter, it would put into doubt her whole working relationship with Ted Wallis: she simply couldn't do it.

She parked outside and took one of the bottles with her. She knocked and waited, half of her hoping that Wendy was already fast asleep in bed.

The door opened.

'Hi, love!' It was a pleasingly normal greeting, and Kelly kissed her mother with genuine affection. She held up the wine and walked through to the back kitchen.

'Are you all set for Christmas?' Wendy asked. It was something that people asked each other every year, as if Christmas was some kind of lockdown, when the world changed completely. Shelves were emptied, cupboards were stuffed, miles of tinsel was hung, and plastic wrapping consumption was higher in one two-week period than the rest of the year combined. It was all kind of crazy.

'I think so. You remember I'm on call?'

'Yes, but it's usually quiet, isn't it?'

'Usually, but we're still looking for that girl.'

'Her poor mother.'

'I know,' Kelly agreed.

Wendy closed the front door and followed her daughter into the kitchen. The house smelled of Kelly's childhood, and she caught her breath.

'I didn't really come to talk about Christmas, Mum.'

'No, I don't suppose you did. I'm surprised it's taken you so long.' Wendy took the wine and opened it, reaching up to get two glasses.

'Are you allowed?' Kelly asked. Her mother's cancer treatment had dragged on for months, but at the moment, she was relatively healthy. She was still considered terminal, and that would only change if they discovered a new treatment, but she was in good hands. Dr Yanni was world-renowned in the field and had a soft spot for her.

He was always on the lookout for new drugs, but Kelly wasn't sure that was necessarily a good thing. Her mother looked exhausted.

'It might take another minute off my life, or even a day,' Wendy said drily. Her stoicism had developed over time, it hadn't come naturally. 'Are you driving?'

'Yes, but I can have a small glass.'

The noise of the wine swirling into the glasses filled the room.

'Come on, let's sit down.'

Kelly followed her mother into the small lounge. The hospital bed had gone, as Wendy was now able to manage the stairs with a cane. That, like everything else about a long-term illness, had become normal. It was amazing how they'd all adapted, Wendy most of all.

'Have you seen him?' Kelly asked. She couldn't say his name for some reason, but she didn't have to.

'Yes.'

'Did you tell him?'

'No.'

'How long did you two, er... have, er...' Kelly struggled with the words and hated herself for it. She felt ten years old again, and awkward. She was asking her mother about her sexual habits, and it was excruciatingly embarrassing.

Wendy sipped her drink and watched her daughter.

'We used to meet up occasionally, when we could, and it lasted about five months.'

'What did you do with Nikki?' Her sister had been a toddler.

'Babysitter. Friends.'

Kelly nodded. 'How did you convince Dad I was his?'

Wendy raised her eyebrows and a curve developed either side of her mouth. Kelly looked away.

'God, sorry, Mum. I can guess that one. Are you sure? I mean, dead sure?'

'Yes.'

'Why didn't you tell me sooner? Like after Dad died?'

'I never thought it necessary until you started soul-searching and questioning everything.'

'I know, I do that a lot.'

'You need a baby.'

'No, I don't, Mum, but thanks for the advice.'

'I'm serious. You're not getting any younger; time is running out. How are things with Johnny?'

'Surely I don't need a steady relationship to get knocked up.' It was a stinging delivery. 'Sorry.'

'You're saying sorry a lot lately too. It's worrying.'

'Thanks.'

Wendy chuckled to herself.

'I just can't imagine you sneaking around, keeping all of this secret. I'm struggling to picture it,' Kelly said, playing with her hair.

'Please don't try and conjure an image. Goodness, all that huffing and puffing. I liked him.'

'What was wrong with you and Dad?'

'I don't know really. Truthfully, there wasn't one event or even an argument; it was a slow burner, and then I realised that I was unhappy, and he didn't want to discuss it. He thought having another baby would cure me of my malaise.'

'Christ, you were young enough to leave him, Mum. Why didn't you?'

'Oh Kelly, people didn't get divorced back then, well, not that I knew of. Women couldn't survive without the man's wage. There was no maternity pay like now. I was a housewife, I never worked. I couldn't have supported you.'

'What about Ted?'

'He was married with his own children.'

'And you never told him.'

'And I never told him.'

'Cheers.' Kelly raised her glass and Wendy clinked hers against it.

'I need to tell him, Mum.'

'I knew you would. But perhaps I should warn him first.'

Chapter 22

Egremont police paid Bobby Bailey a visit at St Bees. He had his head stuck under a low loader when they turned up. At first, his heart did a small flip, thinking they were onto him about his recent activities, or that they wanted to question him about the little girl in Dalton-in-Furness again. But it wasn't either of those. They wanted to know about the missing girl from Keswick.

While he was still on his back, they showed him a photograph of her. He recognised her instantly. He wouldn't forget that face in a hurry: her full lips and that distinctive sway, indicating her cocksureness, or else the fact that she'd been drinking. Sweet one, she was. He'd never seen her before and certainly couldn't recall selling her any of his finest little sweeties. He knew he would have remembered that.

'They all look the same.' It was true; they all dressed like boys, and covered up their figures. It was a crying shame.

'Can I get up?' he asked. The coppers stood aside.

He slid out from under the vehicle. He was one of the few who could always be relied upon to fix it quickly. He wiped his hands on a cloth that was stuck in his back pocket, then cupped them and blew into them. The snow had reached St Bees, and the seaside town was covered in a thick layer. Even the beach was white, and the fair had set up close to it, on a patch of corporation land that in the past was used for access to the lighthouse.

Bobby stamped his feet and gave the two coppers his attention. They asked the same stupid questions that the last lot did, except this time it was about a different piece of candy. They showed him another photo, and it was Luke, but he shook his head again. They asked him about his movements on the night of the Keswick fair, and he lied, saying he was working the generators. They asked him who else he saw; he lied again and named a few pals who'd moved on. They asked him what time he went to bed, what he did after work, who he talked to and if he fantasised about little girls.

'She wasn't little; she was fifteen, you said.'

The coppers looked at one another.

'It's underage, Bobby.'

'Didn't look it,' he muttered under his breath.

'What did you just say?'

'Nothing. On her photo; she looks older.'

'Was she behaving as though she were older?'

'Course she was, they all do.' Shit. He'd just put his foot right in it.

'So you do remember her?' The coppers looked smug.

'Well, it could have been someone like her; they all look the same, don't they?'

'No, I don't think they do. Did you see her or not?'

'Maybe. I think she might have been drunk.'

'What makes you say that?'

'Well, when she got in the car, she had to be helped.' Shit.

'What car?'

'Dunno, it was dark.' He'd said enough, he had no desire to get dragged into this one. He was an idiot.

'Who helped her into the car?'

'I dunno. There was a group of them.'

Each time they pushed him, he let slip more information. He was growing anxious.

'Fucking leave me alone. I know my rights. I'll get a lawyer.'

The uniforms nodded. 'All right, Bobby, calm down. It's just a few questions. Who pays your wages?'

'Maria.' The pieces began to fall into place in his head: they were threatening to go to his boss. 'Are you arresting me?' He jutted his chin out.

'No, Bobby, we're not. We'll leave it for now, but you might want to contact your lawyer.'

The police officers walked away and Bobby stared after them. He tried to stay calm, but he couldn't help thinking that it wasn't the last time he'd be seeing the coppers. He thought about the news reports he'd seen on TV in the pub about the missing girl. No one had mentioned a car, and that meant one thing: the police were either withholding the information, or they didn't know. And if they didn't know, then it wouldn't be long before they came back and pushed him for more details.

He was so angry with himself for letting such a vital detail slip that he kicked the side of the thirty-ton lorry, and then jumped up and down because it hurt like hell. He swore loudly and decided to walk to the pub. The axle was fixed, he wasn't needed until tonight, and he needed to think.

He smiled as he headed off along the seafront. The coppers thought him a lowlife; travellers, fairground workers, vagrants, gypsies – call them what you wanted, none of them were loved up with the rozzers. That said, it could work to his advantage, in that it would be assumed he was an unreliable witness, and so he could change his story and say he'd made a mistake.

Yep, that was what he would do.

The air was freezing and the beach looked like it was covered in salt; it was weird, and something you didn't see every day. He stopped to take a picture on his phone, and then remembered that he'd done the same on the night of the Keswick fair, when the girl had got into the car. As he walked, he scrolled through his photos. He went too far and there was a picture of the little girl in Dalton: nice. He went forward again and found the most recent ones from Keswick. There she was. She was made for a bit of action, she was. Her tits barely stayed in her top and the boys around her couldn't take their eyes off them. Another photo showed her from behind. He had been sorely tempted to follow them, but he'd had work to do. His contact from Manchester to meet. Nedzad had been good to him, giving him generous cuts, and it was always wise to stay on the right side of someone who looked like a mean motherfucker.

He'd managed to source some little blue angels from the Bosnian that were worth a fortune if he could shift them to the kiddies. Roxies. It wasn't often he came across them, but when he did, they sold like candyfloss. Crushed and snorted, or, by the serious smackheads, dissolved and injected, they offered highs like the purest heroin. The comedown was vicious, but he didn't give a fuck about that. Shifting them had distracted him for a while, until that posh twat had called him, terrified, not knowing what to do. It was down to Bobby to clear up again, and the good-looking ballsack dripping in Mummy and Daddy's money owed him big-time. The idiot was always on the lookout for packets of K2. Fuck that. He had no idea how heavy the pigs had got on that stuff. It'd killed a couple of kids in the USA, and now every drug squad in the UK had taken it upon themselves to wipe it off the streets. It was easier to source Xanax or Vicodin.

If the coppers found out the girl had been spiced, it could change everything.

Chapter 23

Luke Miles reminded Kelly of an all-American jock. He was tall, tanned, square-jawed and muscular, with a wicked smile. He lived with his parents in an enormous pad on the shore of Derwent Water, just outside Keswick, tucked away from the road; Kelly reckoned it must be worth a couple of million quid. He was cocky and confident, clearly comfortable in his own surroundings. It was what she had expected. In an interview room, things would be different, but she first had to determine if that was necessary. Interviewing a minor under caution could be tricky. She needed to be sure.

She and DS Will Phillips had been taken into a spacious lounge and offered hot drinks and biscuits. Mrs Miles was present; the father was at work. She sat next to Luke and leaned towards him in a protective manner. There was no history of trouble connected to the family.

First impressions showed an only child who'd been mollycoddled since birth. But when Kelly looked closer, it was a different story. She couldn't put her finger on exactly what bothered her; just that his eyes looked as though they belonged in a much older face. His statement, given on the night of Faith's disappearance in the Shaw living room, mirrored Sadie's almost to the word.

From the snippets of information they'd picked up so far, however, Kelly suspected there was more to the story.

'How well do you know Faith?' she asked.

'I met her at a party. I didn't know her very well.'

Immediately, the boy's use of the past tense made Kelly bristle. She wrote it on her pad and circled it.

'So why were you hanging out with her at the fair?'

He ran his hands through his hair. 'I said all of this in my statement.'

'I know, Luke, but a few things bother me and I'm sure you're only too happy to help.' The mother nodded and glanced at her son, who looked irritated. Kelly reckoned the boy had worked out that the detectives weren't here to make friends. He looked worried, too, and that was the point.

'If you didn't know her very well, why were you happy to help her search for her brother?' Kelly continued.

'He's a little kid. Of course I was gonna help.'

His mother beamed at him.

'Aren't you concerned that you and Sadie were the last people to see Faith? That would really bother me. I'd have to go out looking. Have you tried to find her yourself?'

Luke's mother looked at him, waiting for him to answer. He didn't.

'Was she supplied drugs on the night of the fair?'

'How would I know?' Luke had become the sum of his real age, and his swagger had departed.

'Did you know Jenna Fraser?'

'No. She was a loner.'

Mrs Miles's head swung from Kelly to her son and back again.

'What was Faith's mood like on Sunday night?'

'She was mad at her brother.'

'What was she wearing?'

Kelly darted around the subject, trying to force an inconsistency out of the boy, but he stuck to his story, until she mentioned what Bobby Bailey had told Egremont police.

'So this guy Bobby, who works for the fair…'

Straight away, Luke's demeanour changed, and he sat up and coughed into his hand. It was an epic body cue. Kelly knew that she had something. She paused, holding his gaze until he looked away.

'You know Bobby Bailey, right?'

Luke coughed again. 'Er, kind of, he hangs about, you know. He's a sort of regular feature. I don't know much about him, but some people say he deals.'

That was quite a lot of information they'd just been given. It was clear that Luke Miles was a talker, something that might come in handy in future interviews. She hadn't expected it to be so easy to coerce him into admitting that he knew Bobby. She could tell that he was panicking about the extent of her knowledge. The atmosphere in the room had turned sour, and she ploughed on.

'How did you two meet? It seems a pretty unlikely pairing given that he's a dealer.'

'I said I *thought* he dealt.'

'Luke? What are you doing hanging about with people like that?' his mother demanded.

'I don't really know him; he's just known by a lot of people. I never bought anything from him.'

'Were you offered drugs?'

'I don't know.'

'What does he sell?'

'Everything.' Luke forgot himself and laughed.

'Is it funny?'

Luke remembered who the woman in front of him was and closed his mouth. His cheeks turned pink. He was floundering now and showing signs of desperately wanting to flee the room. His mother glared at him.

'Roxies?'

Luke's mouth opened. He looked at his mother. 'I heard so.'

'Boy, horse, Special K, acid, Lucy, blow, China, hug, study buddies, ice, joker?' Kelly reeled off some of the street names for drugs that she'd researched, and it had the desired effect. Luke nodded slowly and she could tell that he was trying to work out how this middle-aged woman knew so much about the underworld. Dunderhead, she thought. It was enough to puzzle the mother into silence for a few minutes too. The longer she stayed quiet, the more they could push her son.

'Quite a market trader then. Did you see Faith talking to him?'

Luke didn't answer, so she fired another question at him.

'Did Sadie buy stuff from him?'

He was staring at her with the discomfort of a boy who knew exactly what had happened to his school friend. He nodded.

'I think she got stuff for her mum.'

'Luke! Who are these people?'

'Bobby also told us that a girl answering to Faith's description got into a car.'

'No, I don't think that's right.' It was said with real panic and accompanied by erratic head movements.

'Is it possible that Faith had been taking drugs that night and wandered off with a stranger?'

'Yes. I think it's possible.'

'Thank you. Mrs Miles, I think we might need to speak to Luke again, and if we make it formal and interview him under caution, we'll need an adult to accompany him to either Penrith or Keswick station.'

Mrs Miles nodded.

They hadn't even opened the car doors before they heard her screaming at her son. Luke Miles was in trouble.

Chapter 24

Kurt Fletcher was easy to talk to. He and Johnny sat inside the Pheasant and Gun, with the windows steamed up, surrounded by the noise of youths playing pool, the news on the TV and the jukebox. It was a kind of informal job interview really. Johnny knew that Kurt would make an excellent volunteer for the mountain rescue: he had the skills, the knowledge and the attitude. They had a steady stream of applicants, a lot of them from the cities, in love with the romantic notion of being at one with nature, and most of them were rejected. Ex-services were always welcome, and generally did well during the training, which was rigorous.

They'd spoken about it before, and recently Kurt had enquired seriously.

'No sign of the bloke who went missing up there then?'

'No. Time's running out, I don't need to tell you that,' Johnny said.

'I know. It's easily done if you're not careful. I bet he's in a B&B somewhere, next to a roaring fire, with some bird he met, and he didn't even go hiking.'

'But his car was at Revelin Moss.'

'Was it? What day was that?'

'It was found on Monday.'

'I saw a couple of cars up there on Sunday night, but I don't think they were hikers, just kids messing around.'

'What were you doing up there?'

'I'd done Grisedale Pike. I go up there when I need to think.'

'I'm sorry about what you saw, mate. It's not easy.'

Kurt nodded.

'The weather came in and I came down sharpish. But it cleared my head.'

Johnny nodded and they sipped their beer. Bursts of laughter echoed around the pub, and the landlord sat at the bar, watching his staff. He could have been a local nursing his half-pint, but Johnny knew better. He also knew that the pub profits would probably improve twofold if the landlord didn't replenish his glass so often.

'All quiet on Sunday, was it?' Johnny asked.

'Yes. I didn't see a soul, apart from those kids – though I didn't actually see them. They were playing music, probably up to other stuff too. I remember it because it kind of ruined my peace a bit, you know? It didn't sit right with my mood.'

'Glad I'm past all that.' Johnny winked. It was true. He didn't envy the young now. If social media had existed in the seventies and eighties, the shit that could have been posted on Facebook about him could have landed him in serious trouble. Josie spent hours in front of her phone in an effort to catch the perfect shot. She proudly told him, as though it was a fascinating and important fact, that Kim Kardashian took an average of three hundred selfies to capture one perfect post.

'She must get cold,' he had said. 'She's always starkers.' Even Josie found that funny.

'So you're settling up here permanently then?' Kurt nodded. Johnny wanted to know how long he could commit for; they ideally preferred a good stint on the job, say five years. He knew that Kurt had always travelled from Manchester to get his fix of the fells, but now he'd bought a little cottage near Keswick.

They'd met on the top of Scafell Pike, when Johnny was helping to carry slate up there to repair the cairn. It was a First World War memorial, and worth the effort. Kurt had offered to help, and had done so for three days. He worked in Manchester as a landscape gardener, but was desperate to relocate to Cumbria.

'Plenty of demand for your skills, mate,' Johnny said, his mind already made up.

It was true, and Kurt knew it, but a troubled ex-girlfriend had kept him in the city. He hadn't said much, but Johnny had worked out that they'd been together for a long time, until her drug addiction took over and he had to be cruel to be kind and dumped her. She'd spiralled out of control and he'd ended up looking after her anyway. Then she'd relapsed again, and Kurt had hinted on a subsequent night out that she was on her last chance.

'You still together?' Johnny asked now.

Kurt shook his head. 'I've got to leave her to it. I can't help her any more.'

'I'm sorry about that, mate,' Johnny said.

'Yeah, it's fucked up. She was beautiful, look.' Kurt took his phone out of his pocket and scrolled through his photos, stopping at one and showing it to Johnny. It was true: she was stunning.

'How old is she there?'

'That's five years ago, so she was thirty. This is her a year ago.' Kurt showed Johnny another photo.

'Christ.'

'I know. It's fucking killing her. I would've married her.'

'Why doesn't she stop?'

Drug addiction was something Johnny knew little about. They were regularly tested in the army and so he'd never bothered. He believed it was all in the mind, like alcoholics; they could stop if they really wanted to. Kurt shook his head.

'Imagine wanting something so badly that you'd kill for it. You told me once about thirst. Not regular thirst, say for a pint on a Saturday, but swollen-mouth thirst after being deprived of water for three days. You know what that feels like. What would you do for water then?'

'Anything. Are you saying it's like that? But why crave something you know is killing you? Water is vital, it doesn't kill you.'

'Because our brains are programmed to give the body everything it wants to remain happy, and when you're an addict, your brain would rather crave the drug than face withdrawal. She can't help herself. It's not a disease like fucking AA says; that's all bollocks. It's a basic biological response to introducing a mind-altering substance to the body.'

Johnny thought about what Kurt had said. It sounded very scientific. He'd never given addiction much thought. He saw addicts as losers, not victims; he simply assumed they had poor self-control. He'd never heard it explained like Kurt just had.

They sat in silence, then Johnny offered to get another pint in. The photo of Kurt's girlfriend's demise had shocked him, and he thought of Josie: at the beginning of her young life and potentially exposed to chemicals capable of frying her brain. Hard drugs seemed to have become the equivalent of nicking liquor from the drinks' cabinet in his day: everybody seemed to do it, and no one seemed to notice. Until it caused problems.

Johnny had brought people off the mountains high, spaced, stoned, cabbaged, smacked... or whatever they called it from one fad to the next. He'd had conversations with Josie, who'd laughed it off, saying that she wasn't interested. But everything changed when trying to impress your mates, and the difference between the two photos that Kurt had showed him demonstrated how quickly the poison took hold and started to rip through the body.

Kelly said drugs were rife in the Lakes. Whether it was a side effect of dealers moving out of the cities to avoid detection, or because there was fuck all else to do, it didn't really matter. They were out there, and kids as young as primary-school age were being offered them on a regular basis. The Derwent Academy had a reputation for producing zombified teens fit for nothing much but NHS prescriptions. In his day, kids had hung around the bandstand in the local park smoking fags bought in singles; nowadays, even here in the Lakes, it was something injected, and way more serious, and nobody seemed to give a flying fuck.

Kelly said there wasn't the funding to go after every smackhead in the north of Cumbria, and the sentencing wasn't worth it: the CPS focused on rehabilitation rather than detention, and they were talking about legalising drugs for private use. It was the dealers they needed to catch, and then the suppliers, but they were like ghosts, and as Kelly had proven before, big fish were slippery fuckers. It was a dark world, centred round tight gangs, capable and skilled at avoiding detection.

'So you found a place?' Johnny asked Kurt once he'd sat down with fresh pints.

'Yeah, I've been looking for something quiet. I fancied somewhere out of the way, like Borrowdale or Thirlmere, but then I saw this absolute peach only five minutes from Keswick.'

'Nice?'

'Yup. Pub down the road, and a fell at the foot of the garden.'

'Perfect.'

They sipped their drinks. The pub fell silent and all eyes turned to the TV. The landlord turned the sound on the speakers down and the TV up. There was a piece on the search for Faith Shaw.

'Concern is mounting for a missing teenager in Keswick, Cumbria. It comes as the news that a man missing in the same area for three days has been found safe and well in a guest house in Thirlwell, near Keswick.'

'I told you,' Kurt said.

'No shit!' Johnny thought of the time they'd spent searching, but it was good news; just a pity that the girl was still out there.

A photograph of Danny Stanton came up on the screen, and then the link turned to Faith. The screen filled with images of members of the wider Keswick community searching together in the snow. Some had dogs; many wore full waterproofs and others were soaked through; all were downcast and serious. A photograph of the girl accompanied the piece. No one said a word.

A statement released by the police was read out, and Johnny thought about Kelly. It urged people to come forward with information about the girl. The newsreader continued: 'The community has come together here in this northern market town just before Christmas, but hope is fading that Faith will be found safe and well, as the region has seen a nasty snap of icy conditions recently and no one could survive for long exposed to such inclement weather. The idea that she wandered off or went with someone she knows is the focus of police efforts in Cumbria at the moment, and they still hope that she will make contact.'

A photo of a small faux-leopard-skin backpack appeared on the screen and the news reader explained that it was similar to the one Faith carried. Next, a young girl, slim, with brown hair, modelled a pair of jeans, a long green jumper and a baggy khaki cargo jacket.

'Police are hoping that these items might jog somebody's memory. Faith's family are growing increasingly fearful for their daughter's safety.'

Like most of the people in the pub, Johnny was thinking of Faith's family and what Christmas would be like for them if she hadn't turned up by then. Kurt, though, was thinking of another girl's family, and the needle in her arm, her blood sticky under his hand as he tried to wake her up.

Chapter 25

Sarah Peaks glanced furtively over her shoulder. The weather meant that she could get away with wearing a woolly hat and scarf and a bulky high-collared coat. It wasn't that she was being deceitful or treacherous; it was just that she wanted no more trouble. Her association with Tony Blackman was well known enough already, and she was regarded as the friend and lover of a kiddie fiddler. It had turned nasty, and she'd begun to return to the tragic texts of her postgraduate degree with renewed melancholy. A hero treated badly, wrongdoings unpunished, and the innocent fallen. It was romantic and foolish, she knew, but it was the only thing that soothed her.

She hadn't told Tony that she was coming to see one of the detectives working on the prosecution case. He would go ballistic, and she couldn't blame him. It was a long shot. She was here to appeal to rational intelligence, and she hoped her gamble would pay off. She didn't expect much; only to give another viewpoint. Stories of young women accusing men of assault only for the case to be dropped due to unsafe evidence were gathering attention in the press. Sarah wanted to keep Tony out of prison, and though she wasn't sure she could achieve that, at least she could try. The charges were serious, and could see him on the sex offenders' register for the rest of his life, not to mention the inevitable hefty prison sentence.

Sarah had never thought that such a miscarriage of justice would happen to somebody she loved. She knew that it wouldn't be long before the police turned their attention to Tony with regard to Faith. They always looked at paedophiles when young girls went missing, and it made her guts turn over. But it was human nature: paedophile in the area, ergo, he must have done it. The sense of injustice overwhelmed her sometimes, and it took all her strength to continue with her own job and not punch Sadie Rawlinson in the face. If she ever snapped and did such a thing, she'd never work again, and Tony needed her.

She was to meet two female detectives, DI Porter and DS Umshaw, and she was unsure how she felt about this. She was betraying not only a fellow woman but a schoolgirl, suggesting that she'd made up a complex and detailed tale of despicable deceit, wholly and knowingly on purpose. She had racked her brain for a motive, but all she could come up with was that it was for kicks. Stimulation was so instant, cheap and disposable now that youngsters continually searched for bigger highs. How cool would it be to orchestrate a puppet show, ruin real lives in the process and watch the drama from afar?

It didn't sound convincing. Unless you knew Sadie Rawlinson.

There was also the problem of bias. Sarah would have to admit that yes, she had slept with Tony Blackman. That made her motivation questionable, because she had an emotional connection to the accused. The simple answer would be to lie, and she trawled through her memory to try to count up how many people actually knew. Not the kind of knowing that came from gossip and hearsay, but true knowledge that could be proven, and that number was zero. Except for Tony himself. She'd also have to find a believable story for why he was staying at hers so often. Of course, she could be an accommodating and empathetic colleague. It was a quandary, because at some point it would mean she'd have to ask him to deny, on oath, their true relationship. It was too much, but maybe she could tackle it later.

She walked up the stone steps and pushed open the large wooden door, swallowing hard. Her mouth was dry and she'd brought no water. She checked her bag for chewing gum; she found Tic Tacs and popped three into her mouth.

The sight of police uniforms increased her heart rate, and she instantly became aware of eyes upon her, as if she'd committed an offence. Just being in the vicinity of law enforcers was enough to make some people sweat, and it was happening to her. She hadn't been this nervous since the assembly she'd delivered two years ago. She wasn't a natural public speaker, even though her audience was just kids, and she'd developed a rash on her neck for days before the big day. It was only an assembly about a proposed poetry competition in support of the poppy appeal for the British Legion, a subject she could speak on for hours, but nonetheless, her adrenalin got the better of her, and it was only when it was over that her heart rate returned to normal. Tony said it was because she cared. No one seemed to notice her terror, but the physical symptoms were utterly unpleasant, and she hadn't volunteered for anything similar since.

The woman behind the desk checked her computer and said that somebody would be along to meet her soon. Her uniform was smarter up close. The jacket was more pristine and the white of the shirt purer somehow. The woman's shoes were shiny and impeccable, and her tights a perfect shade of dark grey. She almost looked like cabin crew on a major airline, but Sarah forced the thought away, as if someone might be able to read her mind, and with it, her lack of respect.

A lift opened and two women walked out. They looked serious, and tough. The younger one had long brown hair, tied back, and she was effortlessly attractive. The older one was more haggard and worn. Given the choice, Sarah would opt for the younger one to argue with. She guessed that the older one was more senior, but she was wrong, as it soon became clear that the younger woman, who introduced herself as Kelly Porter, was in charge.

Porter introduced DS Umshaw and they shook hands. Sarah was led along the corridor and into what she assumed was an interview room. It was like those she saw on TV: sparse, functional, cheaply decorated. They pulled out chairs and the two detectives explained how they conducted a formal interview. They told her that she was entitled to have a lawyer present at any time. She confirmed her address and her personal details, and finally she was asked if she'd like a drink. She said she'd love a coffee, and Umshaw left to get one for her.

'You understand, Sarah, that anything you say can be submitted as testimony and you may be summoned by the CPS to give evidence, under oath, in court?'

'Yes, I understand.' She fiddled with her fingers.

'Good. Have you spoken to a lawyer?'

'No, should I?'

'The only reason we ask is because you might, at a later date, want to check what we've discussed. Everything you tell us will be recorded and you'll sign it as a statement. None of it can be taken back.'

'What if I change my mind?'

'Facts are facts. You can change an opinion, but not a statement of truth. Of course, we can't avoid recording opinions, but facts are entered as such. That's if you have any for us.'

Sarah nodded. She knew the difference between facts and opinions.

Umshaw came back into the room with a plastic cup of coffee and placed it in front of her. She plopped a couple of sachets of sugar on the table too, and a stirrer.

'Sarah, you requested this interview yourself. Can you explain to us, and for the purposes of the tape, why you did that?'

Sarah didn't know what to say; or rather, she didn't know how to start saying what she had to say. She looked at the two women. They both sounded like locals. She herself had come to Keswick from Lincolnshire. She'd spent most weekends as a child hiking in the Lake District with her parents, and had fallen in love with the place. Her first teaching job had been in Louth, in a tiny school, and she'd scoured the *Times Educational Supplement* monthly for jobs in the Lakes. Then one came up and she applied. Property in Keswick wasn't expensive, and on her wage she could afford a three-bedroom cottage. She still hiked every weekend, and now the top of a mountain was about the only place Tony wasn't hounded.

'I believe that Tony Blackman is innocent of all charges.'

Porter watched her, and Umshaw took notes.

'And why are you of that opinion?' Porter asked.

'Half fact and half opinion.'

'Go on.' Porter held her gaze and Sarah knew that she was being taken seriously.

'I'll start with my opinion. Tony is the gentlest, most caring teacher in the school. He wins Mr Popular every year.'

She faltered, and blushed; it sounded pathetic. She took a breath and carried on. She wanted to communicate how difficult it was to endear oneself to teenagers.

'Kids aren't stupid. They're treated as if they're half-people with undeveloped brains, but they're not. In fact, sometimes they're cleverer than us because they're not tainted by outside influences like incomes, mortgages, politics and experience. Their beliefs are raw. You need to see one of Tony's English lessons…'

Sarah sipped a mouthful of coffee. The detectives said nothing. Her hands shook slightly. There was no going back now.

'I'm prepared to be a character witness for Tony, if I have the chance. It's the least I can do. The kids love him.'

Still silence.

'Time for the facts. Tony is useless on computers. He sucks. He has to be shown how to use the whiteboard virtually every week. I've used his home computer before; it's like a dinosaur, and the software is so old-fashioned. I reckon he hasn't updated it since he bought it ten years ago. He wouldn't have a clue what a firewall is, or encryption.'

This seemed to garner more of a response from the interviewers. She went on.

'What makes you think that's what we're looking for?'

'I know that the files you found were sophisticated ones and I'll say on oath that Tony hasn't the capability of creating them.'

Kelly and Kate swapped glances. 'Alright, carry on.'

'Sadie Rawlinson was invited to Tony's flat to collect a poetry book. He shouldn't have done it – God, he shouldn't have done it – but it was done innocently. I've never, ever seen him aggressive, whereas I have seen Sadie Rawlinson show hostility and physical force scores of times. Fact: she's also promiscuous.' That was a mistake, and she instantly regretted it. It seemed like she was implying that promiscuity was akin to deceit. But it was too late.

'So in your opinion, is it acceptable to assault those girls who experiment with sex, let's say?'

'I didn't mean it like that!'

'Is your information about the events of the evening in question directly taken from the testimony of Tony Blackman, or do you have extra evidence for us?'

'No, I don't.'

'Did Faith Shaw ever visit Tony Blackman's house for extra poetry texts?'

'No! Oh no, no. I knew it!'

'Did Tony Blackman supply his students with anything other than poetry texts?'

Kelly laboured the word *supply*, and Sarah understood her implication. 'No!'

'Miss Peaks, please calm down. DS Umshaw, turn off the tape, please.' Umshaw did as she was instructed. 'That's what you'll get in court, Sarah. Now, let's go through it again, shall we?'

It took Sarah a few seconds to realise that she was holding her breath. It dawned on her that the detectives might actually have been listening to every word she'd said, but not so that they could ridicule her, or call her a liar, or accuse her of wasting their time. Quite the opposite: they wanted more. Before they turned the tape back on, they asked her about the suicides of the two students a few years previously.

'I didn't work at the Academy then.'

'But you heard about them, right?'

'No, not until a student told me.'

'Why not?'

'It's not something a school mentions when they're trying to fill a vacancy. Besides, neither suicide was connected to the school. It was my understanding that the first one, four years ago, was a domestic abuse case, and the second was connected to drugs.'

'What drugs?'

Sarah was nonplussed. 'I'm not entirely sure, but I did hear a mention of some sort of prescription pill that was becoming popular. We get memos now and again in our pigeonholes letting us know the current names for the common drugs.'

'And?'

'What has this got to do with Tony?' She was wary.

'Nothing. But I'm acutely aware, as of course are you, that Faith Shaw attends your school, as did Jenna Fraser, and it's indisputable that drug abuse and suicide are closely linked. I want to know what you think.'

'About what?'

'The role of drugs amongst teenagers. Is it something you've seen increase?'

'Detective, with respect, they don't use at school. It's a social problem that happens elsewhere.'

'I accept that, but their brains don't change as soon as they leave the classroom; surely it affects the child's life in and out of school.'

'There's no study on it. It's uncharted territory, I'm afraid. Our government is way behind on accepting that drugs affect the vast majority of teenagers, and younger children, at some point in their lives.'

'What's the school policy on it?'

Sarah looked between the two detectives.

'I don't think we have one, but the head would say that we're anti-drugs, like all schools.'

'Is it raised in assemblies and lessons?'

'No.'

'Have you witnessed the effects yourself?'

'It's shaky ground. I recognise the signs of abuse, but I wouldn't be able to prove anything.'

'Did Faith Shaw ever display such signs?'

'No, but Sadie Rawlinson does, all the time, and I've heard that her mother is an addict.'

'DS Umshaw, please turn the tape back on.'

Chapter 26

Building a detailed picture of Faith Shaw was vital to discovering where she'd gone. The narrative of her life hinged around her social media accounts, and they were mind-bogglingly vast.

She'd been reported missing on Sunday evening, and it was now Wednesday. Sky News had been in touch with Cumbria Police HQ, who were preparing a new statement. Kelly and her team had explored all the possibilities, ruling out running away from home fairly quickly, as well as latent drug use, or an underlying medical condition that might cause insomnia or memory loss. She had decided that Faith's disappearance was not only unusual, it was also unexpected, and given her age, they had to assume that she was at risk. That bit was pretty standard. What they did next was the tricky part.

Profiling a victim took time. Sometimes a character trait or a traumatic event could cause a change in behaviour, triggering physical absence, but this didn't seem to be the case with Faith. There was nothing missing from her bedroom; she hadn't packed a bag. She didn't drive, she hadn't been diagnosed with mental illness, there hadn't been a fight at home or at school, and no one had noticed any unexpected conduct. Thus the suicide profile was ruled out.

After three days, it was obligatory to enter the case with the Missing Persons Bureau and log the details on the PNC, the police national database, but the fact that she was now on the computer system said nothing about the girl herself; they were merely jumping through hoops. Of course, they all hoped that she'd hitched to Blackpool and she'd be picked up by local police there tonight, but they also knew that most missing persons turned up within forty-eight hours, and Faith was still gone. Every constabulary in the land knew that, statistically, after that first forty-eight hours, the victim was usually dead.

A knot formed in Kelly's stomach as she thought of Michael. And of Josie. It was what continually drove her forward: justice for the family and protecting others.

Johnny had been at home pretty much every night since the weekend. He'd driven his daughter to the point of despair with his incessant questions about where she was going and who she was seeing, and Kelly suspected the same thing was happening all over the north Lakes, and possibly further afield. It was a normal human reaction.

As senior investigating officer, Kelly didn't really have to visit the Shaw family at all. She was obliged to keep them updated, but a junior officer could do that. But she wanted to see them. She needed to see them. Every time she looked at Maggie's face or watched Colin's sunken shoulders, it galvanised her to work another hour on the case. Every time she saw the dark circles around Michael's eyes, it made her want to bring Faith home for Christmas. But in her gut, hope was decreasing hourly.

Faith's mobile phone signal had died on Monday. It had last pinged off a mast in Keswick, so they knew that up to that point, her phone at least had been in or around the town. There had been several calls to Michael before nine o'clock on Sunday night, and they had been accounted for: he had gone missing after an argument with friends, and Faith had searched for him frantically. The last one was at 8.47 p.m. and that was corroborated by what the boy had told them about it being close to his pick-up time. The last signal was at 11 p.m. Michael had said that Faith had berated him in one of her calls because her battery was low.

But despite not having Faith's phone physically in front of them, Rob's Manchester mole had been able to access all her social media accounts. It was new technology, and Kelly could barely contain her excitement, as well as her trepidation, over what they might find.

As soon as the printouts were ready, she and Rob glanced over them to see if anything stood out. They could tell from the amount of data that getting to know Faith Shaw might take some time: she was active for an average of almost nine hours per day on her phone, communicating with her mates on FaceTime, Snapchat and WhatsApp. Instagram was all photos, then there was Facebook, and texting. There were mountains of the stuff.

They sat either side of a large desk at Eden House. It had soon become clear to both of them that combing through someone's social media posts was akin to rifling through their personal diaries: they were looking at the very essence of the girl. They soon became used to her tone of voice, her presence, her manner and her humour. They laughed intermittently and showed each other photographs. Faith was a beautiful girl. Kelly could see both Colin and Maggie in her, as well as young

Michael. She was at her most captivating when not posing, which was probably true of most people. She regularly used the app that put dogs' ears or Harry Potter style glasses on faces, and the images were cute, innocent and fun. But overall it was draining, and desperately sad.

They sat quietly concentrating, looking up to share details, but after a while, both of them fell silent, and grimaces of concern spread across their faces. There was an overriding impression in these accounts of image being all-important. Twenty years ago, photographs captured real-time moments, people and places portrayed exactly as they appeared. Now, looking at these photographs, Kelly and Rob noticed that they weren't snippets, or amusing prints of points in time; they were staged arrangements, contrived impressions or notions, giving off a certain message. They were make-believe and illusory. It was depressing. But it was obvious to see the motivation behind such fiction: the pressure to be liked. Literally, with a tick or an emoji.

'Is it just me, or is there a veiled sense of desperation here?' Kelly asked.

'I agree,' Rob said.

Kelly chewed her lip and decided that a lot of what she was reading she wouldn't be passing on to the family. She thought about Josie, and considered picking her brains about the way youngsters spoke to one another. Some of the language was mere bravado and hyperbole, tediously and endearingly teenage. But some of it was downright vicious and offensive. In fact, it could be seen as criminal.

'Do you think they all speak to each other like this?'

'I hope not.'

'She handles it well; rarely bites back. Look at this: there's a gorgeous photo of her on top of Skiddaw with her brother, and three people comment on her stomach, her arse, and her brother's goofy teeth. They are absolute bastards; how do people put up with this shit?'

'I've got a WhatsApp group here called "Bitches Yo!"'

'Nice. Who's in it?'

'I recognise some of the names from her year at school, including Sadie. A few references to Roxie.'

'Roxie? Let me see.' It was the street name for the opioid OxyContin, and too much of a coincidence considering what they already knew about the potential role of drugs in the case. It was also what Jenna Fraser had been prescribed.

'It doesn't look like a profile, does it? It's just somebody they're talking about, if it's a real person.' Kelly rubbed her eyes. Hours of reading adolescent coded messages was sending her dizzy. 'Did you speak to your mates like this at school?' she asked.

'Boys are different.'

'Not any more. A lot of these comments are from boys. Admittedly, it's mostly girls, but the boys are just as bad. You know Maggie Shaw said Faith was bullied?'

Rob nodded.

'She never said that it had stopped.'

'I thought Faith had made friends with them?' Rob said.

They continued to talk and search at the same time, then Rob paused suddenly and looked up.

'Guv?'

'What is it?' Kelly asked.

'Read this. I don't trust my own eyes.' He passed her an A4 piece of paper, a printout of some Instagram posts.

'What am I looking at?' Kelly asked.

'Look at who has commented on the third photograph down.'

'Fuck.'

Chapter 27

Danny Stanton had been recognised by the landlady of a small establishment in the village of Thirlwell. The young man had initially found it amusing that there'd been such a fuss about his disappearance, but when he turned up to claim his car, which had been impounded from Revelin Moss car park by Cumbria Constabulary, he was less jovial. Kelly and Rob were there to greet him.

Apparently he'd met a young woman, and they'd walked over the fells together, ending up drinking pints of ale in a tiny tavern nestled along the Whinlatter Pass, after which they'd staggered back to her room in the guest house and begun a three-day shag fest.

'You have to admit, it's quite funny,' Rob said to his boss.

'Of course it is, but I'm not going to show him that. Christ, it's no wonder the mountain rescue guys are volunteers, is it? No company with profit in mind would fund this crap. They all raised their glasses that he'd been found safe, that's the main thing. You said that the officers who went to the guest house conducted a search because they suspected drug use?'

'Yes, guv. I think the two of them had been halfway to Mars for three days.'

'I've not heard that one before. What did they find?'

'Nothing except a recently flushed toilet and plenty of alcohol and fags.'

'How old was the woman?'

'Eighteen.'

'Right. My concern is how he knows Faith, so let's stick with that.'

Rob agreed.

Danny Stanton's black Ford Ka was in a warehouse in Penrith where the police stored and searched vehicles suspected of being involved in criminal activity. It had been towed there on Tuesday, mainly to get it somewhere secure should they need it in future. They had no reason to search it, but Kelly had secured an extra twenty-four hours from HQ, and she'd managed to find a forensic officer based in Carlisle to come and have a look over it. Her own forensics guys in Penrith weren't free: they'd been working on a particularly disturbing domestic case, combing a double bed for the DNA of a girl allegedly raped by her father.

Stanton knew none of this. He simply thought he was going to swan in and collect his wheels, having caused chaos for three days. Valuable resources had gone into looking for him that could have been used to search for Faith, and Kelly was irked by it.

She waited with Rob outside the warehouse door. The snow had stopped for now, but the sky was light grey and expectant, confirming that more was on its way. Rob wore a black overcoat over his black suit, with a white shirt and dark grey tie. His attire matched the current mood of Eden House, or at least the incident room. He was clean-shaven and his hair was neatly trimmed. He might possibly have been mistaken for a car salesman or a bank clerk, but his eyes gave away the fact that he was a copper. Detectives had eyes that pierced; that seared into people and didn't let go. Kelly had seen that the day she'd interviewed Rob Shawcross.

Yes, she was lucky. Her team was fucking awesome.

Danny strode towards them with a young woman by his side. Kelly assumed this was the girl he'd spent the last few days with.

'Mr Stanton? I'm DI Kelly Porter, and this is DC Rob Shawcross.' She stepped forward, aware that her nose was red.

Danny looked wary, which Kelly took as a sign that he had at least some respect for authority. They shook hands.

'Miss, could you wait in your car, please?'

The girl nodded and glanced at Danny, who shrugged as if to say he was fine with it. Kelly reckoned she looked high: her eyes were red and her nose was running, and she hadn't been outside in the cold long enough for it to be the result of the freezing temperature.

They went into the warehouse. Danny began talking.

'Look, I'm really sorry for all the fuss I've caused. I had no idea.'

It was no warmer inside the building, but at least there was no wind. The door clattered shut behind them and Rob walked towards an office kitted out with a few chairs and an electric heater.

'Take a seat,' he said. Danny looked nervous for the first time.

'I thought I was here to collect my car,' he said.

'We need to keep your car a little longer, Danny,' Kelly said.

'Coffee?' Rob asked.

Danny looked from one detective to the other, trying to suss out their agenda, but their faces were blank; they'd done this a thousand times. He sat down slowly.

'Yes please. Black.'

Rob went to the machine in the corner of the small office and made three small plastic cups of coffee. He handed them round, then sat down.

'So, Danny, can you tell us again why you left your car at the Revelin Moss car park?'

'I wanted to go hiking on my own, for an adventure, you know? I needed to get away for a while. I thought just heading off would be a good idea. And it was, it was amazing. I didn't tell anyone my plans, and I know that was dumb.'

'But you posted on Facebook. That doesn't really fit with wanting to "get away", does it?'

'No, I guess it doesn't. Facebook's a habit. I can't stay off it.'

'It's addictive, isn't it?' said Kelly. 'Like a drug.'

Danny shifted in his seat and sipped at his coffee, which spilt as he jerked the cup away from his mouth.

'Shit, it's hot!' he said. Kelly and Rob didn't move.

'Where did you meet the girl?'

'Halfway down Grisedale Pike. I was looking for somewhere to camp, but I don't know the area, so I just wandered off and I had no idea where I was.'

'But I thought you'd been there before; at least that's what your sister told us.'

'Well, not exactly the same area. That's what I meant.'

'So the girl happened to be there? The weather was awful, wasn't it? No one in their right mind would go wandering up there in that snow. She doesn't look like a hiker.'

'She's a songwriter.'

'What?'

'Free spirit. Wanderer, you know; she kind of just gets out there and sits and writes and stuff. She said I could go back with her to keep warm.' Danny looked around nervously.

'She went out in the snow to write poetry? On her own?'

'She works here, she knows the area well. It was only when she showed me where we were on a map that I realised how far I'd gone in the wrong direction.' Danny's hands were shaking slightly, and he forced himself to try his coffee again: anything to avoid the stares of the two coppers.

'What do you do for a living, Danny?'

'I'm a student.'

'Your sister told us that you dropped out two years ago and now she doesn't know where you get your money from. She's worried about your health.'

'I get a grant, I'm still studying. My sister doesn't know my hours. I have random lectures.'

'Danny, have you heard of Faith Shaw?'

Danny stopped sipping and brought his cup down. He looked from one detective to the other and shrugged. 'The name rings a bell. I don't know why, though.'

'Instagram?'

Kelly showed him the picture that he'd liked and commented on.

'Oh.'

'That's you, right?'

'Er, yeah, but I don't know her, as in *know* her.'

'I'm glad about that, Danny, because she's only fifteen.'

'Shit! No way!'

'Did you ever arrange to meet her?'

'No!'

'So this message asking her if she'd like to "hook up sometime, babeeee" is referring to what?'

Danny's eyes grew wider; the skin around his neck looked pink. Rob sat up in his chair.

'Everybody does it. It's not serious.'

'But it is serious, because Faith's been missing since Sunday. Which is why we have a warrant to impound your car for an extra twenty-four hours. Are you stating categorically that Faith Shaw has never been in your car, Danny? How could she be, you've never met her, right?'

Danny didn't answer straight away, which was all the answer they needed.

'Do you know this man?' Kelly showed him a photograph of Bobby Bailey.

Danny showed a flicker of panic, but he was no kid, and he was able to control his responses.

'No.'

'Are you absolutely sure? His name is Bobby Bailey and he's a known drug dealer working out of the charter fair.'

Danny swallowed and glanced towards his car.

'Definitely not.'

'Where are you staying this evening?' Rob asked.

'I was planning to go home as soon as I got my car back.' His voice had grown desperate.

'You might like to rearrange your plans. We'll need you back here at the same time tomorrow, unless we decide to extend the twenty-four hours. For now, you're free to leave.'

Danny paused, then got up and walked quickly across the warehouse floor to the door, which slammed behind him.

Chapter 28

When Kelly and Rob got back to Eden House, the team was assembled in the incident room. During a complex case, they met daily, sometimes twice. Everybody was busy and pushed for time. The briefings were a way of coming together and sharing thoughts. Kelly liked them to be a casual affair, because that was how people relaxed and made connections.

'Afternoon, everyone. I had an interesting conversation with the daughter of a friend of mine this morning,' she began. Her team listened intently. They were all used to the way she zipped through the agenda. Everyone got a say, no matter how irrelevant it might seem. Kelly believed in getting a feel for an investigation, and chatting about minor details often brought about the best leads.

She and Josie had talked amicably on the phone about the way in which children and young adults spoke to each other online. Josie confirmed that abuse, insults, name-calling and humiliation was all absolutely normal. She came across as helpful, mature and engaging; it was one of the most satisfying conversations Kelly had ever had with her, because it was calm, unloaded and utterly equal, though she wished they could have celebrated such a triumph over a different topic.

'All the pressure on these kids seems to make them miserable. They pretend to be "hashtag fine", but the reality is something else, otherwise the suicide stats would tell us a different story. My friend's daughter confirmed that it's not just normal but acceptable, because it's habitual. And it's habitual because it's acceptable.'

Kate Umshaw nodded. 'The girls' social media accounts drive me nuts. They're continually taking selfies and watching how many likes they get.'

'Kids being generally obnoxious to one another is not a new thing, right?' Kelly said.

'Right,' they all agreed.

'It's the accessibility that has changed. Anyone, anywhere, any time can be got at. The kids can't stand up for themselves, and so it becomes ingrained and more common, and then you've got yourself a habit. There's never a break from it,' said Kate.

'I was bullied at school, but I think it's worse now.' Emma spoke up. She was the youngest on the team and at school barely more than ten years ago.

'I'm going to the Derwent Academy for the rest of the day. Kate, can I steal Emma to come with me? I think everyone knows what they're doing. Anything new?'

'Just thinking about what Danny Stanton told us, guv. How easy is it really to wander off the north-west side of Grisedale and end up almost at the end of the Whinlatter Pass, where it hits Thirlwell?'

'It depends which way you descend.' Will spoke. 'If you go all the way down Hobcarton End, then it's pretty easy, but Thirlwell is a way off to the west, and it's all forest and crag that way.'

'And in shit weather?' Kelly added.

She got up and drew a diagram on the whiteboard. She added three names: Danny Stanton, Luke Miles and Bobby Bailey. 'Didn't Stanton look shifty as hell when we asked him about Bailey, Rob?'

'Definitely, boss.'

'And then there's his comment on Faith's Instagram post. Though with today's social media web, I suppose it could be entire coincidence that he follows her account.'

'But it doesn't feel like that,' Emma said. 'And we have his sister saying that he comes to the Lakes regularly.'

'I reckon we bring Bobby in. He's the one with previous; he's the oldest and likely to be calling the shots. He lives a rough life according to the DI in Barrow that I spoke to, and he's been in trouble before. I think the fair goes to Ulverston next. I'll talk to DI Lockwood.'

Kelly's personal mobile rang: it was Johnny. She toyed with ignoring it, but Johnny rarely disturbed her for a social call; he preferred face-to-face. She excused herself and moved out into the corridor. As she glanced back towards the incident room, she could see her team standing around the board, pointing and adding detail.

'Josie said you spoke today.'

'Johnny, I'm in the middle of a meeting, sorry.' She was slightly irked that he'd called to ask her about her conversation with his daughter.

'I wasn't ringing for that; it's just she said it was good to talk.'

'That's positive, but I really need to go.'

'Wait. I was with Kurt for drinks last night.'

She sighed, itching to get back to the incident room. 'Who's Kurt?'

'Mountain rescue guy, climber, moving here, girlfriend is a drug addict…'

'Oh Christ, I know, the one who found Jenna.' The memory stabbed sharply at her and made her even more eager to find out where Faith was.

'Yes. Same. He was doing Grisedale Pike on Sunday, late, and saw two cars in the Revelin Moss car park. He reckoned it was kids partying. I just thought I'd better tell you, because that's where the bloke who went missing left his car.'

'Johnny, you're a legend.'

'Well, I know. Many thanks. Is it that important?'

'It could be. Can you give me Kurt's number? We'll have it somewhere, but that would be quicker.'

'I'll WhatsApp it to you.'

'Why didn't he come forward sooner?'

'It was just a car; why would he?'

'So why did he tell you last night?'

'He was asking if the man had been found yet, because he was out himself that evening.'

'Can he identify the cars?'

'I did ask him if he remembered and he said it was dark, and the snow was heavy, but they could have been dark grey or black in colour and they were both fairly small models, like a Fiat or a Ford.'

'Great.'

'What are you up to later?' he asked.

'I'm in Keswick all day.'

'Should I bring Josie over and we'll go out for dinner?'

'Yes, I'll call you when I'm done.'

She hung up and walked back into the incident room.

Chapter 29

Kelly had been assigned twenty uniforms from all over the north of Cumbria to assist at the Derwent Academy, and the interviews had been well under way since Tuesday. They'd prioritised them depending on how close a pupil or member of staff was deemed to be to Faith Shaw and her daily routine.

Despite the weather, the academy had remained open all week. Many schools across Britain had closed, and northerners had ridiculed them for being pussies. With a few sweeps of a good spade and an extra layer of warm clothes, every teacher, bar two, had made it in. Of the two who didn't, one lived at the top of a hill in Little Broughton, which was completely cut off, and the other on a farm in Buttermere. Neither was a priority for their inquiries.

Kelly's Audi was four-wheel-drive, so she didn't really give a second thought to people all over the country struggling to navigate the roads. The school's driveways were freshly ploughed and clear of yesterday's snow, and she found a parking space. DC Emma Hide was always good company, and they chatted about the significance of the car sightings by Kurt Fletcher.

Kelly hadn't been inside a school for years, but she figured that lessons were in full swing, because no one was milling about. They entered the reception and she made the introductions. The woman behind the desk was pleasant enough, and led them through a labyrinth of corridors and airless foyers into a hall where uniformed police sat at desks interviewing adults and children. A few parents had turned up to supervise, as was their right, though it made the officers' job a little more challenging, because sometimes the innocence of youth meant that children had more truth in their earwax than an adult possessed in its entire body, and that was a good resource to tap unchecked. Those days were gone, though, and minors were now protected, making transparent inquiries harder. The kids whose parents sat beside them looked embarrassed and kept their heads down.

Kelly approached an officer who was between interviews to ask how it was proceeding.

'Two hundred and seventeen so far, boss.'

'Anything?'

'We've built up a fairly standard picture of her typical day, and as far as character goes, she's a well-liked kid, very polite and respectful, well behaved, punctual and conscientious.'

'Star pupil?'

'Pretty much.'

'No changes in the weeks leading up to last weekend?'

'None of note. Quite a few of her teachers commented on her lack of confidence, though.'

'Issue?'

'Potentially. It indicates that she might not be the sort to take risks or get into trouble.'

Kelly agreed. 'Is the head teacher around?'

'Somewhere. She's pretty much left us to it.'

A bell rang and the corridors echoed to the banging of doors, the thundering of feet and the sound of scuffles and general mayhem. A few pupils ran through the hall, having specifically been asked not to by a tannoy announcement, and several teachers followed them, admonishing them. The kids blatantly ignored their adult supervisors. The parents accompanying their children to interviews looked on horrified. A water bottle was thrown like a missile over their heads and exploded on the wooden floor, sending water everywhere.

Eventually the anarchy subsided and students carried on to their next lesson. Several teachers entered the hall, Sarah Peaks among them. She was Faith Shaw's English teacher.

Kelly waved, and Sarah approached. The teacher looked uncomfortable, and Kelly surmised that it couldn't be easy working in this environment when she was so involved with Tony Blackman. She introduced Sarah to the uniformed officer.

'We're taking general statements about Faith today,' she explained.

Sarah nodded. 'She's one of my favourite pupils. I don't mean that I don't like others; it's just that Faith is one of those kids who hangs on your every word. Her love of learning is infectious.' She sat down.

'A lot of people have said the same. She sounds a lovely girl,' Kelly said. She decided to hang around for Sarah's interview, while Emma went to check on a few of the others.

'She is. Her ability in English is remarkable – very advanced for her age. She writes poetry, and her stories are very deep and richly crafted.'

'And what does she write about?' the officer asked.

'Bullying mainly. I brought some of her work for you. I think it says a lot about her experiences.' Sarah pushed the books she'd brought with her towards the PC, and Kelly leaned in, interested.

'Did this impact her at school?'

Sarah nodded.

'How?'

'She seemed more mature than others in her age group, as if she'd grown up quickly. When it was really bad, her mother actually said to me that she didn't know if Faith would make it. That was in confidence.'

'Why wasn't it reported if it was a safeguarding issue?' Kelly asked. 'You're obliged to pass on such information.'

'It wasn't specific and it was more the mother relieving her own anguish. I wish I had now. Can I be blunt?'

'Of course.'

'I'd rather stick a red-hot poker up my arse – excuse my language – than have Sadie Rawlinson as my friend. If anyone knows where Faith went that night, it's her.'

The PC looked at his pad and wrote the statement down. There was nothing quite like good old-fashioned honesty, Kelly thought.

There were a few more questions, and then Sarah was allowed to go. The PC glanced at Kelly and raised his eyebrows.

'I'm not sure that Faith's choice of friends was to everyone's taste,' she said. 'I think it's important to explore this thread with the teaching staff and her year group. Make sure you do that.'

He nodded.

Chapter 30

Kelly and Emma were shown to the maths department, where Sadie Rawlinson was in class. Kelly wasn't taking any chances, given what Rob had told her. The sixth-former guiding them knocked on the door, and Kelly went inside and approached the teacher. He didn't ask for ID, and seemed thankful to get rid of the student she'd asked for.

'Sadie, get your things. You're to follow the police detective right now.'

Kelly glanced sideways at him, incredulous that he'd made such a meal out of his simple task, but she was quickly beginning to understand why. The students looked thoroughly entertained, and it was a small momentary pleasure for the teacher, as if he prayed for moments like this to punctuate his day. She walked to the doorway and waited while the girl packed her bag.

Sadie Rawlinson was a surly creature. She was small, with pointed features and mousy hair. She rolled her eyes at the teacher, then at Kelly. Kelly stifled a smile and her incredulity at such brazen behaviour. The girl would be a nightmare on the witness stand, and her first thought was that the Tony Blackman case probably wouldn't go to trial.

'Hurry up!' the teacher boomed. Sadie rolled her eyes again before following Kelly out. Kelly nodded her appreciation to the teacher, who looked more relaxed than he had when she'd first gone in.

'This way, please, Sadie.'

They made their way to the sixth-form block, where Justin Cain was waiting for his interview.

'We're not allowed in here, it's sixth form only.' Sadie stood in the doorway.

'It's your lucky day. Will you be staying on here to do your A levels, Sadie?' Kelly beckoned her in and shut the door.

The girl clocked Justin and stopped; he shifted position in his seat and looked bashful, despite his six-foot frame. There was no doubting that they knew each other.

Kelly took Sadie into a side room. 'Sit down,' she said. Sadie sat, and Kelly studied her. It was no wonder that Rob had felt uneasy. Sadie was a disappointing example of a well-worn stereotype. She wore too much make-up, her skirt barely covered her thigh gap, her blouse was undone so her tie wouldn't stay up, and she chewed gum. Kelly couldn't really believe what she was seeing. She'd thought characters like this had died out with Trisha Yates in *Grange Hill*. The girl's northern accent was thick and unfortunate, making her sound even rougher.

'It's good to meet you at last, Sadie. Well, we are in the middle of a few scrapes, aren't we?'

Sadie chewed her gum with her mouth wide open. 'What do you mean?'

'You're the main witness in a assault case, and now you're the last one to see Faith Shaw before she disappeared. Terrible coincidence.'

Sadie blew a bubble. Kelly observed that she couldn't sit still. She was either ADHD or desperate for a stimulant that the gum couldn't provide. She sniffed a lot too.

'So tell me in your own words exactly what you did on Sunday evening, Sadie. Please try not to miss anything out.'

Sadie rolled her eyes again and began her story. It was told in a monotone manner, with few pauses, and delivered as though reading from a script. Kelly took notes and didn't look at her; she found that it put some witnesses off, and she wanted Sadie to have no interruptions so the chances of her getting carried away would increase. The girl gave the same simple statement that she had on Sunday night in front of Colin and Maggie Shaw: Faith had said she was visiting the Portaloo, and they never saw her again. Today, though, she embellished it by mentioning some shady characters hanging around the rides, one of whom had taken a particular interest in Faith.

Kelly scribbled, *Late forties or fifties, white, scruffy, lechy...* It could have described any one of twenty workers at the fair; she should know, she'd seen their photographs.

'Name?'

'Bobby.'

Kelly sat back. Sadie carried on chewing.

'And why didn't you mention him in your original statement?'

'I didn't want to scare Faith's mum and dad, you know? They're going through enough.'

Compassionate wasn't the first word Kelly would have used to describe the girl before her. The whole story stank, but as a lead, it threw more shit Bobby's way.

DI Lockwood was visiting the fair in Ulverston later today, or tomorrow morning, to speak to the man.

After ten minutes of going round in circles and Sadie not changing her story, Kelly decided that she'd get Justin in.

'Do you care that your friend is missing, Sadie?'

The girl stopped chewing and changed her demeanour. It was as if she'd forgotten this bit: the part where she showed sorrow.

'Yeah! Of course. I was closest to her.' Her chin wobbled slightly and she wiped an eye. Kelly thought she might break into full-blown hysterics.

'You can wait outside now.'

Emma escorted her out and brought Justin Cain in. His story was delivered in the same fashion, centred on the toilet visit, and had also clearly been rehearsed; with whom, Kelly had no idea, but she guessed it was Luke, after she'd caught him out over Bobby. Sure enough, Justin also mentioned Bobby and described him in detail.

'And why didn't you tell us this before now, Justin?'

'I didn't want to worry Faith's mum and dad. They're going through enough.'

Kelly recorded the words carefully. But Justin had more to say. He was a fidgeter and silences didn't sit comfortably with him. This was always a bonus when interviewing a witness. He told her that in his opinion, Sadie was jealous of Faith. He looked to the door several times as he did so and Kelly said nothing, just listened. He didn't strike her as the sharpest tool in the drawer, and was perhaps the weak link in the threesome. Perhaps he'd forgotten his brief. Either that or he had an axe to grind.

She remained calm when he mentioned that on Sunday evening, Luke Miles had taken them all for a drive in his black Hyundai i20.

Kelly dismissed the teenagers, and she and Emma walked back to the main hall.

'Do we have CCTV for the town centre yet?' she asked.

'It's going to take another few days. There are two cameras in the centre: one at the top end of town and the other outside the old corn exchange. They both cover the area of the fair quite well.'

'What's taking so long?'

'They're outdated systems. All the information is stored on discs, then sent away to head office. They haven't been located yet.'

'I think I want to check footage on the circular as well. If Luke took our little group for a spin, they might have left town.'

Emma nodded. 'That should be easier, guv. I'm sure the highways CCTV has all been updated, though I do remember that the bypass roundabout was having work done.'

'Find out, will you?'

Kelly's phone rang. It was Kate Umshaw back at Eden House.

'Kelly, can you talk?'

Kate never called her boss by her first name. Kelly walked a distance away from her colleagues and pulled out a chair.

'What's up?'

'The toddler, Dale Prentice, from the Greenside lead mine two years ago?'

'Of course, I know who you mean.'

'His foster parents reported him missing yesterday. He was taken from a car park in St Bees.'

Chapter 31

Craig Lockwood drove through Dalton-in-Furness on his way to the fair. The medieval town was one of the oldest in Furness. The castle keep on the market square was lit up brightly, and a huge Christmas tree bent gently under a mass of snow. The old stone houses had mostly gone now, but the facades of some of them could still be seen in the tiny heart of the town, where the valley would have been hundreds of years ago. He could have taken the bypass from Barrow, but he wanted to take his time. It had been a long day, and the fair wouldn't yet be open.

He didn't personally know Bobby Bailey, but he had his description, his photograph, and a few contacts to point him in the right direction. Kelly Porter was his counterpart in the North Lakes, and he was more than happy to work alongside her inquiries. Cumbria was like a vast mound of rock that you could penetrate either from the south or the north. Kelly's patch was the north, from Carlisle down to about Coniston and Ambleside; his was everything between the southern tip of Barrow, on the Furness peninsula, to St Bees and across. Often they overlapped, and this was one such time. At Kelly's request, he'd contacted a few old drug squad pals in Manchester and asked if there'd been any prior surveillance on Bailey for dealing.

There hadn't. He'd need to get his own evidence.

Craig had enjoyed working with Kelly Porter the last time around, more than two years ago. He'd never expected to uncover something so vast, stretching from Workington Port, south to Barrow and then north to Penrith. The operation had been colossal, and that was just the beginning. What they subsequently unearthed abroad, and how far the money trail spread, was staggering. In the end, they uncovered people smuggling, prostitution and modern slavery resulting in several convictions. Unfortunately, one of the ring leaders was already dead but they nailed his accomplices. Generally, though, they each had their own patch to adhere to, and it meant that moments like these, which might always lead to something bigger, were something to relish. Like Kelly, he had spent time out of the Lakes; in his case, fifteen years in the Manchester Met. Stints like that changed an officer's approach; made them less shockable and more resourceful. He wasn't denigrating local officers at all; it was just that operations in the cities were slightly different and gave teeth to fledglings.

And now there was the missing toddler. He'd agreed to get South Lakes on it, as Kelly had her hands well and truly full with stuff going on up in Keswick. They'd liaise regularly. Because of the age of the child, it was vital to get cracking straight away, and he had officers trawling CCTV in the area, interviews being carried out, descriptions logged. He was also following up a lead on the woman who'd spoken to the foster mother in the car park. Egremont police were working flat out collating everything, and a liaison team had been sent to the family address. Kelly had explained to him that Dale's details had been discovered on the teacher's computer – and that Nedzad Galic, the boy's father, had never been found.

Kelly was surrounded by a good team, but a few of them needed to spread their wings. He knew Kate Umshaw from a secondment he'd done in Keswick many moons ago, and she was going nowhere. Young Will Phillips had been promoted, and that was fantastic for him; Craig just hoped that now he'd take the next step and get out of Cumbria. Emma Hide had masses of potential, but Kelly called her a plodder; she was the type of officer who would soldier away in the detail and come up with an explosive little nugget every now and again that brought another dimension to an inquiry.

He wasn't wishing Kelly's team away from her; it was just that he didn't like to see talent stagnate. As for his own team, he encouraged fluidity wherever possible, and he'd lost some fine officers to the Met. He didn't mind; he'd cut his own teeth years ago and was happy now to chug along at the pace that Barrow offered him. Mind, if Kelly Porter had anything to do with the progress of this particular inquiry, Craig suspected it was about to get punchy.

This was the third time she'd called and asked about Bailey, and he knew she was on to something. The drugs angle came up each time, and he'd arranged for her to chat to his contact in Manchester. The city had long been the drugs conduit of mainland Britain, ever since the days of the Quality Street Gang and the Crazy Face Gang. Shipments couldn't go straight to the provinces; there was too much money at stake, and the business was run by large groups of thugs who would have stood out in backwaters like Ulverston. Instead, they hired individuals who couriered the gear out from the city like a spider's web. Perhaps Bobby Bailey was a runner, who happened to conduct a lucrative trade through the fairground.

Ulverston was a twenty-minute drive from Barrow, and Craig had just added a pleasant ten minutes meandering through Dalton. He drove up the hill out of the valley, and carried on through Lindal and Swarthmoor. Cumbria slate and stone houses dotted the route; you were never far from the illustrious quarrying past of the golden county. Many a rich lord had made his millions from what lay underneath the glacial deposits, millions of years in the making. New industry was rare, and the old ones had all but gone, but Furness still had something that nowhere else had, whether it was the Duddon Estuary on a day like today, when you could see all the way to the Isle of Man; or the mountains to the north of Black Coomb, covered in snow.

Bobby Bailey was from a travelling family, and had little in the form of a paper trail to his name. Craig had found virtually nothing on him in the archives, apart from the fact that he'd been employed as a mechanic for a few years in Askam-in-Furness; he'd also popped up on a credit search as owning a debit card registered to a bank in Newbury, near Reading. He'd got off with a caution for the indecent exposure, served a two-year suspended sentence for the indecent images, and the attempted rape charges had been dropped. They had his fingerprints and DNA, but they had no reason to arrest him. Kelly wanted him watched. Craig fully intended to put as much pressure on him as he could.

He turned off to Canal Foot, where the fair was already set up, ready for its opening night, and looked for a place to park. In the daylight, fairs always looked like a sadly neglected toy: discarded, shabby round the edges and out of date, the colours faded and dirty. Only the cape of the dark and the accompanying neon bursts of light would clean the place up and turn it to magic once again, and that was when it became exotic and alluring.

Even the fairground workers, who during the day looked mangy, unwashed, malnourished and up to no good, became inexplicably attractive to the hordes of girls waiting to be given a free ride. Nothing had changed since Craig had attended the fair thirty years ago, following the love of his life around from ride to ride, only to watch her be wooed by some oily nineteen-year-old with dirty fingernails and bad breath who promised her another go on the waltzers while he stood like Rambo on the rear of the carriage. Craig, in his clean shirt and pressed drainpipe jeans, money enough in his pocket for five such rides, was powerless to compete with such heady nonconformity.

Bobby Bailey was unlikely to conjure any of this allure, day or night. He was a misfit. Craig's first impression was of a boy wandering through life and suddenly finding that one day he had to go out and get a job. His demeanour was that of a teenager, and a shifty one at that. Craig could tell by his clothes that they were probably slept in every night, and he'd bet his life that the guy didn't wash. He fitted the classic stereotype of a pervert: a man trapped in a child's world. But – and there was a sizeable but – there was something about him that meant he had successfully evaded the law, and there was always a reason for that. Either Bobby Bailey was lucky, or he wasn't the down-and-out dimwit he looked.

He'd been easy to spot.

Craig recognised him straight away from the photo he'd shared with Kelly over the Dalton incident, and now he watched Bobby yawn and scratch his head as he listened to another man saying something. It could have been instructions, or it could have been a bet on this afternoon's horses; it didn't really matter. Bobby Bailey was a yes man. Ostensibly.

Craig spent the next hour in his car, watching Bobby come and go. One thing was for sure: the guy wasn't afraid. He wasn't a man on the run, and he didn't seem to be nervous or expecting trouble. He wasn't looking around like someone might if they had something to hide, so he was either arrogant or stupid. He did very little apart from follow people around and carry the occasional box.

But as the sky darkened, and the lights were switched on, and the first paying punters arrived on the scene, all that changed. It wasn't just the way the shadows fell, or the fact that more people were now crowding into the small space on the edge of the sea; it was that Bobby Bailey had morphed into a different character entirely. His shoulders lifted, his eyes were alert, his swagger was purposeful; he had intent, and he had an agenda.

Craig got out of the car.

Chapter 32

Luke Miles sauntered into the station with his father, who wore a suit and carried a briefcase. He was clearly affronted at having to accompany his son to a place frequented by the criminal underclass, and he glanced around the place like a lord surveying his land. Kelly had learned that both Luke's mother and father were governors at Derwent Academy, and huge influencers in the town. Philanthropists. She had come across plenty of those in her time, and never fell for the holier-than-thou facade.

They were escorted to an interview room and Will Phillips operated the recording equipment.

'Good afternoon, Luke. Mr Miles. Please take a seat. We've called you in for formal interview as there are several inconsistencies in your original statement.' Mr Miles went to intervene, but Kelly shot him a sharp look.

'Mr Miles, you're here as the responsible adult for your son, but I must gain answers only from him. Thank you. Let's get straight to it, shall we? For the purposes of the recording: DI Porter and DS Phillips interviewing. Luke, please recap for me exactly what happened on Sunday evening after eight o'clock.'

Kelly's shoulder blades ached from sitting hunched over notes. She watched the boy as he took a breath and prepared to begin his speech. It was well rehearsed, and a word-for-word regurgitation of what Sadie and Justin had said. She showed him a photograph of Bobby Bailey.

'That's him. He was watching her.'

Kelly sighed. Luke had already admitted knowing Bailey, but now he was changing the story again.

'And why didn't you tell us this at the time?'

'Well, I didn't want to upset Mr and Mrs Shaw. They've been through so much.'

Kelly rolled her eyes inwardly.

'I believe you drive a brand-new Hyundai. How blessed you are. Was it a gift?'

Mr Miles shuffled indignantly but kept his mouth shut.

'Yes, from my dad.' Luke was wary.

'Ever take it up Whinlatter Pass? Or through the forest, perhaps?' Using the information from Kurt Fletcher was a long shot, but anything was worth a go.

'Sometimes. I go all over. It's my car.' He sounded like a toddler.

'Has Faith Shaw ever been in your car? And be very careful how you answer this.'

'I beg your pardon!' Mr Miles interjected. 'That sounds like a threat.'

'Mr Miles, please. You're merely here as an extra adult. Luke needs to answer the question. Unless you've forgotten, there's a missing girl who we're desperate to find. Someone's daughter.' Mr Miles looked at his feet and Kelly turned again to Luke.

'Faith's last-known whereabouts are crucial to us, and Justin Cain said that you all went for a drive in your car. Now, you can verify that or deny it – I don't mind. Or you can waste my time and perjure yourself in court.'

Luke's face went pale.

'I took the girls for a ride.'

'Luke!'

'Mr Miles, this is the last time. I'll have to have you removed. Your son can be chaperoned by another officer.'

'Sorry.' He turned to his son, pain etched on his face.

'What time, and where?' Kelly continued.

'It was about nine. We went over the Whinlatter Pass and back.'

'Who?'

'Me, the two girls and Justin.'

'For the record, you are stating that Faith Shaw was in your car when you left the fair at around 9 p.m.?'

'Yes.'

'Do you realise how important this is to our inquiry? It changes everything. Why did you withhold it?'

Luke's father glared at his son, waiting.

'We came back!'

'What time?'

'I don't know.'

The boy in front of Kelly was poles apart from the one she'd visited at his home.

'So when did she wander off to the toilet on her own? Before or after the drive? Or was there no Portaloo stop at all?'

Luke swallowed, and Kelly knew she had him on the ropes. He was floundering, but she didn't need an answer, because she already knew that they were all lying about the toilet. She couldn't help wondering what else they were lying about.

'I can't remember.'

'Luke, you're an intelligent boy, that much is obvious. How hard is it to comprehend that if I think you're not giving me everything, that's going to raise my suspicions? All I want to do is find Faith. We have a witness saying he saw two parked cars at Revelin Moss car park, and it's likely that one of them was yours. Do you know Danny Stanton?'

He stared at her. Kelly stared back. Mr Miles looked between the two of them. He held up his hand as if in class, needing to ask an important question.

'Mr Miles has requested to make a statement,' Will said for the recording.

'What is going to happen to my son? Are you charging him with a crime?'

'At the moment, we're looking for consistency. So far, none of the kids with Faith on Sunday evening have been straight with us. Luke was the driver of the car in question. We will investigate the importance of that and he may well be charged. At that point, he would be remanded in custody.'

'Could I speak to him in private?'

Kelly nodded, and they turned off the tape. Video recording equipment monitored the room and they went to the screen to watch, leaving father and son to have the most important conversation of their lives. Kelly knew it wouldn't be long before one of the teenagers broke their silence. Justin was a weak link, but in time, they'd all want to save their skins.

Chapter 33

Craig Lockwood walked along the back of the rides, navigating his way around electrical cables, bottles of oil, plastic chairs, cardboard boxes, bits of wood and litter. He'd watched Bobby go to the bar for the fourth or fifth time, and in all that time, he hadn't done any work. Craig was having a hard time working out exactly what Bobby's role was other than to loiter.

It didn't take long for him to witness the first act of lewdness. He could tell that Bobby had had his eye on a young girl wearing a yellow coat for quite some time: he'd spotted her buying a stick of rock with her friends by the hall of mirrors and had followed them all the way down to the haunted house. The journey had taken the girls forty-six minutes, and Bobby had stopped every time they did, watching them covertly, then moving off when they did, never straying more than about fifteen feet away from them. It became obvious that his tried and tested method was to learn the habits of individuals and wait until they were alone; as the girl in the yellow coat was now. She must be around twelve years of age, Craig reckoned, and she was buying a drink while the others went on the magic carpet – she didn't seem to want to participate on this particular ride.

Bobby made his move. He was next to her in a matter of seconds and chatting to her as she waited for her Coke. He pointed to somewhere in the distance and the girl nodded, then to Craig's utter astonishment, she walked off with him and disappeared beyond the end of the drinks van. Craig sprinted after them, careful not to slip on the snow, looking round frantically for the yellow coat. When he finally spotted it, the pair were almost at the edge of the fair, close to where the dark replaced the lights. Craig shouted. The odd couple stopped and turned around. The girl was nonplussed, but Bobby dashed away. Craig went to her and breathlessly asked what she was doing.

'That man said my friends told me to meet them.'

'And you believed him?'

'Shouldn't I? Anyway, who are you?'

'Police,' he panted.

'Police? Let me see your ID.'

'My ID! You go off with a complete stranger and you ask to see my ID! Jesus! Look, here it is. What did he give you?'

'Nothing.'

'Bullshit, turn out your pockets.'

The girl rolled her eyes and brought out a clear bag containing what looked like tea leaves. Craig took it; he figured it was skunk.

'That cost me ten quid!'

'Piss off, and don't do drugs!'

'You're letting me go?'

'If you leave now.'

The girl had a local accent and wouldn't be difficult to find if he needed her. Not with that coat. He walked away shaking his head. Bobby had disappeared. The guy was a pervert and a weirdo, but was he a criminal? Whether he was or not, he'd need to be cautioned.

Craig walked towards the back of a trailer. He turned the corner and searched behind it both ways, but saw found nothing.

'Bobby!' he shouted. Out of the corner of his eye he saw movement, and spotted Bobby running across the wasteland towards the sea. He rolled his eyes and gave chase for the second time in a night, dodging patches of ice. He regretted not keeping up his gym membership.

Craig wasn't fast, but he was fitter than Bobby, who tired quickly. He caught up and stuck his leg out. Bobby fell with a thud and rolled over, ending up face down in the snow-covered grass, with the waves crashing on the beach just metres away.

'Police,' Craig announced. 'Pleased to meet you, Bobby. Why were you running?'

''Cause you were fucking chasing me!'

'What did you want with that very underage girl in the yellow coat?'

'Nothing!'

'Didn't look that way to me. You gave her this.' He held up the bag and Bobby rolled his eyes.

'No I didn't!'

'Get up, Bobby.'

He got up.

'I'll be watching you. I know about the family who dropped the charges. Stay away from little girls.'

'I didn't do nothing!' Bobby marched away, back towards the fair, and disappeared among the trailers.

Craig followed him, hanging back a little. He moved under the open window of a caravan. The smell of weed wafted into the night air. He heard Bobby's voice, but no other; he must be on the phone. He moved closer to the window and picked up the odd word – 'money', 'kid' and 'gear' – but that was all.

He called Kelly.

Chapter 34

Nedzad hung up the phone. There was a problem, and he wasn't in the area to take care of it. He was in Manchester, eating Chinese food in his favourite restaurant. There were a couple of people he trusted to deal with these things, and he called one of them now. Bobby had ceased to be necessary and would have to go. No one got away with threatening Nedzad, and he'd heard the panic in the gypsy's voice clearly. He wouldn't be missed.

The man he was dining with spread his hands as if to say 'What the hell was that all about?'

'Bobby, whining again. I'm tired of it.'

His dinner partner agreed.

'He's scared of the police. It won't do.'

The man opposite him raised his eyebrows.

'It's good to get out of Keswick, yes?' Nedzad asked him.

'You have no idea. Thank you.'

'Not at all, it is my pleasure. You have to lie low for a while, I understand. You can help me here. How is the case progressing?'

'Slowly. I'm confident that I can pull it off, though.'

'You have been around for a long time, my friend. You were highly recommended to me and you've never let me down. These little men who simply cause problems are like gnats biting at your ankles in the middle of the night. Do you want me to take care of the girl?'

'I think she'll hang herself if she's given enough rope. I've got a few ideas. My colleague – the one I told you about – has given a statement on my behalf. The girl is an unreliable witness and I can diminish her credibility.'

Nedzad smiled. He appreciated control and command, and his companion was holding his nerve. He liked that. He was a happy man tonight. His son slept soundly in his cot, and he'd even got a smile out of him. The poor child was clearly used to being passed around, but not any more. No one would separate them again.

'I have to go to Europe. Do you want to come with me? There's a lot of money involved.'

'I can't. I have to stay local because of the investigation.'

'No one will know. You're not tagged.'

'It's too risky.'

'Are you going cold on me?'

'The charges were completely unexpected and I don't think you appreciate the atmosphere. Crime in the North Lakes is low. It's not Sarajevo. If another girl goes missing who's connected to the other one, it'll raise suspicion.'

Nedzad smiled and forked some more dumplings onto his plate. They were delicious. 'The girl could be distraught at the loss of her friend and wander off...' He walked his fingers across the table and whistled. 'Besides, I have business in the area too. The woman who first took my boy is investigating, yes? I still have business with her.'

'Hold on there, she's a police officer. You can't harm a copper: that's taken extremely seriously here.'

'Who said I want to harm her? She has family. I know all about her. I've waited a long time for this.'

'For God's sake, will you at least wait until I know what's going on with my case?'

'Of course, my friend, for you I will do that. Let's have a toast to the gypsy, God rest his soul. He found my boy, with your help, of course.' They raised their glasses.

'To Bobby. Sleep well.'

They chinked the glasses together and drank. It was an expensive bottle of Chablis that was on the menu for over ninety pounds, but Nedzad didn't pay for his food and drink here.

'When everything calms down, you can come and work for me here in the city. You must get very bored up there with all the lakes and sheep. Unless you like sheep? Which reminds me: I have a private room just for us at the Taurus Club tonight.' Nedzad winked.

The Taurus Club was the smartest strip club in Manchester, and many a footballer had been caught with his pants down there. Unlike at cheaper joints, the girls were beautiful, and the punters got their money's worth. Nedzad's guest smiled broadly: he knew that when Nedzad was paying, it always included a private dance, followed by extras on top.

They ordered dessert.

There was no rush.

Chapter 35

Emma packed up her things and prepared to leave the school. Everybody else had gone, and the hall was quiet.

She'd spent an hour looking up the details of the two students who'd committed suicide in the last four years. One was a boy who'd been in Year 10; his was considered a case of drug abuse. The other, a Year 9 girl, was recorded as a case of domestic abuse. Sarah Peaks had said herself that neither incident had anything to do with the school, but Emma wondered.

A man who looked like some sort of caretaker came in and eyed her suspiciously. She smiled, and he softened his demeanour.

'Hello there, I'm just finishing up.'

He nodded. 'You been talking to the kids about the missing girl, then?' he said.

'Yes, we have. We're doing everything we can to find her.'

'I bet you are. I take my hat off to you lot. They don't make it easy, these teenagers, do they? You got kids?' He glanced briefly at her abdomen as if it would answer his question.

'No. You?'

'Three. They're all here, all pretty sensible, thank God, not like some of 'em.'

'Do you know Faith Shaw?'

'Not really. Seems a nice enough girl, though.'

'How long have you worked here?'

The man laughed and did a calculation in his head. 'Twenty-two years.'

'So you knew the two kids who took their own lives a few years back?'

'I knew the boy, for sure. Same age as my lad. They were mates. They said it was drugs, but that was only the half of it.'

'What do you mean?'

'He was miserable as sin. Hounded, he was. Picked on till he could take no more.'

'In school?'

'Of course in school. I was just glad it wasn't my kid; we all were.'

'Why wasn't it reported at the time?'

'He didn't tell. They call 'em gay, you know. If they snitch. They'll take anything, they will. I've told my lads that if anyone ever gets at 'em, they can punch back, just make sure it's harder.'

'So you didn't know the girl so much? The one they said was a domestic case?'

'Her dad hit her, that's for sure, but some violence you can't see, can you?'

'No, you're right. Did anyone come and question their school pals or teachers at the time?'

'I can't remember. The head was keen to play it down, that's for sure. My lads weren't asked anything about it. Sometimes the kids who have problems get forgotten, don't they? They're not missed, if you know what I mean. One was into that stuff he smoked, and the other hardly turned up. If it had been a governor's son or a Little Miss Perfect getting A's in everything, people might have taken notice, that's all.'

Emma thought about Jenna Fraser. She'd been a model student, a fine athlete, and as clean as a whistle until she'd taken her first pill.

'You think this one's done herself in?' the man asked.

'Do you?'

'Probably,' he said.

Emma carried on packing her things, deep in thought. 'Your boy who was in Year 10 when his friend killed himself, would he talk to me?'

'Don't see why not. He'll be here any minute. He sits in here till I've finished for the day. He don't like me walking home, so he drives me.'

It was touching.

The head teacher entered the hall. 'Are we done?' she asked.

'There's only you left, if now is a good time?' Emma smiled at her.

'I've already given a statement.'

'Not to me.'

'What do you need to know?'

'Will you take a seat?'

'No, I'm fine standing.'

'In your opinion, was Faith Shaw suicidal?'

'I've already answered this. No, she was the absolute opposite. Bubbly, happy, communicative, inclusive; a model student.'

'Have you read any of her English work?'

'If you're referring to the usual teenage angst about boyfriends, loneliness and pop stars, then I've got news for you: that's what they're all like.' The woman was condescending.

'What is actively done in this school for the mental health of your students?'

'Oh, the messages are very clear: we support one another as a community, we promote compassion and we will not tolerate inconsiderate behaviour; everybody is invested in as a whole child.' It was like a well-rehearsed speech for Ofsted.

'But what about the ones who don't feel included?'

'There aren't any.'

'I did notice that you have no bullying incidents logged in your policy documents. That's quite a record.'

'I know, we're very proud.'

'Isn't it rather unrealistic?'

'Perhaps you're referring to low-level behavioural issues. They don't count as full-blown bullying. There is a real difference, you know.'

'Ah. Can you explain?'

'Well I should have thought it was fairly obvious. We would log incidents of a violent, repetitive nature, for example.'

'Only if there is a complaint?'

'Of course.'

'And you receive none?'

'A lot of petty squabbles are dealt with on the spot. It's rarely what you would consider bullying. You need to be very clear about the difference; that's why we have expert training on the subject.'

'How often?'

'I beg your pardon?'

'Your expert training – how often, and who is involved?'

'I can't remember the figures. I'd have to look.'

'Right. You do that for us. And the two kids who took their own lives, Jake Trent and Laura Briggs: they were happy?'

'Now they were tragic cases, but nothing to do with us at all. Jake was a drug addict and Laura was abused by her father. They were very unhappy children.'

'But all was well at school? They didn't attract negative attention?'

'Well, it was ruled at the time, by people much cleverer than me or you, that their mental health problems were extra-academic.'

'But those problems don't cease to exist because children are at school.'

'That's where you're wrong. Often unhappy children lead separate lives at school because it's where they feel safe.'

Emma looked at the head, trying to read her. She spoke like a politician: confident and self-assured, even when the ship was clearly sinking.

'Thank you for your time. That's us done, I think.' Emma held out her hand, and the head took it, visibly relieved.

'I'm glad you got what you wanted. I'm looking forward to returning to normal.'

'It's not really normal, is it, when you've got a member of staff suspended and a child missing. Plus three suicides.'

The head blushed and was clearly about to say something, but thought better of it and turned to go, heels clicking on the laminate floor. It was only then that

Emma noticed that the caretaker had listened to the whole exchange.

A young man approached him, and they high-fived.

'Is this your son?' she asked.

The man nodded and introduced him.

'She wants to talk about Jake,' he added.

'Dad!' The boy was angry, but more than that, he was hiding another, more potent emotion – pain.

'I don't want to upset you. I just wanted you to tell me about Jake, that's all,' Emma said.

Emma was thirty years old, but she looked much younger, and the perceived small age gap helped. Her warmth made the boy relax, and he looked between her and his dad, then down at his feet.

'OK,' he said, and sat down.

He spoke to Emma for over an hour. She caught Kelly Porter on her mobile phone at five o'clock.

'Guv, did we pull the Jenna Fraser's mobile phone records?'

'No, why?' Kelly said.

'I think we need to.'

Chapter 36

Sadie Rawlinson was on a downer.

She approached her home with the usual trepidation about seeing her mother, but something else was shaking her ordinarily hard and impenetrable exterior.

Sadie couldn't remember the first time she'd found her mother slumped in a chair, or passed out on the floor, or staggering into a piece of furniture. It had always been so. It was her mother who'd encouraged her to try her first joint. She'd been eleven years old.

She couldn't remember her father, either. There'd been plenty of men who hung around the house, but none who stayed for any length of time. They were usually dealers or scroungers. Sometimes they slept in her mother's room; sometimes they tried to sleep in Sadie's. She hoped that today, her mother would be alone. Passed out would be even better, as well as being highly likely. Sadie needed to get high, and to do so in peace, with no shouting matches, no harassment and no one trying to cut in on her gear. Her head was banging and she was desperate to drift away from the demons threatening to derail her. She knew that she was a statistic, and a bad one at that. She wasn't stupid. She was perfectly aware that her spiralling addiction was ruining her life. But she didn't care. She needed the high more than she wanted to break the cycle.

She opened the door.

The top-floor maisonette, courtesy of the local council, was silent.

She checked the kitchen and the sitting room. She'd been jittery since she'd filed charges against Mr Blackman. Then she went to her mother's door and pushed it open. The room stank. Her mother lay slumped on the bed, and for a moment, Sadie felt pain. It was in her chest, and she imagined it to be her heart. There was once a time when her mother would be surrounded by cans of Special Brew or Breaker. Now it was tiny plastic bags, mirrors covered in powder residue, and the smell of burning heroin. Brown sugar.

The stupid fuck had left the needle in her arm again. Her mother would kill herself one day, Sadie knew it. Maybe then she'd be free to start over. Fat chance. She removed the needle and released the elastic strap cutting off the blood supply. Her mother groaned and rolled over. Sadie pulled up the covers and left her to her slumber. Now she could isolate herself and blot out the images plaguing her mind.

She didn't want to think any more. Thinking hurt, because it made her feel. She'd lied to the police and they knew it. She'd tried hard to keep it together, and for a while it had seemed to work. The plan all along had simply been to get Tony Blackman off their backs. But it had spiralled out of control. He wanted too much, he demanded too much and he wouldn't leave them alone. She regretted going to the party with him and getting involved in the first place. Now he could use it to control them.

At first it had been fun: the parties, the free gear, the thrill of being treated as part of something, hanging out with the coolest teacher in school; but then it grew risky and she was the first one to defy him. His temper shocked them all. It wasn't a game any more. Mr Blackman wasn't the man they thought he was, and they became scared. They were in over their heads and couldn't think of a way to get him to leave them alone. It had been Faith's idea, bless her. She was always the bright one.

Before Sadie faced the toughest decision of her life – whether to tell the truth – she was going to get high and forget. The truth was something she was unfamiliar with. She'd need to sit on it for a while.

She went to her room and put her bag on her bed. Her pulse rate quickened as her thoughts turned to the small plastic bag in her coat pocket, and her hands shook as she unwrapped it. In these moments, something inside her just took over, and she allowed it to. It was like the most intense kind of need she'd ever felt. It was better than childhood Christmases; better even than outsmarting the police.

In her drawer, she found a lighter and her mirror. It was already covered in the residue of powder long crushed and snorted. It was never cleaned. She carefully began breaking the little pill apart with the butt of the lighter until it resembled fine crumbs. Saliva filled her mouth. The tablet should really be completely crushed, but she couldn't wait, her need was too great. She discarded the lighter and searched for a banknote, finding a new tenner. These plastic ones were epic for snorting.

A moment of time took her away from herself, and Faith's face filled her mind. Her friend had tried the odd joint, a bit of PCP, even an Ecstasy tablet, but she'd never got hooked. She said she needed to try stuff to give her the knowledge to dismiss it. And she did. That was why Sadie hated her, though, at times like this, the hate turned in on itself and self-loathing took over: the real cause of her pain.

Tears stung her eyes as she bent over the mirror and used the edge of the tenner to order the powder into two lines. She took a deep breath and snorted one line, and then the other. Her nose tingled instantly and she rubbed it. Her eyes watered and she shook her head.

It was good stuff.

Her body numbed and she began to smile. She curled her legs up onto the bed and lay down. Her eyes flickered and closed as the drug entered her brain quickly, thanks to the tiny vessels of the nasal membrane, which made the pathway to the bloodstream almost instantaneous. But the biology didn't really matter. Only the deadening of thought and sense mattered.

The line between life and death no longer existed; only the escape from the noise.

Chapter 37

Kelly walked towards the centre of town, passing groups of kids throwing snowballs, and hardy walkers soaked from their day on the fells. The weather showed no sign of improvement; in fact, more snow was predicted. She listened patiently to Emma as she briefed her on what the caretaker's son had said. He'd agreed to sign a formal statement.

Jake Trent had first come to befriend Mr Blackman at a party. It was usual for the teacher to turn up at parties; it added to his reputation as a statement teacher with swagger. It hadn't taken long for Jake to begin to show all the signs of being a full-blown addict. The caretaker's son claimed that it was Mr Blackman who'd given Jake Trent his first opiate pill.

Kelly swirled the information round her head as she headed to the restaurant she'd agreed with Johnny. An officer had been sent to confront Mr Blackman with the accusation, and he'd strongly denied it, meaning that if Kelly wanted to pursue that particular angle, they'd have to investigate it separately. Not only that, but when his flat had been searched when the computer was seized, no drug paraphernalia had been discovered. But at least it gave her a new idea about why Sadie Rawlinson might have been at the teacher's flat. Though if he was her supplier, what was she doing accusing him of sexual assault?

She'd assigned Emma the task of further digging, but they were already stretched, and resources were buckling under the strain. Her whole team was putting in longer and longer hours as the Blackman case and the search for Faith intensified.

She spotted Johnny and Josie across the road and waved. The Skiddaw Bistro was a new addition to the town; it served funky Mediterranean food that was supposedly healthier than a standard Italian or Spanish restaurant, or that was how it was advertised. Kelly just loved her food. So did Johnny. Josie was a little trickier to convince.

'I'm on the bikini body diet,' she said.

'What's that?' Kelly asked. Johnny flashed her a look that said, 'Behave.' She winked.

'I follow this vlogger from New York. She's amazing, but I'm finding the vegan bit hard.'

Johnny covered his face with one hand and made himself busy asking for a table. As the waitress led them away, he glanced at Kelly.

'Vegan? Why would you do that? You need protein.' They wove in and out of chairs and Josie tutted. Kelly checked herself. The evening was supposed to be about bonding as a threesome, and it had got off to a bad start. 'And there are no beaches in New York.'

'I don't think that's the point,' Johnny said.

'You have a fabulous figure, Josie.' Kelly tried flattery.

'You old people always say that. Look – *she* has a figure.' Josie held up her phone and showed Kelly a picture of a woman in a bikini. She was tanned and glorious; she had clearly had work done, and the photo had been airbrushed. It made Kelly desperately sad for these teenagers.

'God, she looks like she needs a big fat steak,' she said. Johnny winced.

'She's got five million followers on Instagram.'

None of these kids lived in the real world. They just didn't compute the difference between reality and fiction. Kelly knew she'd said enough.

'So what are you allowed to eat? Is this menu all right? There's salad,' she said.

Josie studied the options. Kelly watched her. Josie was fairly grounded and resilient. If she was racked with this perverse sense of perfection, more fragile kids didn't stand a chance. She remembered what she and her team had come to perceive Jenna Fraser: perfection on the outside; dying on the inside. But thoughts of the dead girl didn't help and she pushed them away.

The investigation had been thorough: there was no foul play, and no one else was involved. The parents had been asked specifically if they thought Jenna was coerced or bullied into her decision, and they'd stated categorically that they didn't believe that had been the case.

Case closed. 'I'm starving. It all looks lovely,' Kelly said.

Johnny was always quiet when he played umpire between the two women in his life.

'I'll have a Diet Coke, the no-dressing Caesar salad with no bacon or chicken, and a strawberry sundae,' Josie announced.

Kelly opened her mouth, but Johnny squeezed her knee under the table. She got the message. She ordered squid, and Johnny went for paella.

'How's school, Josie?' They settled into a typical parents-take-teenager-for-dinner conversation. Kelly laughed at Josie's anecdotes, and Johnny relaxed.

'You know I was asking you about the way kids speak to each other?' Kelly asked.

Josie nodded, tucking into her plate of lettuce.

'I was amazed. I had no idea. Doesn't it hurt? I mean, in between all the insults online, and the crushing necessity to conform, where's the fun?' Kelly shovelled in a mouthful of carbs loaded with Parmesan cheese and seafood.

Josie looked confused. 'We don't conform,' she said.

Kelly didn't know what to say. All she could see from social media searches was a bunch of identical robots acting like sunflowers, turning their heads to the latest star with three million likes.

'Right. So what are you into at the moment, Josie? What's the latest thing?'

Josie looked horrified. 'There isn't a "thing". That would be weird.'

'So what happens if you don't like *Love Island*, or Ariana Grande?'

'How can anyone not love her after Manchester?' Josie said in disgust.

'Of course, very brave. Er, I mean, what if someone likes different music?'

'It's not about her music. She's an icon.'

'Right.'

Johnny was going purple trying to keep a straight face. Kelly sipped her glass of wine and realised glumly that her questions were falling off Josie like blossom in summer. The whole premise of the conversation was useless. She worried that if she asked any more, she'd completely lose the girl, and she was supposed to be here to improve their relationship, for Johnny's sake. She changed the subject.

When Josie's sundae arrived, Kelly had to bite her lip. The temptation to give her a lecture on veganism was strong, but she resisted. Almost.

'How's your cream?'

'Yum.'

Johnny squeezed Kelly's leg again.

'Can Dad stay at yours tonight? I'm loving his sixty-inch TV, and I'm not a kid. Kelly, tell him, he's suffocating me!' Josie pleaded.

Kelly felt flattered that the girl was asking for her help. It was touching. She looked at Johnny. 'You've been told.' She turned to Josie, 'You know he only cares about you. The missing girl hasn't been found yet. It's serious, Josie.'

'I know, God! But I've got you two down the road. If anything ever happened to me, Dad would kill them!' Josie giggled. It wasn't funny, but Kelly and Johnny pretended to see it for the quip that was intended.

'What about a compromise?' Kelly suggested. Father and daughter both looked at her. 'Your dad can come and stay if you answer your phone every hour and then he comes and checks the locks before you go to sleep.'

'Deal,' Josie said.

Chapter 38

'Where are you taking me, Ted?'

'It's a surprise.'

Ted held the door for Wendy while she fastened her coat. The air was fresh, but both of them were prepared for it. She wore a hat and she'd applied her make-up carefully. Her handbag matched her silk scarf, which she tightened round her throat.

'Ready?' he asked. She nodded.

Ted had turned into a kind man. Not that he ever hadn't been, but some men hardened with age and regret, while others, like John, fell ill and became impenetrably cantankerous. Ted, though, had mellowed and matured. The lines round his eyes were soft, and the portals they framed were twinkly and bright. His speech was as deliberate as his hands, and he was even more of a gentleman than before. The night they'd met, at the fountain on the earl's estate, he'd shown the same qualities, but then they had been accompanied by a cheeky wickedness. They'd been attracted to one another straight away, and it had scared her. She'd never strayed from John, and never thought she would. It was only when she was presented with an opportunity so delicious that she even contemplated it.

She hadn't set out to hurt anyone, least of all her husband; it wasn't like that at all. To Wendy, the fact that John had never noticed the change in her spoke a thousand words. Guilt wasn't something she'd felt until she'd faced her daughter, and even then it was momentary, and she'd prepared to be unapologetic should Kelly challenge her morally. To Wendy's surprise, she hadn't. Despite being childless, Kelly was wiser than she'd allowed for, and she felt sad about that. Wendy always figured that Kelly would do her growing up when she had a family of her own, but that had never come, and now, even if it did, she was unlikely to see it. The drugs could only keep her alive for so long.

She had read about miracle cures for cancer in magazines. In Florida, a woman had eaten plates of steaming broccoli and cured her breast cancer. In Russia, bread products made by hand with local wheat had cured a man's bowel cancer. In Canada, a woman had cured her leukaemia by only consuming raw milk. The list was as endless as it was extraordinary. Wendy had no time to dedicate to such quackery; she was ready to be off, and she was determined to enjoy herself until her time came. She'd lasted much longer than anyone had predicted. Her initial prognosis had given her six months, something she'd kept from her daughter. Then she'd started the trials. That was over a year ago. Her body ached more these days, and she was on a break from drugs, letting nature take its course. The deterioration had begun almost straight away, but it was her choice and hers alone; she hadn't discussed it with the girls.

When Ted had turned up out of the blue, and Kelly had found out the truth, Wendy had known this day would arrive. Kelly was her father's daughter all right: her analytical brain, her desire to seek answers, her unshakeable belief in herself; and those kind eyes, full of naughtiness. She felt a twinge of shame when she thought about John, the man who'd brought up her daughters. But she'd said sorry enough. Neither of them had been saints; goodness, if they were courting nowadays, they'd both be caught red-handed on those iPhones that were everywhere.

She felt sorry for the youngsters now; they were imprisoned by their screens. What made it worse was that they used them for their work, and then they came home and used them for their rest. There was no escape; it was madness. She wouldn't miss it. The accountant had been and sorted her affairs. John had done most of it anyway, and nothing much had changed since he'd gone, only the amount that was left. The girls would have the house. They'd no doubt disagree over what to do with it, but that, thankfully, would no longer be her concern.

Ted held her elbow as they crunched through the snow. The sky was blue, the air crisp. There was no better place to be in the world than the Lakes on a day like today. The mountains glowed in the distance and Wendy wished she was a climber. She never had been, but that wasn't the point. She'd started dreaming about lots of pastimes that she'd never get to try.

Ted helped her into his car. It was very smart indeed. He kept it clean and tidy, and she liked that. Kelly could learn a thing or two from him; her car was a disgrace. He got her settled, then went to his own side and climbed in. He turned to her and smiled. Life was a funny old thing. No one could predict what might be around the next bend. She smiled back.

He drove towards Keswick, and she thought he might be taking her to a nice café, or perhaps a pub with a roaring fire. The main road was clear, but piles of snow were stacked high at each side. The mountains, as they drew closer, looked majestic, and all of their millions of years old.

He drove through Keswick and on down the east coast of Derwent Water. Cat Bells looked inviting and gentle, and Wendy wanted to dive into the lake. They'd swum in Ullswater, off the shore of Wasdale Hall's grounds, drunk and frivolous. Everybody did it, and without phones, no one was self-conscious or worried. Wendy had stripped to her bra and knickers, but she might as well have thrown them off too, since soaking wet they were see-through anyhow.

'Remember swimming in Ullswater, Ted? At midnight?'

'Good heavens, that's brought back memories! I don't think I could manage that any more,' he joked.

'We'd be on the front page of the *Daily Mail* now, you know. It was scandalous.'

'Yes, I suppose you're right. The youngsters think we didn't know how to live, or have fun.'

'I wanted to talk to you about that, Ted.'

'Hmm?' He concentrated on his driving.

'What we got up to.'

He gripped the steering wheel. 'I haven't forgotten, Wendy. I just wish I could have made you my wife.'

His words came as a surprise. She'd never felt like a floozy, or used in any way, but she hadn't thought about the flip side either.

'Kelly has been asking certain questions.'

'About what?'

'Us.'

'Well that makes sense. She has been rather tetchy lately. Do you think she minds?'

'No, not at all. That's not what I meant, Ted.'

He negotiated a milk tanker in the road ahead and they came to the Lodore Falls. He pulled off and parked at the hotel.

'Oh lovely! I haven't been here in years.'

'We're booked in for lunch.'

Ted got out and went to Wendy's door to help her out of the car. He was still strong, and she leant on him.

The foyer was warm and there was a well-tended fire in the bar. The smell of food and Christmas spices was intoxicating, and Wendy decided that she'd have a drink before dropping her bombshell on Ted. She ordered a sherry, and they were escorted to their table, which overlooked the lake. The sun shone into the dining room and Wendy was reminded of another meal she'd had in an expensive hotel, with Kelly. Father and daughter had the same certainty, the same self-possession when in company: nothing fazed them. Nikki was different. John's daughter was more reserved in company and hesitant about her place in the world, not convinced of her path. Kelly had built her own path, as had this man before her.

She sipped her sherry and perused the menu. It was thankfully simple. Her tolerance of food was intermittent lately. She prayed that her digestive system stood the test today. She didn't want to embarrass Ted. She wished to be dignified to the end, and if she wasn't, she'd make sure that he didn't see her.

'What takes your fancy, Wendy?'

'I'm thinking the chicken, it sounds lovely.'

'Starter?'

'No, that's too much; I think I'd pop.'

Ted ordered, then reached across to take her hand.

Maybe she'd wait until after they'd eaten, she thought. She chastised herself. She'd promised Kelly that she'd do this; in fact, she'd insisted. Kelly had been more than willing to give Ted the news herself, but that wasn't right. It was Wendy's job. What happened next was up to them. She wouldn't be here. She couldn't wait.

'The reason I mentioned Kelly is that I need to tell you something.'

'I'm listening.' He sipped his pint.

'She's your daughter, Ted.'

He didn't react in any of the ways she'd been prepared for. She'd imagined herself alone, phoning a taxi, being called a liar; she'd seen raised voices and histrionics. But none of those things happened. He was about as calm as anyone could be; she should have known. She saw Kelly in him when he looked at her and cocked his head slightly, thinking about the perfect question to ask but testing it in his brain before presenting it to the world.

'I did wonder,' was all he said. He didn't question it or doubt it. Wendy's hand shook slightly as she drained her sherry and asked for another.

'Did you?'

He nodded. 'Does Kelly know?'

'Yes, that's why I'm telling you.'

'How did she take it?'

Wendy looked at him. She could see that he cared for Kelly. He really wanted her to be receptive to the news.

He looked like a man who'd been given a second chance; or at least hoped for it. Her throat tightened.

They'd be all right.

'She wants to see you.'

Chapter 39

Rob's Manchester mole sent his report on Christmas Eve.

It was not what anyone had expected, and it blew a hole through the Tony Blackman case. Most of the report was computer jargon that only Rob understood, and when he read it out to the team at Eden House, they had to stop him and request that he explain what on earth he was talking about. They understood the straightforward English, such as 'download', 'input', and 'keyboard', but when it came to things like firewalls, spyware, encryption and steganography, they were baffled.

Rob apologised and tried to translate the report for the laymen in front of him. They'd hit a similar kind of web of confusion when they'd tried to unpick the mass of bank accounts and files connected to a money-laundering case a few years back, run from the Isle of Man. They hadn't had Rob then, and they'd relied solely on computer buffs sitting in dark rooms.

Apparently it was really easy to conceal files on computers; you just downloaded an app, or used the computer's own system for hiding data from prying eyes. However, most of the tricks available freely online weren't anywhere near good enough if you were contemplating hiding information from the police.

Rob explained that on Friday 1 December, between 6 and 7 p.m., close to eighty JPEG images had been downloaded from a removable device onto Tony Blackman's computer hard drive. Alongside the images, nineteen videos, including audio, had also been downloaded. The process had taken fifty-nine minutes and the pathway had been cleared by a cleaning device that had to be plugged in manually. So what the mole had uncovered was that rather than try to conceal the graphic content, the user had tried to conceal how it had gotten there.

'You can never erase the hard drive memory. What's a red flag is that the images were there in plain sight, and paedophiles usually go to great lengths to firewall and encrypt the actual material. In this case, what took time is finding out how all the images got on to the computer at the same time, and we now know that it was done via the removable device.'

Rob also explained that at the same time as the device was running, the user had also been searching Lakeland poetry. But that wasn't all. During the fifty-nine minutes, several Instagram and Facebook accounts were logged onto, and posts were deleted and liked. The accounts belonged to a user called 'SadieSadie1234' and were registered to a mobile phone in the name of Miss B. Rawlinson. Everybody in the room knew that Sadie Rawlinson's mother was called Belinda, and it didn't take a genius to work out that Sadie probably didn't pay for her own phone.

'Jesus, we're talking contempt and wasting police time,' Kate Umshaw said.

'We can say goodbye to the CPS wanting the case,' Kelly agreed. 'Kate, you and Emma need to go and pay mother and daughter a visit. I'll get Blackman in. It still doesn't prove that he didn't download the images; just that Sadie was in his flat at the time it was done. We need to get a statement of her competence in computer science from school. She also needs to be asked how Mr Blackman managed to assault her when she was cruising Instagram and Facebook. What was she looking at?' Kelly asked Rob.

Computers had changed the face of policing. They had created a labyrinthine pit of other worlds to hide in. The police were always playing catch-up as more sophisticated and impenetrable spaces appeared in cyber land. It was a minefield, and Kelly was glad to have Rob. It didn't matter how many times he explained how it all worked, she would never get it. But when he translated it into her language, she knew that they could use it. None of that helped Mr Blackman, though. He'd been inextricably linked in the public mind with sex offences against children. He'd never teach again.

'She was liking photos and commenting on pages. Typical social media activity.'

'Right, so she was sitting at his computer, Lakeland poetry pending on Google, presumably as a red herring, and checking her social media. Can we prove it?' Kelly asked.

'In a court, you could argue that whoever was sitting at the computer was the same person who downloaded the material, otherwise they would have had to have taken turns. Either way, Sadie Rawlinson was using the computer when the images were being downloaded.'

'What would a defence team argue?'

'That she had no idea what was going on and that Blackman was the one using her social media accounts.'

'And the assault?'

'All planned. He's an unstoppable pervert with a lust for young girls, and he lured her there, showed her some poetry and gave her the name of some handy websites to search, downloaded the images, then assaulted her.'

'Bullshit. How likely is it?'

'You can never tell with lawyers. She hasn't got the means to pay a shit-hot barrister, that's for sure, but you also never know with Legal Aid. It all depends on her performance in court, against a perceived predator. If it were to go to jury, they'd have most likely seen him in the press already.'

It wasn't the police's job to prove guilt or innocence in a court of law – that was up to the legal process – but the lawyers and barristers could only use what the police had provided, and it needed to be watertight, or else the CPS wouldn't entertain it.

'Emma, have you heard from your mole?' So much of their investigation now depended on digital footprints. Emma had got Kelly's go-ahead to examine Jenna's iPhone records more closely, and had passed them to another computer geek who sat not three desks from Rob's contact in the Manchester office.

'After talking to the caretaker's boy, I can't help thinking that a helping hand over a cliff comes in many different forms. Jake Trent, the boy who killed himself two years ago, injected himself with so much fentanyl that it could have felled a five-hundred-pound bull. The boy had been a consummate and skilled drug user; there was no way he'd get his calculation so wrong. Or that's what

215

the caretaker's son said. North Lakes Serious Crime wasn't even involved after the coroner ruled an overdose, and the boy's past indicated a miserable downward spiral of self-destruction, confirmed by the parents and the school.'

Kelly went to the whiteboard. 'So, we've got Tony Blackman potentially supplying drugs, as well as Bobby Bailey and Luke Miles a question mark. I think Sadie is the common denominator here, and she's fragile as hell: her mother is a drug addict, with a history of low-level warnings from the police, including prostitution in Barrow, and Sadie's veneer is too tough to be real.'

Chapter 40

Ted sat on a bench overlooking Derwent Water. He'd walked through snow to get to this particular spot and had wiped it off the bench so he could sit down. He pulled his coat tight around him and caught his breath, which came in great white clouds. The snow made the Lakes brighter somehow; it provided the perfect light for the sky, water and fell to shine.

He and Wendy had spent the night at the Lodore Falls Hotel. He'd dropped her off reluctantly at home this morning, and left her to rest. She'd looked happy, but tired. The last thing she'd said to him was that she wished they'd done this years ago. He wished for the same thing, but ever the pragmatist, he looked forward, not back.

He already had two daughters. A third was an unexpected surprise, but one that didn't perplex him. On the contrary, it made him happy. He'd asked Wendy a hundred times why she hadn't told him; why she'd kept it to herself for all these years, but he knew the answer. He thought of his own ex-wife and questioned the paternity of their daughters: perhaps Mary had done the same. He'd never know.

He'd driven back to Derwent Water because if he couldn't physically be with Wendy, he wanted to be where they'd last been together. The bench, under the trees, overlooking a pebble beach and with a view of Cat Bells and Grisedale Pike beyond, was dedicated to 'Dear Ada, Wife, Mother, and dearly beloved Grandmother. Always in our hearts and taken too soon. 1987.' He fantasised romantically that Ada used to sit here with her husband, with Walla Crag behind them, gazing out onto the lake, planning their retirement; a retirement that never came because she died suddenly of some awful disease.

Pain was such a constant visitor to life that pleasure should be scooped up and bagged at every opportunity, and that was just what Ted intended to do. He was no fool. He'd trained in medicine, and he knew that Wendy was gravely ill. She'd been battling for the best part of two years, and had been in and out of the Penrith and Lakes Hospital more times than he'd cut open bodies, but it didn't diminish her resolve, or indeed her sense of fun that he so fondly recalled.

He thought about his new daughter. It was rather late to assume the role of loving and supportive father when almost forty years had passed, but he was willing to give it a go. There was, after all, nothing to lose. Their working relationship was coming to an end, as he had finally made the decision to retire, and Kelly would have to get to know a new coroner. Perhaps the impromptu pints in the less salubrious establishments of Penrith would continue, but that might be too much to hope for. All he could do was stand by Wendy now, and wait to see what Kelly wanted of him, if anything.

She was quite something, Kelly Porter. Just like her mother. Last night had been wonderful, an experience Ted had never thought he'd get to enjoy again. A night in a Lakes establishment with a beautiful woman was something that didn't happen every day, particularly to a man in his sixties. He felt like a youngster who'd conquered the best-looking girl in the school. But with age behind them, there was no demure stalling, or crippling embarrassment, or need for Dutch courage; it had been spontaneous, thrilling and one of the most exciting nights of his life.

He looked out across the lake.

The fact that the bench upon which he sat was situated not two hundred yards from where Jenna Fraser had ended her life was not lost on him. Those youngsters saw nothing ahead, only what was behind them, and they despaired of a future they thought they had lost before it had even begun. How wrong they were! The wastefulness hit him and he looked down at his hands: the hands that had cut open Jenna's body, to reveal that her heart was the only intact part of her. It had probably gone on beating for minutes after impact because it was so cleverly designed by its maker. The same maker who had crumpled these hills and fells; the same maker who drove one man to kill another. Ted had had plenty of corpses on his slab, but none quite like that of Jenna Fraser.

He'd had two missed calls from Kelly. One this morning, as he was asleep next to her mother, and the other when he'd been dropping Wendy off. Was she spying on him? Did she know that he knew?

He'd been too nervous to call her back, but now he felt silly, and took his phone out of his pocket.

When she answered, he began to ask how she was, but Kelly was in work mode and wanted to talk about suicide. Ted sighed and realised that he'd have to make an appointment with his daughter, rather than the detective, to have a proper conversation with her. She was asking about two teenagers who'd taken their lives two years apart, both from Keswick.

'Of course I remember them,' he said.

'Jake Trent was a drugs overdose, correct?'

'Yes, pretty straightforward. Fentanyl, it's a cheap heroin substitute.'

'And Laura Briggs, four years ago, she was a domestic case.'

'Yes, as I recall.'

As always, Kelly didn't draw breath when she was onto something. Ted had no idea why she was raking up old suicides, but he was sure that she had good reason. She was an excellent detective; probably the best he'd ever worked with.

'The case was harrowing,' he told her. 'She'd cut her wrists in the bath and gradually bled to death. She was being sexually abused by her father.' Ted wished he could have some time alone with child abusers in his mortuary, with a saw, a scalpel and some blunt rusty shears. A few slow hours would do it.

'I know, Ted. They were open-and shut-cases, handled by first responders and your office. There was no need to involve the serious crime department. At least that was what was thought.'

'What do you mean?'

'I'm doing something that I don't think has been done before, Ted. And I want your advice.'

'Of course, Kelly. I'm here for you.'

There was a pause.

'I guess Mum has spoken to you now. She said you were taking her out yesterday.'

Ted blushed a little, remembering his tryst the night before.

'We went for lunch at the Lodore Hotel.'

'Nice! When are you taking me?'

'Whenever I can catch you. You're always busy.'

There was a short silence, and Ted wanted to fill it, but he was in uncharted waters.

'Ted, we need to sit down and have a pint. I don't see you as my father. John Porter was my dad. But if you would like to, I think we should spend a bit of time together.'

'I should like that very much,' Ted said. Kelly couldn't see the grin spreading across his face.

'Right. Good. Like I said, I'm doing something that hasn't been done before. I've come across too many suicides of school kids that simply shouldn't have happened.'

Ted grew serious once more. 'No death should occur, Kelly, apart from expiry from old age, but you can't control it, I'm afraid. You know that.'

'But if I can catch the dealers, I can get them for murder because the victims were kids. In the eyes of the law, that's like pulling the trigger.'

'It's a grey area. Suicides are notoriously difficult to overturn. The government doesn't like the statistics; it makes them look bad. Are you asking me if there are any links between the cases?'

'Yes. Is there any way of proving the source of the drugs from what you gathered at the autopsy?'

'Possibly.'

'That'll do. Remember the Baby Dale case from two years ago? He was found behind Greenside lead mine.'

'Yes, indeed I do. Was he reunited with his parents?'

'Not exactly. His father was a wanted criminal from Sarajevo and the mother disappeared from hospital.'

Ted looked across the lake. He could listen to Kelly all day long and live off her infectious passion for solving riddles. He smiled and waited.

'He's gone missing from his foster home and I think our Nedzad Galic is back in town.'

'Is this related?' he asked. 'I'm confused. I had one of your officers asking questions about Jenna Fraser's file yesterday. How is that linked to the child?'

'Emma Hide?'

'Yes, that's her. We had a chat about fentanyl and the OxyContin that Jenna was prescribed, amongst other substances, and whether batches can be traced. I told her they could, of course.'

'What are you doing tomorrow?' Kelly changed the subject yet again. 'Mum is coming to mine; would you like to join us? I know it's late notice and I'm sure you have plans already...'

Ted paused, and remembered that today was Christmas Eve. The girls were with Mary this year. It would be the first Christmas he'd spent entirely alone.

'If it's all right with your mother, I would love to,' he replied.

'We'll eat at one o'clock. Do you know where I live?'

'No. You told me you'd moved out of your mother's.'

'It's Pooley Bridge. I'll send you the address.'

Chapter 41

Christmas Eve was perhaps the worst and best time to record a TV appeal for a missing teenager. It would reach those preparing to spend time with their loved ones, and at the same time hopefully trigger some recollection of the girl who would be absent from the festive day. A day of family, a day of love and peace on earth: the phrase made Kelly baulk. If there was peace on earth, she would be out of a job. If humans could live together without killing one another, she'd be cosied up in a retirement home with Johnny, sipping cocktails and planning their next trip to the Bahamas.

Fat chance.

Kelly hadn't seen Maggie and Colin Shaw all week, and she felt as though she'd been through some sort of time warp when she first caught sight of them: they both looked as though they'd aged ten years. They'd lost serious amounts of weight, their shoulders were hunched, and dark circles haunted their eyes.

She greeted them in a back room, away from the press. There were camera crews here from all over the country, as well as one from the USA and another from Italy. The plight of the beautiful, innocent girl had caught the imaginations of people thousands of miles away. Kelly had to admit that it bore all the hallmarks of a front-page story, regardless of which language it was written in.

She spoke to the couple about what to expect from such an event. They'd had liaison officers with them all week, who'd remain for as long as the money lasted. Kelly would fight to keep them, but the reality was that at some point, their resources would have to be redirected.

She asked the Shaws to stay on afterwards to chat about something to do with Faith. She hadn't briefed them at all, and neither had the liaison officers. She didn't want to affect their TV appearance by bringing in the spectre of the possibility that Faith might have harmed herself, or giving any hint that she was considering a full investigation of the Derwent Academy. It was controversial, but Kelly had looked into it until late the previous night, which was why she felt somewhat groggy today.

She'd read precedents going back ten years on the mental state of suicide cases, and had found countless instances where a single person, not even a group, was implicated in the deterioration of a victim's mental state just before they took their own life. But none of those mentioned were ever legally held accountable. Not one. It bugged her.

She'd fallen asleep somewhere around 3 or 4 a.m., only to be woken by the bin lorry beeping its horn for someone to move out of the way. The familiar nausea of lack of sleep had punctuated her day ever since. The team brief led by Rob this morning on computer anatomy had almost killed her off entirely.

Now, the sight of Michael Shaw woke her quicker than any strong Italian coffee. He looked lost, but determined at the same time. He had wanted to be involved, and no one was about to tell him he couldn't be. He sat between his parents, Maggie Shaw clinging onto him.

Kelly had explained to them about when they'd get their opportunity to speak, after which the press would file out and vacate the room. There would be no questions at this time. A liaison officer from HQ would sit with them during the statement and the showing of the photos chosen by the family. In all of them, Faith looked so alive that she almost jumped off the paper. Maggie had said she was certain about what she planned to say, but Colin simply stared blankly ahead. Michael wanted to make a speech, but the liaison officer said it was probably best that he wasn't given too much exposure, else the media would make a meal out of it; in addition, there were certain protection issues that needed to be adhered to with a minor appearing on a live feed. Michael took it well. Kelly knew that simply his presence would have a huge impact on viewers.

As requested, one of the liaison officers had gained a copy of all the paperwork kept by Mrs Shaw relating to Faith's school life, and collated it, ready for Kelly to have a look. She was handed an envelope and put it to one side.

They were ready.

Kelly watched them leave the room and heard the cameras whir as soon as the door opened. It closed again and she was left alone. The silence took her by surprise, and she felt injustice rise up inside her. It threatened to suffocate her, and she swallowed hard to fight it. She'd been in the same situation countless times, but she couldn't get Michael's face out of her head. The memory of him sitting on Faith's bed telling Kelly about his sister's make-up.

She sat down and opened the envelope. Everything was ordered by date. Phone calls to the school, letters written to teachers and the head, copies of texts, WhatsApps, Instagram posts, Snapchats and emails. There were literally hundreds of communications between Mrs Shaw and the school. It seemed that Faith had been hounded daily for the best part of two years, and no one at Derwent Academy had done anything about it.

She stood up sharply when the door opened once more and the family filed back in. Maggie Shaw was sobbing, and Colin bumped into a chair. Michael walked out of the room into the corridor. Kelly didn't know which one to see to. Liaison officers surrounded the parents, so she slipped out after the boy.

'Hey,' she said. He was kicking the wall; not hard, just a rhythmic *tap, tap*.

He nodded acknowledgement.

'What was it like when you moved here? It must have been tough.'

Michael nodded. 'It was fine. It was Faith who lost it.'

'Lost what?'

'The plot.'

'Oh.'

'Now *they're* losing it.' He indicated the room where his parents had disintegrated after facing the press.

'They're not losing it, they're suffering. But that doesn't help you.'

'I don't want help.'

'What do you want?'

'I want Faith back so everyone can act normal again.'

'I understand,' Kelly said. 'How did she lose it? I mean, when you moved here?'

'She ran away, she said she wanted to kill herself, she went crazy, she had no friends. Mum and Dad drank a lot of beer.'

Kelly loved that about kids: ask them a straight question, and you got a straight answer. Kids should be coppers, she thought. 'How did she threaten to kill herself?' She wanted to be as gentle as she could with him.

'She got knives out of the drawer and she said she'd meet a stranger.'

'What kind of stranger?'

'I dunno. Someone online, you know, stranger danger and all that.' Michael spoke as if he'd been to a hundred lectures on child protection and was considering changing jobs.

'Do you think she was serious?'

He shrugged.

'I thought she was happy now?' Kelly tried a different angle.

'It was an act. Children are very good actors, you know.' When he said this, Michael looked her straight in the eye, and Kelly felt thoroughly outsmarted. She couldn't work out whether Michael Shaw was a very clever twelve-year-old, way ahead of his years, or if he'd been listening to his relatives talking, supposedly out of earshot.

'Did she see a doctor about being unhappy?'

'She saw a shrink.' The American word jarred with Kelly, but she guessed he heard it a lot if he watched American TV, like most kids did.

'You know what a shrink is?'

'Course I do! She stopped going, though; it made her worse. I could have told everyone that, but no one listened

227

to me. There was nothing wrong with her, she just chose crap friends. And she's a girl.'

'I don't know much about what her friends did, Michael, do you?'

'Yeah, they used to take her places and leave her there. Mum used to go out looking for her in the park and find her on her own. They said we'd move again. I kind of expected it, but we didn't.'

'She has different friends now?'

'No, they were always the same.'

'Can I get you a Coke?' Kelly asked. There was a vending machine downstairs, and she wanted to process what she'd heard. Michael's parents needed some space to calm down before they were driven home. Michael nodded and followed her.

'So I met Justin this week,' Kelly said. 'He was nice, right? The night of the fair?'

'He only did it because he fancied my sister.'

'So he was nice to you to gain favour with Faith?'

Michael nodded again. They took the stairs.

'And what about Luke?'

'He liked her too. But I told her Mum and Dad would freak if they found out.'

'Why would they do that?'

Michael looked at her, and a smile began to form at the corners of his mouth.

'You don't know a lot for a police detective, do you?'

'For me to know stuff, I have to have people tell me, and for that they have to trust me.'

'Everyone at school knows about Luke. All the teachers and adults think he's amazing and clever and he's this kind of cool person. But he's not.'

'So what is he really like?'

Michael looked at his shoes. 'He's in charge. He always knows how to get stuff, and people will do anything for him, to get out of owing him money.'

'Why do they owe him money?'

Michael gave her another look, but she persevered. She guessed what he was hinting at, but she needed him to say it.

'What can he get, Michael?' she asked.

'Everything.'

'Are we talking posters of Coldplay? Cans of Fanta?'

Michael raised his eyebrows, reminding Kelly of her mother expressing disappointment at one of her daughter's moral choices.

'What about, let's say, illegal substances that cost quite a lot of money? I'm guessing a bit of skunk, possibly some MDMA or ketamine.' Kelly went for gold.

Michael's eyes widened and he leaned in close. 'Yes. I told Faith not to.'

'Has he asked you?'

'Course! Everyone does it.'

'But not you?'

'I don't like being out of control, and I want to join the army.'

Kelly wanted to hug him.

At the vending machine, she bought him a Coke. He guzzled it thirstily, and they went back upstairs. She wished she could take him home. It was like watching a programme on TV where you were drawn in on purpose, but then the door slammed in your face and there was nothing you could do apart from shout at the TV, believing foolishly that they could hear you.

'Did Faith do drugs?'

'I don't know. She never looked whacked.' Kelly winced at hearing a twelve-year-old speaking in such a way, so confident and knowledgeable.

They went back to the room where the officers were comforting Mr and Mrs Shaw. Michael went to his mother's outstretched arms. She looked like an empty vessel. The boy was on his own from now on; Kelly knew that to be the truth. And there was absolutely nothing she could do about it.

She said goodbye, and gave Michael a card. No one noticed; she did it subtly.

'I'm here,' she said.

He looked at her and nodded in the stoical way that endeared him to her so much.

Once the Shaws had left, Kelly looked through her iPad to find the number of Luke Miles' insipid excuse for a lawyer.

It was Justin who'd told her two days ago that Sadie was jealous of Faith. Jealous because Luke Miles was infatuated with Faith Shaw. It was another wedge to drive between the friends. Friends who, it would appear, were shaping up to be the epitome of modern counterfeit relationships.

The possibility that Sadie Rawlinson simply wanted to cause damage wherever she could sat further at the forefront of Kelly's mind. As the law stood, it was the most appalling waste of their time, and nothing else. To date, no one had ever gone to prison for being a bitch.

But there was another scenario. Perhaps Faith was anti-drugs and had refused Luke's gear too many times.

He wouldn't be best pleased.

Chapter 42

Craig Lockwood drove to Barrow Park. A forty-five-acre haven of peace and tranquillity in the middle of the town, the park had fought of late to get rid of down-and-outs, drug dealers and otherwise shady characters, and was beginning to win the battle. Rangers now patrolled the grounds, thanks to green-flag status and lottery money; and the smell of piss, the graffiti and the smackheads had all but gone. It was the perfect stage for a liaison.

He was on his way to meet Maria, the madam of the fairground. Travellers had frequented Furness for centuries, and Maria was fourth-generation Romany, originally from Lithuania. Her family had decamped to Britain when Hitler started gassing Jews and gypsies. She and Craig had spent a few years together at the Ramsey secondary school back in the eighties; that was, when Maria attended. She was destined to run the fair, as her mother did, and her grandmother before her. O levels were never going to change that. They weren't friends, as such, but they respected one another, and these days swapped the weather forecast and the state of the EU whenever their paths crossed.

It wasn't often that Craig had actively sought her out, but she'd given him more than a few nuggets over the years, and he'd turned a blind eye to some of the scrapes her sons had found themselves in. Not that he could get away with it any more. Computers, accountability and the death of good old-fashioned judgement left them with little smudge factor these days. It was health and safety combined with political correctness on speed, and it made for a sterile, often sluggish investigative process. But Craig still kept old contacts.

Snow covered the grass and the topiary looked like mounds of marshmallows. The birds were silent in their cages, and the boats were moored until the spring. There was no one around. Maria waited for him in the band-stand. She wore a full-length black North Face quilted jacket, and her dark features made her look like an Eskimo planning some Alaskan fishing quest. The cigarette she was smoking smelled as though it was imported. But that wasn't Craig's concern; he wasn't here for HMRC infringements.

They didn't acknowledge one another, apart from a shift in body position.

'Whatever it is, we'll find it eventually. It's out of my hands, Maria. It's a North Lakes investigation too, and it'll get bigger. We could close you down entirely, and all because of one guy dealing to kids.'

The wind blew her hair gently, and she dropped her cigarette to the floor and stood on it. She exhaled the smoke, and Craig was reminded of all the years that he'd bought twenty a day. He'd kicked the habit nine years ago, but he still adored the smell.

'His mother was a dear friend of mine,' she said. She never looked at him.

'I understand.'

'I don't turn over kin. You know that.'

'Children are involved. You know what that means. I know about the previous, Maria. It's time to stop protecting him.'

'Are you threatening me?' She looked at him, and he stared back. It was a game. A very old, familiar game, in which both sides' poker face had seen better days.

'No. I'm just appealing to the mother in you. I need a reason to sniff around.'

'I don't want you in my face.'

'Not necessary. It could be anywhere.'

'His trailer?' she asked.

'That'll do,' he said.

'How about supplying prescription pills?'

'To kids?'

'This conversation's over.' She walked away, but stopped and turned when she reached the top step. 'Bobby Bailey was the name of a horse I bet on when his mother was hit by a car on the A595. She died. That bet was bad from day one.'

Craig nodded his head slightly and acknowledged what she'd just done. They had to witness a deal, identify his digs, and be ready to move. Bobby Bailey wouldn't skip prison this time round.

Chapter 43

Nedzad looked at his son tenderly as he rocked him gently back and forth. He'd waited for this moment for two long years, and he studied every inch of the boy intently. He was just as he'd remembered him: dark eyes, a square jaw and large fists. He was a Galic.

The child was quiet, as if aware of his clandestine origin and the need to remain silent. He was dressed well and had been looked after; that much was obvious. His body was covered in a respectable layer of fat, and his wrists were marked by deep creases. Nedzad burst with pride that he'd sired such a strapping lad. He was heavy and thickset, unmoving as his father rocked him into a deep slumber.

Nedzad knew everything about him. He'd been moved five times in his short life, before being placed with the family in St Bees, on Cumbria's windswept coastline. He looked as though he'd benefited from the blast of fresh air that he took in on his daily walk along the beach. He'd been watched for months, but Nedzad had been patient and waited for exactly the right moment.

He sang to him in Serbo-Croat. A song his own mother had sung to him a long time ago. Looking at his son made everything worthwhile. The hardship he'd endured, and the long periods of uncertainty and conflict that he'd overcome to get to where he was. Manchester was like a goblet brimming over with possibility, and only one person could possess the vessel at any one time. It was world famous for its brutality, its labyrinthine housing estates and its drugs and guns. *Gunchester*. Nedzad laughed, but quieted himself so not to wake his son.

People thought the drugs had died with acid house, but they were wrong. Another, more lethal generation of dealers had filled the places left by the sprawling gangs of the nineties, and a more ferocious, mostly foreign, and highly digitalised species had sprouted and prospered. Everything was operated online, from tracking shipments to ordering prescription pills. It was easy. Getting there hadn't been easy, but that was why he'd waited until now to snatch his son.

There was a knock on the door, and Nedzad spun round, anger flashing in his eyes in case whoever was on the other side of it disturbed his son. The door opened silently and a man put his head round it. Nedzad nodded. All was well.

He was a decision-maker. Ruthless and absolute, but effective. It hadn't taken him long to reach the decision about Bobby Bailey, and now the visitor told him that the task had been carried out cleanly and easily. Nedzad held his son up, and the man smiled and stroked the child's head gently, with the same hand that had put a kitchen knife through Bobby Bailey's heart. It had taken him less than a minute to die. The kill was clean, the park was quiet, and the clean-up straightforward. Bobby had served his purpose and Nedzad didn't like loose ends. In his experience, loose ends unravelled the garment eventually.

There were always couriers and dealers to fill job vacancies, and he had more than he could count. Bobby Bailey was a tiny lab rat, useful for a time, but expendable and replaceable. Nedzad's time was better spent on the business end of his growing operations. But for now, he deserved a little break with his son, who would never leave his side again.

Bobby Bailey had been born into poor stock, and as such, had met a filthy end. It was the inevitability of life that kept Nedzad's resolve strong, his unswerving belief that one pursued a birthright. He would teach this to his son, in the absence of his mother, who had succumbed to the grief of losing her child. She was easily replaced, and a boy only had need of a father. A man who would teach him to thrive and win.

In a week, Nedzad would have forgotten Bobby Bailey's name.

Chapter 44

Kelly read the report on Danny Stanton's car.

The vehicle had been full of crap, but any piece of crap might yield a shred of DNA or bodily fluid, and so crap was the forensic scientist's best friend. There were fag butts, crisp packets, a pair of women's knickers, an empty deodorant, a stinking bag of Tesco BBQ chicken, and, tucked away under the driver's seat, wrapped in a Greggs paper bag, a small plastic sealable bag containing twelve blue pills. They were slightly larger than paracetamol size, and they had the number 47 on them, just under the diameter line. They were well made but not perfect, and they matched a memo sent out by the constabulary drug squad about a batch of prescription pills that had killed a seventeen-year-old in Bolton.

Kelly informed the drug squads in Kendal, Bolton and Manchester, then turned her attention to Luke Miles' car. Meanwhile, they were bringing Danny in for formal interview.

Luke's car had been towed to the facility from the school car park, under warrant. This vehicle was well looked after. It was clean inside and out, and there was no litter present whatsoever. The mats had been vacuumed, and the dash, along with all the other plastic surfaces, had been wiped. A new air freshener dangled from the rear-view mirror, smelling of forest pine. So they got on their hands and knees and looked through magnifying glasses. Several hairs were found in the footwells, where vacuums couldn't reach, and placed in tubes. A stain on the back seat was swabbed, and a packet of cigarette papers was bagged.

One interesting find was an acrylic woman's nail, brightly painted, found underneath the driver's seat. It didn't belong to Faith, as her mother had already confirmed that she didn't wear acrylics. Sadie Rawlinson, however, did. If it turned out to be Sadie's, it proved that she'd been in the car, though they already knew that.

Statistically, ninety-nine per cent of forensic finds were worthless, but it was a job that was worth every man hour. The other one per cent might give the investigators a fresh lead, or consolidate what they had. The work had to be meticulous and thorough, with times, dates, locations and signatures all logged so that some jumped-up 'expert' couldn't dispute the integrity of the potential evidence if it went to trial.

The two officers searching Luke's vehicle had been thorough, that was for sure. They'd checked cavities, the inside of soft furnishings and any concealed air pockets. They were given specialist training to do this, though damage did sometimes occur. Air-bag cavities had become popular in recent years as places to hide stuff: illegal stuff. Generally, where there was a soft cover, there was a potential hiding place behind it. It was painstaking work, but they might not get the chance to search a vehicle twice, so they had to get it right the first time.

Kelly looked at the photographs of a set of snow chains that they'd taken from the boot. The set had been sealed with cable ties, and they'd been cut. Every stage of the process was carefully logged. A tiny seam within the snow chain case had been cut with a scalpel, and a search inside had revealed her best evidence yet that Luke Miles was dealing in illegal substances. Forty-three small plastic packets had been pulled out, each the size of a small strip of matches. On the front of every one was printed the same smiley cartoon face, underneath which was printed: *K2 SMACKED*. It was synthetic marijuana. Further exploration yielded twenty-two packets of Adderall, seventeen boxes of OxyContin, and a sizeable quantity of MDMA: a count of the tiny white pills, stamped with a minute hand print, came to one hundred and seven. MDMA used to be known as Ecstasy, but the name had gone out of fashion. Whatever the trend, Luke was in possession of Class A drugs, and the quantities could easily be argued as evidence of dealing.

It puzzled her what the boy's motive was. He had everything: a happy, comfortable home life, solid grades at school, and, she had to admit it, good looks. And yet here he was, willing to throw it all away. She made arrangements to haul in his bank accounts and get a warrant for the family home, especially Luke's bedroom. She doubted that he dealt in e-payments, and so they'd need to find the cash.

She received a phone call from Johnny. The helicopter had been out today for almost three hours. It wasn't the news anybody was hoping for: they'd found nothing. Kelly's heart sank. From everything she'd learned about Faith, it was becoming clearer that the girl had come to harm. Sending the helicopter out was expensive, and the investigation costs were mounting. It was hugely frustrating.

It was Christmas Eve, though it certainly didn't feel like it. The office was decorated with some hanging bits and baubles, and they'd put a synthetic tree in a corner and decorated that – or at least Emma had. They were even playing festive music, but the mood was low, because no one wanted Faith's family to have to face tomorrow still not knowing. The same was true of Dale Prentice's foster family. Police from Egremont to Workington were working extra hours trying to locate the toddler, but Christmas inevitably slowed things down: man hours, lab closures and magistrates' holidays. Kelly was hoping to get a few warrants before close of play today, but she wasn't banking on it.

Rob put his head round her door.

'Guv, we're finding it difficult to locate Tony Blackman. We've tried Sarah Peaks and his own flat, but she hasn't seen him for two days. She said he was feeling poorly and expected that he'd taken himself off to bed because of all the stress. She's got a key to his flat and we accompanied her there, but there was no sign of him.'

'Phone?'

'Not answering.'

'Shit.'

Chapter 45

Near the crazy golf at Hope Park on the south side of Keswick, a man was throwing snowballs with his two young sons. They ran around like lunatics, gathering snow and compacting it so hard that had their mother been there, she would have told them off and ended the game. One of the boys received an ice ball in the face and clutched his nose; his brother bent over laughing, only to be rugby-tackled by his father. The injured brother forgot his injury and pounced on his sibling, rubbing snow in his face.

They rolled around in the snow, getting covered in it, and Dad scooped piles of the stuff up, dumping it on both of them. The older brother escaped and jumped over a row of small bushes. The father performed a pincer movement with the aid of the younger boy and ambushed his son, felling him and falling on top of him.

The scuffle spilled over to what, underneath the drifts, was a flower bed in summer. The snow was softer here, where it hadn't been disturbed by excited children on holiday for Christmas. There was only one more sleep until the big day, and it looked as though it would be snowy and cold; just time to dry their clothes overnight and start all over again as Mum cooked the turkey.

The boys turned on their father and he feigned surprise as they held him down and shoved snow down his jacket collar. He squealed and roared as the clumps of ice melted on his skin, clawing for handfuls of snow for his revenge. The boys ran away.

His hand caught on something and stopped his frolicking. He turned to see if it was a root or a discarded glove. It was neither. At first he thought it was simply litter, and he cursed the youth around here. But as he tugged, he realised that it was a bag. A huge ball of snow hit his head and his boys cheered their victory.

'Wait! Wait! No, I'm serious, hold on, I think someone must have lost this,' he said. The boys were wary, not knowing if it was a trap, but then they realised they were thankful for the rest, and went to see what their father had found. They knelt down, oblivious to the cold and wet, and he held it up: a small backpack, distinctive because it was made of faux leopard print.

'It's a girl's,' said one of the brothers. The dad nodded in agreement, because he'd seen it before. An overwhelming sense of grief hit him as he looked at his boys and back at the backpack. He'd seen it on TV. It was just like the one the police said the missing girl was carrying at Keswick fair.

A snowball landed on his head and slid down the back of his jacket.

'Stop!' The boys were taken aback by their father's tone, and stopped fooling around. They watched as their father opened the bag. There was a green jumper inside, and a mobile phone, along with some make-up.

There was also a wallet, and he opened it, not knowing quite what to do other than search the thing; it was as if he was on autopilot. Later, he would tell his wife that it was almost as if he might find the girl herself in there. His heart raced as he came face to face with Faith Shaw's student ID.

'What is it, Dad?' his sons asked.

He turned to them and realised that he'd zoned out, and that had scared them. He gathered everything together and put it all back in the bag.

'We need to take this to the police,' he said.

'Why?'

'Because there's a family out there that won't be enjoying their Christmas like you guys tomorrow.'

The boys looked at each other, realising that whatever their father had just uncovered was important. They didn't like the way it felt, but they knew it was serious.

'Do you think it belonged to that girl, Dad?'

No one spoke of anything else at school. It had even made the national news and Facebook. The girl was in Year 11, and she'd been missing all week.

'Yes, I think so. I saw the bag on TV. I think this is it.'

The father stood up and brushed the snow off himself. The boys copied him, then they walked in silence back to the car. They'd come out ostensibly to gather twigs for their snowman back at home, and pick up last-minute beer for Grandad. The lure of the snow-covered park had proved too much for them and they'd missed three calls from an irate mother and wife.

She would soon calm down once they told her why they were late.

Chapter 46

Kelly hid her head under her pillow. Christmas Day was just another day and she didn't know why so much fuss was made of it.

She felt sick to her stomach.

It was about the worst possible outcome they could have wished for. Johnny stroked her back. He knew what it meant. A fifteen-year-old girl missing in freezing weather, very probably using drugs, and now her backpack found abandoned. These stories never ended well. The area around the find had been searched until they ran out of light. Wherever Faith was now, she was nowhere near her bag. Michael popped into her head, and she told Johnny.

'Kids are more resilient than we give them credit for,' he said.

She nodded, but continued to stare out of the window next to the bed. She knew that already. But she struggled to shake the sense of dread, on a day when she should be able to forget her job for at least a couple of hours.

The house was quiet, as were the streets outside. Josie hadn't wanted her dad to bounce on her bed on Christmas morning like a five-year-old, so he'd spent the night with Kelly. It was early, and Josie would either still be asleep, or surfing Instagram, no doubt checking what various celebrities had posted to give their millions of fans further racking insecurities about their normal dull lives. Johnny had woken Kelly with a tray on which he'd put a cup of tea and a gift. He wanted her to open it. She sat up, trying to push away the negative thoughts crowding for space in her head.

'Merry Christmas,' he said.

Butterflies trembled in her stomach. The package was ring size. *Surely not.*

Shit.

She sipped her tea and took the small present in her hand, tearing off the paper to reveal a velvet box. Her hands juddered slightly as she opened it. Inside, sitting on a velvet cushion, was a ring, but it wasn't what one might consider an engagement ring, and Kelly breathed easier. It wasn't that she didn't know what to say; more that they hadn't discussed it. She was relieved, but still needed to check.

'It's stunning.'

'It was my granny's. I wanted you to have it. You two would have got on well.' He smiled at her. He'd told her this before, and Kelly wished she'd met his grandmother. Now, more than ever, she wanted to connect and belong. It was as if the ring would give her some balance today: the day when both her mother and father were coming to lunch. She took it out of the box and he rushed to tell her about it.

'My grandfather was based in India and he had it made for her. It's rubies all the way round, and Indian gold. That's why it's so yellow. It's softer than African.'

Kelly held it; it was delicate, but heavy from the stones.

'It's beautiful.'

'You can wear it on whatever finger you like, no pressure.' He smiled.

She tried it on the middle finger of her right hand, and it fitted.

'I love it, thank you. I can't compete, I'm afraid.' She got out of bed and put a dressing gown over her nakedness. He watched her go to a drawer and take out a wrapped present the size of a shoebox. She gave it to him and he ripped the packaging open. It was a pair of Ramses Birkenstocks.

'Wow! Who knew flip-flops could be so heavy!'

'Put them on! You'll never go back to Sports Direct, I promise.'

He slipped them on and nodded his approval. 'Nice. Can I wear them in bed?'

'Do what you want.'

For the next forty minutes, Kelly forgot about what her brain wanted to wire to her to-do list. Johnny commanded all of her attention. Everything else – her mother, Ted, Faith, suicide, drugs, bullies and mangled bodies on mortuary slabs – melted away.

And he kept his flip-flops on.

The last thing she wanted was to get out of bed and start cooking and setting the table. It wasn't going to be a formal affair, but it had the potential to turn into a fairly punchy afternoon. As long as Josie was sitting near Wendy, and as long as there was no drama with Nikki, then the day should go as planned. Nikki didn't have an invite but that didn't stop her from generating some crisis, with her at the centre. She had a huge turkey, hand reared locally, some vegetables and potatoes, and shedloads of alcohol.

She lay back on the pillow and studied her ring. It was something reassuring to have on hand; more than that, it made her feel safe. Should things go awry this afternoon, she could always fiddle with the ring and take deep breaths.

'I don't want to get up,' she said.

'I know. I need to check on Josie. I'll call her first, then peel some potatoes. Come on. Fancy a run?'

To her surprise, Kelly realised that she did in fact fancy a run. Christmas Day was always quiet: there were no cars, no tourists and no phone calls. It was the perfect time to get out and enjoy the solitude. She looked at the ring again. 'Do you think I should wear it?'

'I think it's there to be worn. It's up to you, but it shouldn't be seen as only for special occasions. Is it comfortable?'

She nodded.

'Wear it then.'

She did.

He called Josie first and received a few grunts in return. She'd be round before midday to open her presents. Kelly had spent two weekends driving to Glasgow and trawling the shops there for what a teenage girl might find cool, and then there was the lovely trinket box from Keswick fair – a night that seemed weeks ago now. She hadn't expected shopping for a teenager to be so difficult. Josie wasn't into any of the things Kelly had liked at her age – running, live music, *National Geographic* magazine and *Top of the Pops* – and she'd been stuck for ideas. Finally they'd decided on vouchers. It was dull, but anything else was risky.

They had just over an hour before they'd need to welcome their guests, and so they decided on a short jog up through Waterfoot and on to Soulby Fell. There was no one about; it was as if the human population had been stricken by some lethal virus and had vacated the planet just for their convenience.

'Do you think you might have to go in?' Johnny asked her.

She didn't know. 'I've got a few calls to make. I don't need to go into the office unless I'm called. I'll keep my fingers crossed. What about you?'

It was the same for Johnny. He wasn't on call like she was, but that didn't mean the mountain rescue might not need him. Lunch was to be kept simple – a glorified Sunday roast with a few trimmings – and they'd leave the drinking to Wendy and Ted. Josie would be allowed a couple of bottles of beer.

The sky had turned brighter, and the flat light associated with the heavy snow they'd seen for the past week was dissipating. A thaw was predicted, and it looked like the forecast was accurate. The temperature had risen a degree or so, and water dripped from the trees. It ran down the lanes as they ascended, soaking their trainers. Mud splashed up their legs and sweat stuck to them rather than steaming off.

'Look.' Johnny pointed to the peaks: the snowline was a little higher and they could see that some patches in the distance had melted.

By the time they made it back home, Kelly calculated that they didn't have time for a shared bath; they'd have to settle for showers and get cracking on the prep they should have done last night. Clean, and dressed in jeans and jumpers, they listened to Christmas songs and waited for their families to arrive. Johnny wore his new flip-flops and Kelly wore her ring proudly. It was very feminine and made her feel somewhat adorned. Of course, her mother would tell her that it was on the wrong finger, and Johnny would go along with it. The day wouldn't be that bad, she decided.

Until she remembered the Shaws again. And the Frasers, and the Trents…

She pushed the thoughts away and carried on peeling Brussels sprouts.

The time passed quickly and Josie arrived carrying gifts. The girl was smiling more than Kelly had seen in the last few months, and she changed the music to something more upbeat and modern. She even helped set the table. Kelly had made a vegetarian loaf for her. It looked like some kind of gigantic turd, and utterly unappetising, but she'd followed the instructions carefully, and, having nibbled a bit off the end, decided that it tasted quite good. She received an unexpected hug for her pains, and Johnny winked at her behind Josie's back.

Now they were waiting for Wendy and Ted. As Kelly was basting potatoes, Johnny came up behind her and put his arms around her waist. She hadn't realised that she was shaking. 'You OK?' he asked. She couldn't answer. There was nothing to say. She'd had a relationship with a man she called Dad for thirty-five years before he died, and now she was inviting a stranger into her home, into her life, and she had his blood flowing through her. Johnny took the spoon off her and told her to get a drink and check the table.

'Josie wants to wait to open presents; she's got your mum something too.'

Kelly raised her eyebrows.

The doorbell rang and she jumped.

'Why don't I get it?' Johnny said. She listened as Johnny went to the door, and Josie greeted her mother. She heard Ted's voice and it didn't panic her. Hearing them together like that touched her. She went into the hall. Her mother and father were dressed smartly, as if on a date, and Josie and Johnny looked at her, waiting for her to say something.

She went to Wendy and kissed her. 'Merry Christmas.'

She looked at Ted. They hadn't seen each other for months. She'd been avoiding him. He looked charming and warm, like she always expected him to. She walked towards him, and he opened his arms and took her into them. She allowed herself to be held.

'Merry Christmas, Kelly,' he said.

It felt good to welcome him to her home, but at the same time, it was difficult to push aside her old relationship with him and accept this new, intimate one.

'Let's get your coats off. Lunch is nearly ready.'

Her mother followed her into the kitchen as Johnny chatted to Ted about the speciality beers he'd bought.

'Thank you for inviting him, Kelly.'

Kelly turned around and looked at her.

'I'm so pleased for you, Mum. I really am. You make a handsome couple. And look at you! You're a new woman. I love your make-up. You look gorgeous.'

She couldn't recall ever saying that to her mother before, and it felt satisfying and natural. But it was true. Wendy seemed calmer, less distant, and chattier. She didn't want to ruin the moment by bringing her sister up, but they would have to have the conversation at some point about whether Nikki should be told. It wasn't a conversation for today, though.

'What are you drinking?' she asked. 'There's sherry, champagne – well, Prosecco – beer, whatever you want.'

'You look happy, Kelly.'

She stopped fussing and looked at her mother, who was staring at her, smiling.

Chapter 47

Emma Hide wasn't officially on call on Christmas Day, but she figured she might as well work as anything else. Andy had stayed over last night and they'd spent the morning together. She liked him; he was uncomplicated and easy-going, unlike men her own age, who seemed to be more into appearance than anything else. Andy dressed well but didn't talk about it. The fact that her boss had introduced them was a little odd, but they'd got over that quickly. She couldn't imagine Kelly at school with him. He said that Kelly always hung about with the boys more, and Emma could empathise with that, because the same was true of her.

He was spending the afternoon with his kids. She hadn't met them, and that suited her for now. They were still having fun. Meeting his children would take it to the next level. Everyone at the office had family to spend the day with, but her own family was complicated. Family gatherings were exhausting, and she avoided them. She'd popped into her mum and dad's in Keswick for about an hour, but no longer. Her sisters would be there all day, with their kids, who were adorable, but Emma had always been the quiet one, preferring to come and go. No one minded, and they knew that police work didn't stop for holidays.

From Ted Wallis's office, Emma had gathered the information one of the traceable drugs that had been found in Jenna Fraser's system: from a batch of Fentanyl. The packets of Adderall from her bedroom had been traced to a specific batch in Liverpool, and the information had been collated and shared with the Merseyside drug squad, who'd informed the inquiry that there were ongoing operations inside Cumbria involving surveillance and infiltration. They were delicate, long-term operations and involved persons travelling between Liverpool and Manchester and the countryside north and south of the M62.

Jenna's mobile phone had been plugged into the relevant sterile machines in the dark and had begun to regurgitate data. The data had been collated and stored, but was never examined; once the suicide verdict came back, it was decided there was nothing to investigate, and Kelly's team didn't have the time to trawl through all the phones they had bagged and tagged. Except it was Christmas Day, and Emma had nowhere to be, and she couldn't stop thinking about what made an athletic sixteen-year-old get sucked so far down the rabbit hole that she jumped off a cliff.

The data had chugged out of the machine and onto readable files. Much of the messaging had been wiped clean, but the mole had managed to salvage an impressive mass of information from iCloud and other mobile forums that was never deleted because it couldn't be. Several clever IT people in the USA had made billions of dollars finding ways to hold and store data without using networks. It wouldn't be long before the information was routinely used in police inquiries, for sure.

The mole had unearthed a series of texts and phone calls between Jenna's phone and one other number, and that was Emma's first lead. On the day Jenna had jumped, she'd been texting and calling right up to when she left her house, half dressed, to run up Walla Crag.

He had also recovered Jenna's movements in the weeks prior to her death, and Emma's attention had been caught by the fact that in the week before her death, the girl's phone had pinged off a mast in Keswick not just a couple of times, but every single day. She had clearly travelled to Keswick for something regular and important. Emma brought up the original report on her computer and went through the statements from parents and friends – though Jenna had few friends. Nobody mentioned her going to Keswick. Nobody mentioned her talking for hours on the phone or texting somebody upward of twenty times a day.

It didn't take long to find out who the number belonged to.

Emma closed her screen and thought about the implications of what she'd found out. It didn't merit disturbing Kelly on Christmas Day, but she couldn't wait to share her findings. Her boss was on call, but that generally meant for emergencies, and she didn't think this was an emergency.

Instead, she turned her attention to the coroner's report on the other two teenage suicides. Four years ago, Ted Wallis had autopsied the body of Laura Briggs, and it made for uncomfortable reading. The fourteen-year-old had been badly abused, and her injuries were consistent with prolonged periods of rape. Old wounds had healed and been reopened repeatedly, and the coroner noted that her sexual organs had been deformed over time. As for her lethal injuries, they constituted several slashes to her wrists, made with pieces of broken mirror. She had bled to death in her bathtub in under three minutes.

Again the girl's phone had been picked apart as a matter of routine, and the records consigned to the bowels of cyberspace, kicking around in the dark until someone came along and sniffed them out. That was where they would have stayed had it not been for Kelly Porter demanding to know why so many school kids were being driven to oblivion. Was it simply a case of modern life pushing them to the limits, or was there something else to it?

Emma turned to the post-mortem report on Jake Trent. The boy was fifteen when he injected himself with a cheap heroin substitute in his father's bathroom. The traumatic part wasn't the fact that it was gory or shocking; it was Jake's age. Fifty-year-old has-beens were supposed to OD; but a fifteen-year-old boy with his whole future ahead of him? No, he was supposed to live. Emma admired her boss for taking the matter seriously, and that was why she was sitting reading reports on Christmas Day rather than watching *It's a Wonderful Life*; because it pissed her off too.

She rubbed her eyes as she studied the chemical composition of certain opioid compounds found in prescription drugs. Adderall was an upper, but fentanyl was a downer, and the danger was in using them at the same time. She thought back to what Sarah Peaks had said about drug education, and wondered if kids were informed about the physical dangers as well as the social ones. That was the problem: the education system was way behind these kids and what they knew. The problem was what they *didn't* know. In the US, there was a different approach, and it was a priority to find out what kids were being exposed to, but here, where romantic naivety diminished the belief that there was a problem in the first place – and claimed that drugs were for losers – the emphasis, Emma found, was on raiding the big boys. In the meantime, thousands of kids were being exposed to ever more dangerous chemicals that no one knew anything about. And no one talked about.

She sighed.

So often with overdoses, a cocktail of several drugs acted together to break down organs. The question was, where had Jake got his supply? Keswick wasn't a large town. There couldn't be that many dealers, and plenty of them were known to the police.

She checked the number found so often on Jenna's phone again.

Maybe there was a new kid on the block, or an old sweat hiding right under their noses, in plain sight.

Chapter 48

Craig Lockwood had little to occupy him on Christmas Day either. The boys were with their mother; he'd dropped them off at their swanky house, complete with matching BMWs in the driveway. It killed him when he saw her with her new husband. He couldn't bring himself to even say his name. But what killed him even more was when the bastard spent time with his boys. They were old enough now not to be swayed by superficial gifts, and they generally came home to Craig telling him what they were or were not impressed with. They also told him how their mother had changed. The marital breakdown had been a cliché. Craig had neglected her and she'd looked elsewhere. The boys had opted to live with their father and she didn't object; she was keener to jet off to villas in the sun with her new fella than be tied to motherhood. The irony was that now Craig spent much more time with his family than he ever had.

His biggest achievement, though one he'd never admit to the boys, was keeping them off drugs. He'd terrified them with videos of overdoses, crime programmes and statistics so that they went to parties turned off the stuff before they even thought about trying it. It amused Craig, but the boys joked that they were more sensible than their dad. They hardly touched alcohol either; again, Craig had showed them pictures from the mortuary of enlarged livers and burst hearts. It wasn't pretty, but he didn't want them to end up as washed-up old losers, dependent on everything from substances to women.

At fifteen, his younger son was the same age as the missing girl from Keswick, and it smarted. All parents must imagine it, he figured: that terror of your kid going missing and turning up dead, knifed or worse. He'd once sat them down and told them they had a hundred pounds each to see how many knives they could buy over the internet. They managed to legally purchase twenty-four between them. He then showed them some photographs of knife wounds.

The elder boy was now eighteen and heading off to the London School of Economics. Craig's worries were far from over, but at least his son had a path to walk.

He'd had a lie-in on Christmas morning, and then showered and dressed ready for his main task for the day: to incarcerate Bobby Bailey. An old magistrate pal had signed a warrant, and now Craig was on his way to Ulverston again. The fair wasn't moving on until the day after Boxing Day, when it would resume in Kendal.

Maria had described which trailer Bobby stayed in; predictably, it was not the one he'd told the police. If Bobby had anything to hide, it would be in the trailer he called home. Only a few people knew which one that was, and that number now included Detective Chief Inspector Craig Lockwood. This was going to be a Christmas that Bobby never forgot.

Craig would have preferred it if policing was still done the old-fashioned way – with a good nose and a punch in the face – but it wasn't and they all had to get used to it.

Every damn thing had to be accounted for, and entering Bobby's trailer might turn out to be crucial for Kelly. He had to do it right. He figured that Bobby would let his guard down on Christmas Day, not expecting the coppers to be out looking for him.

He had taken his son's car and wore a cap pulled down low. He heard music coming from trailers, and a dog pissed up the side of a lorry. A few kids chased each other and cycled up and down on new bikes, no doubt nicked. But he wasn't here for petty theft.

A few fair workers milled about, but no one paid his car any attention. Two men stood by the canal edge, talking animatedly and pointing out to sea. They paused occasionally to shout obscenities at passing women. After an hour or so, a group of four others approached and sat down. Craig was growing impatient. This was where Bobby usually hung out, and he begun to think that he'd been invited somewhere else for Christmas dinner. Either that, or he was sleeping off a hangover in his trailer.

He got out of his car and made his way to the trailer that Bobby called home. The shutters were all down and he tried the door. It was open. He glanced around, but the group wasn't interested in him and carried on laughing and chatting. Craig felt a slight pang of pity: it was a sad sight on Christmas Day.

The stench hit him as soon as the door was ajar. Craig recognised the smell immediately. Either Bobby had a dead dog in there, or he was a goner himself.

He pulled a handkerchief out of his pocket and covered his mouth. He had plastic gloves should he need them, as always. The light was dim and the smell grew stronger. He gagged, but stepped inside. His eyes adjusted and he made

259

out a scene of neglect and disarray, though it wasn't as if the place had been burgled; just lived in by a lazy bastard. He looked around and called Bobby's name.

Nothing.

His eyes watered, but he was becoming accustomed to the reeking air. Then he heard the flies. It always amazed him how quickly the little buggers sought out a juicy dead body on which to feed. It was as if they were the sharks of the air, sensing lifeless flesh from miles around. Even in a closed vehicle such as this, they always found a way in. He hadn't seen a fly for months, but they always appeared when there was a meal to be had. He approached the bedroom, the buzzing getting louder, and braced himself. As he pushed the door open, flies flew past him and he Craig batted them away from his face.

Squinting, he made out a figure lying face up on the bed. At first glance it just looked like someone sleeping. He flicked on his torch. He knew it was Bobby.

The flies were in disarray, having been rudely interrupted; they flew off every time Craig moved, before landing on the body again. He went closer and shone the light all over the corpse. Bobby's face was unmarked. He looked larger than Craig remembered, but that would be the bloat of gas as his insides disintegrated. His clothes moved slightly around his abdominal area, which Craig put down to the hatching and feeding of insect larvae. But it was the chest area that focused his attention.

There was a clear cut in Bobby's shirt, around the heart, and Craig shone the torch into the gash. The flesh had been slashed cleanly and deeply, and after a look over the rest of the body, Craig reckoned this was the only wound.

It was a professional hit.

He went outside and made the call to medics and forensics. He would need uniforms here to begin interviewing. He wouldn't be popular interrupting the dinners of those on call, and he felt a bastard, If only he'd left Bobby for another day, his colleagues could have enjoyed their Christmas. But then evidence might have slipped away, or worse: someone else could have found him.

Maria wandered over when the sirens created a fuss ten minutes later and the place lit up. A crowd gathered close to Bobby's trailer, unwilling to be moved on by the police, who taped a barrier around the area.

'What happened?' Maria asked.

'Looks like a hit to me, and judging by the body, it was a couple of days ago. See anything?'

Maria looked down at her shoes. 'No. But I'll ask around.'

'You do that. If he was dealing, then maybe you could find out where his supply came from. It looks like a clean hit to me, and in my experience, people only get whacked like that for sex or money. My guess is that Bobby wasn't part of any complicated love triangles.'

He went back inside the trailer.

'Cursory search?' he asked a forensic officer.

'Pills, powder, some skunk.'

Craig nodded. It was a treasure trove of illegal chemicals, and had they apprehended Bobby Bailey alive, he could have answered many questions. Maybe he'd died because he was sloppy, though this didn't fit the execution-style homicide. Whoever did this was in and out within minutes, and there was no sign of forced entry. The officers were brushing for prints on everything, and it would take hours, the place was such a den of filthy living.

'Sir, what do you make of this?' an officer asked.

Craig whistled. It was an unopened bag of hypodermic needles, clearly labelled as the property of a doctor's surgery in Moss Side, Manchester.

Chapter 49

In his bedroom in his parents' house outside Keswick, Luke Miles heard sirens. Downstairs, his mother was basting the turkey and probably cursing the local thugs who were disturbing her Christmas carols.

Luke wasn't so sanguine. From the moment they'd taken his car, he hadn't slept, hadn't eaten, hadn't even had a wank. The thing he was most terrified of wasn't the coppers, or his teachers, or his clients, or even serving time. The thing he was petrified of was his father.

He was confident that the snow chains were bombproof, but the police could have used dogs. He still held on to the hope that they'd found nothing. The policewoman hadn't said they were searching for anything in particular; they were probably just doing one of those forensic sweeps you saw on TV, where a man in overalls gathered dust and shit on Sellotape. He'd be fine. So why then had he not slept?

He'd taken too many Addies and he needed to get a grip. It was frying his brain and left him jittery and whacked, but at least it kept him awake, with the odd joint in between to even things out. He looked in his bathroom mirror, pulling the skin under his eyes and examining his teeth. His mother thought him tired and stressed due to revision. He splashed water on his face and paused to listen as the sirens grew louder.

They lived in a detached five-bedroom house at the end of a long drive, surrounded by trees and bushes tended to by a gardener. His dad had worked in London at some point – Luke took little notice of where the money came from – and still dabbled in shares and investments. He wore expensive suits and spent more on a watch than the value of Luke's brand-new car. Life was easy. Luke's mum took care of his comfort and his dad took care of his future; meantime, Luke played the joker. Literally. Though it was the spiced joker that had led to things unravelling slightly. A little too much here, a bit extra there, and a dead girl in a pear tree… though it wasn't pears, it was pine. He shook his head to rid himself of the image. He couldn't possibly have known that she would do something so stupid. Not his problem.

He looked out of his window from behind the curtains, and sure enough, the cop cars were driving up to the house. His brain wouldn't work properly and he didn't know what to do first: flush the shit down the pan, or clean himself up. Panic set in and he realised for the first time in his short life that he was in real danger: a danger that his dad could not save him from. These were uniformed police officers with radios, stab vests and cuffs. There were two cars and they looked as though they were kitted out with tons of extra technology: all to catch him. They kept their lights on but turned the sirens off, and he heard his mother open the front door.

Words were exchanged, and his mother shouted for his father. Her voice was high-pitched, and he heard the tension constrict her throat: her baby was about to be dragged away by the law. Fuck. He needed to get his story straight. Scratch that: stories, plural. He had a decision to make, and that was which name to give them to save his skin. He had several options and he cared little for any of them, but he had to choose the one that would take the most heat away from him. He also had to get his story in first, but he was saying nothing without his dad's lawyer there. A narrative began to form in his head: one for the cops and one for his dad. They both had to be convincing. To be fair, his dad would believe anything he said; the coppers would be harder.

Downstairs, his father was trying to calm his mother and demanding an explanation at the same time.

'Luke!' he shouted.

Luke looked in the mirror for the last time. Shit, he'd almost forgotten to get rid of the gear. He scrabbled around the room trying to remember where he'd stashed it all. The problem was, he had so many hiding places that he'd forgotten some of them. There was no way he had time to get rid of everything. The place was like a fucking geriatric ward with all the tranquillisers and shit he had stowed away. He managed to throw a load down the toilet and began flushing, but that was when he heard footsteps on the stairs.

His door was barged open and he came face to face with six foot of solid law.

'You got the shits, son?' The copper nodded to the bathroom, where the toilet was still whirring away trying to fill the cistern back up.

Luke shook his head but said nothing.

His father appeared breathlessly behind the uniform. 'Luke, don't say anything. I'll have a lawyer there as quickly as I can.'

'Dad?'

'They're arresting you, Luke. They found drugs in your car.'

'With respect, sir, I think we might find a few substances in here too.'

'You can't search without my permission.'

'I have a warrant, sir.'

His dad fell silent. He knew that Luke was in serious trouble.

'There's some other explanation for all of this. Luke, don't panic. Go with the police and do as they say. Don't speak. Are you clear about that?'

Luke nodded.

'That's quite enough, sir,' the copper said.

Luke looked at his father and reality hit him between the eyes. His heart began to thump so fast that it was visible under his T-shirt. Sweat covered his forehead and ran down his back. He thought he might cry. His father put both hands on his shoulders but said nothing more.

–

Luke was cuffed and led downstairs. Mr Miles was asked to leave the room while a search was conducted; meanwhile, Luke was put in a patrol car, read his rights, and made to sweat it out until they were done.

Luke's mother stared at her son from the landing window that overlooked the driveway. Her husband marched up and down in the hallway, barking into his phone. Two police officers left Luke's room with boxes and bags of items, and his mother could only move aside as they filed downstairs.

They'd worn plastic shoe covers and gloves inside her son's room, and she knew that whatever they'd found was seriously damning. She couldn't speak. When her husband finished on the phone, he went out, slamming the door. She heard him telling the officers that he was accompanying his son to the station. That was his right, and they acknowledged the fact.

In the kitchen, the bread sauce caught on the bottom of the pan as the moisture dried up and the starch in the bread began to caramelise. A smoke alarm went off and shocked Mrs Miles out of her stupor. She rushed to the kitchen to find dark grey smoke filling the room. She pushed the pan off the hob and it clattered to the floor, skimming her leg and searing into her skin. She screamed, but no one heard her.

Chapter 50

The day had gone as well as Kelly could have expected. The Garmin watch that she'd helped Josie choose for her dad had been well received, and Johnny was in danger of appearing pretty smart for a local mountain rescue guy. She'd chosen a present last minute for Ted: a vintage brandy. For her mother, she'd bought Estée Lauder make-up and a gift voucher for a spa day at a local hotel.

Everybody commented on her ruby ring, and she almost got away with enjoying a whole day without thinking about work. Until she received a call from Craig telling her about Bobby Bailey, followed by one from the magistrate in Penrith informing her that Luke's arrest was going ahead today. She sighed and informed her guests that she'd have to go in to work after all. They were all welcome to stay, and she wanted them to. Her house had accommodated them comfortably, and even her mother praised her cooking. Johnny had done most of it, in his new flip-flops.

She looked around and was satisfied that everyone was happy.

Having Ted there had led to a mixture of emotions. On one hand it had been easy because they were old pals, but now the parameters had changed. She thought back to how she'd behaved with her dad – well, John. They'd been tactile. They'd lain on the sofa together, they'd held hands hiking up a hill to see the sun set, and they'd hugged when she graduated. Then she'd gone away. Now she looked at her biological father and couldn't imagine doing any of those things. He'd kissed her on both cheeks when he'd entered her house. He'd complimented her taste in furnishings and said that her home was just like her: it felt good to be around. She'd thanked him and meant it. Her mother had seemed tired all day, but despite that, she looked happy.

There were no phone calls from Nikki bemoaning the hardships of life, and even Josie seemed contented. She sat in the round easy chair that spun, glued to her phone and smiling to herself. Kelly reckoned that her job was done and she'd earned herself a massive tick in several boxes; she could slip away quite easily and return to them all later. The TV was on, and Wendy and Ted chose something made fifty years ago. Kelly went out to the terrace as Wendy explained to Josie just how much could be learned from watching old movies.

Johnny sat on a lounger and looked up to the sky. 'It's definitely thawing,' he said.

She sat beside him. 'I shouldn't be too long,' she said.

'I'm sure you will be, but it really doesn't matter. I'll tidy up.'

'Thank God I didn't have any champagne. I need a clear head for this.'

'How old is he?'

'Seventeen. Eighteen next month.'

'You don't build the contacts needed for those drugs overnight.'

'I know. You need cash flow too, which he has in spades, I reckon.'

'Good luck. I feel as though I might have a kip,' he added.

'I'm jealous, enjoy. I'll see you later. Thank you for my present, I love it.' She looked at her ring and moved it on her finger. It sparkled in the light. They kissed and she forced herself to pull away and stood up. She threw him a blanket and he pulled it over himself.

The drive to Penrith was quiet as expected, and she mulled over in her head how to approach Luke Miles. He had swagger, and the last time they'd spoken under similar circumstances, his arrogance had astounded her, but underneath, she'd also seen innocence. Her instinct was telling her that there was more to all this. The drug squad would be involved as soon as Boxing Day was out of the way, but for now, they only had twenty-four hours to keep Luke until they had to charge him or let him go, and Mr Miles' solicitor was on his way. That would do one of two things: make her life easier because he could instruct Luke to come clean; or backfire and go the other way because he could recommend minimum cooperation.

They certainly had him on possession, but they had to prove intent to supply, and that was always the kicker. Possession and supply of Class A drugs carried a maximum of life, and Luke was soon to turn eighteen. His age was surprising, given the apparent sophistication of what he was involved with; something she'd learned from her recent conversation with Emma, who'd been beavering away all day. If they could get him to deliver information on who he knew and how, they might be talking big sentences worth the CPS's time and money.

Over the last few weeks, Luke Miles had either texted or spoken to two people Kelly was very much interested in. One of them was Jenna Fraser, and the other was Faith Shaw. If he'd been dealing regularly for a long time, she wanted to know where he got the gear from.

Chapter 51

Emma was waiting at Eden House for her boss. She didn't know where to start, and babbled about facts and figures, texts and timings before Kelly had barely taken a breath.

'Emma, slow down. Tell me slowly. Start with Jenna. Why were you working anyway? I thought you were with Andy.'

'He's with his kids.'

Kelly nodded and they walked towards the offices. She felt adrenalin in her veins. She knew it. She'd known that Jenna had been pushed: pushed over the edge by an invisible hand. But she had to prove whose hand, and whether it amounted to homicide. Being tormented by phone calls, social media or even a drug dealer wouldn't get the case reopened.

'He threatened to tell her parents.'

'And we have that in black and white?'

'Yes, she kept everything. It's in an encrypted email that was hidden behind popular movie icons on her phone; that's how he supplied her. He wanted her to meet him.'

'What was he going to tell her parents?'

'He said he had a video of her injecting. As well as some sexual photos.'

'And we've got all these messages?'

Emma nodded. Kelly stopped short. 'My God. Do we know how they met?'

'Online. He followed her Instagram page dedicated to her races, then I found some digital messages asking her to meet him, and she said yes.'

'When was this?'

'Last year, around December. But that's not all, guv.'

'What?' Kelly stopped walking again. They were at the lifts and there was no one else around. Of course there wasn't; it was Christmas Day.

'Danny Stanton followed her too, and I found a photo of them together.'

Kelly put her arm on Emma's shoulder and smiled. For the first time, she thought they might have a hope of getting some justice for the broken body of Jenna Fraser.

'Both Luke and Danny closed their Instagram pages after Jenna was found dead.'

'What about the one we found liking Faith's stuff?'

'It was created later. Anyone can do it: you can create pages and make them look as though they go back years. It's easy to keep closing pages and recreating them. It's common, apparently, as kids grow bored of old photos and images.'

'Why don't they just delete them?'

'Because that's traceable.'

'This is too.'

'Only by someone scouring their search history for hours. It's pretty cutting-edge stuff. You really need to know what you're looking for.'

'Who did it for you?'

'I've got my own mole.'

'Same office?'

Emma nodded.

'God, it's scary. I'm so glad I don't have kids.'

'I agree, guv.'

'I take it the lawyer is here?'

Emma nodded. They took the stairs to the corridor where the interview rooms were located.

'Merry Christmas, ma'am,' the uniform on the door said cheerily.

They went inside and Luke glanced up. He looked unkempt and scared. The lawyer stood and introduced himself. He wore an expensive suit and Kelly wondered how much Mr Miles paid him. Money was always the biggest hurdle to justice. Almost any crime could be negated, argued away, diluted and whittled down to very little if huge sums of money were thrown about. Experts, lawyers, scientists, orators, chemists and doctors could all be bought.

'Good afternoon, Luke. Merry Christmas,' Kelly said.

His eyes narrowed and the lawyer sighed.

'I've spoken privately to my client and instructed him to answer none of your questions. We'll hear the evidence against him now.'

Bollocks. The guy knew what he was doing. Kelly looked at Emma; she was the one who knew the chronology. Emma shuffled her paperwork and got everything in order. Meanwhile, Kelly listed the drugs offences.

'Possession with intent to supply all classes of drugs.'

'Denied.'

'The amount of profit will hike up the sentence to maximum. When Luke turns eighteen next month, he'll face fourteen years.'

Luke shuffled in his seat and went to object. His eyes were like saucers and Kelly could tell that he was coming down off something. The lawyer reached out to still him.

'Bullshit. Today he's seventeen and a minor. What have you got on profit?'

Kelly looked at her notes. They'd found around five hundred quid in the car as well as a further two grand in his bedroom.

'Christmas presents,' the lawyer said.

'When did you start using, Luke?' Kelly asked the boy.

'Don't answer,' the lawyer said.

'Why did you threaten Jenna Fraser with telling her parents?'

Luke's mouth fell open. The lawyer stood up. 'Hold on, what's this?'

'Did you do the same to Faith?'

'This interview is over.'

'It's not an interview. I'm charging you, Luke Miles, with possession and intent to supply. Your father can enquire about bail charges, but for the time being, you'll be moving to a cell. Do I need to read him his rights?' she asked the lawyer.

'I want some time with my client.'

'Sure, when you've heard the other charges. Maybe you need to think about talking, Luke. We know you didn't organise all of this alone. And we know that both Jenna and Faith knew Danny Stanton. Oh, by the way, your friend Bobby is dead. Knife through the heart, and I don't think he did it himself. Do you think whoever killed him might come after you next? Any ideas?'

'Don't answer!' the lawyer said.

The sweat on Luke's forehead ran down into his eyes and he wiped it away. Kelly thought how sad it was for a body so young to be in the grip of such a strong addiction. He was dying right in front of her; maybe not straight away, but it was a statistical inevitability that he'd die prematurely. All his father's money, all the hope invested from his middle-class roots, all the opportunity bestowed upon him by virtue of being born into his wealthy family: all of it was slowly slipping away.

Kelly received a phone call, spoke briefly, and hung up.

'Well, merry Christmas. You had MDMA in your bedroom too, Luke, didn't you? That elevates the charges considerably.' She turned to the lawyer. 'For your records, that's Ecstasy, the one that killed Leah Betts: touchy subject with judges.'

'I'd like to speak to my client before he's taken down.'

'Taken down? What does that mean?' Luke spoke for the first time, his voice cracked and terrified. As it should be. Kelly felt sorry for him.

'You're being incarcerated, Luke. You've been formally charged, and until your father can make bail, we're keeping you here,' she told him.

Luke stood up, knocking over the chair. 'No! I can't!'

The lawyer held him. 'Get a grip, lad. Calm down.'

Kelly looked at Emma. 'Detective Hide, be my guest.'

Glancing briefly at her notes, Emma reeled off dates of communications and presented images from Instagram and Facebook. But the clincher was the proof that Luke had encrypted and hidden up to seven accounts, all linking him with Jenna.

'Did you help Sadie Rawlinson infiltrate Tony Blackman's computer, Luke? It looks like you're very gifted in that department. Did you have something against Mr Blackman too?'

Luke looked at his father's lawyer and back at Kelly.

'Isn't it about time you told us what's going on?'

He slumped forward and held his head in his hands.

'Is it true that one of your first customers when you became a supplier two years ago was Jake Trent? You threatened him as well, didn't you, Luke?'

Luke looked up between his fingers.

'He's going to kill me,' he said.

The lawyer stood up, Kelly looked at Emma, and they all waited.

'Who is going to kill you?' Kelly asked.

Chapter 52

The phone woke Johnny and he struggled to find it, not quite remembering where he was. It was mountain rescue calling, and his heart sank.

'Yes?'

'Sorry, Johnny, we need you. We've got three lads on call attending the Whinlatter site, and we've just had another call come in.'

'What's going on up at Whinlatter?'

'They're helping secure the entrances to the forest. There's mountain bikers up there going mad, apparently. Their usual route is barred and they're having hissy fits.'

'Why? What's happened?'

The cycle routes up and down Whinlatter were famous for their risk and unpredictability, as well as, of course, their elevation. The annual Christmas ride was a popular gathering. Johnny had cycled Whinlatter before, many times, and although it wasn't as tough as Hard Knott, it was a leg-breaker, that was for sure. He could imagine the groups of cyclists turning up, looking forward to the deserted peaks on Christmas Day, only to find their way barred. It must be something important.

'A body's been found, and it's chaos up there. A cyclist almost fell on top of it.'

'What?' Johnny sat up. The blanket fell to the floor and he peered over his shoulder at Josie, who was still on her phone. Wendy was asleep leaning against Ted; Johnny thought they looked contented. If only Kelly could see them. He rubbed his eyes, trying to focus. Like Kelly, he was glad he hadn't had a drink. Helen in the mountain rescue office continued talking.

'The thaw exposed her. Gossip is it's the schoolgirl.'

Johnny put his head in his hand and slowly stood up. His first thought was of Kelly.

'Where do you want me?'

'We've had a call from Skiddaw. Someone has taken a tumble on the scree; they fell a couple of hundred feet.'

'How the hell did they do that?' Skiddaw was like the kindergarten of climbs, path all the way and tame even by English Lakes standards.

'Well they're giggling like lunatics. There's at least three of them, and I can't get any sense out of them. All I know is they're lost, and one of them has a bone sticking out of the side of his leg, but, and I quote, "we've toked him up nice and good, and he's out of it".'

That was all he needed. It happened from time to time; the Lake District attracted romantics and rebels, both of whom seemed to enjoy getting high on the top of a mountain. The problem was that it was fucking dangerous. A group of kids had done the same last New Year's Eve and almost died on Scafell Pike. It didn't matter how tame they were, drugs altered minds, and drastically adjusted distance and perception, so that a crevice or drop-off might appear the size of a ditch when it was actually a thousand feet.

He left the decking and went into the house to tell Josie he had to go out. She nodded and yawned.

'You had a good day?' he asked.

'Yeah. Look what Leah got, Dad. Isn't it cool?' She showed him her phone. He presumed that they all posted their presents online and it saddened him. He looked at the photo. Josie's friend was sitting on her bedroom floor, surrounded by boxes and bags labelled with famous names. It made his stomach turn.

He looked at her and almost lost it, saying no, it's not fucking cool to gloat and pose and show off when some people have fuck all. But he bit his tongue.

'Whatever floats your boat. Personally I like my flip-flops.'

At least that raised a smile, and it was genuine. He couldn't help think that Josie's enthusiasm for her friend's labels was laboured.

'I don't know how long I'll be. Stay here?'

She nodded. She seemed happy to hang out with the old folk, whom she found amusing. Johnny nodded to Ted, who stuck up his thumb.

'Something come up?' he asked quietly, not wanting to disturb Wendy. Johnny nodded.

'I'll tell you later. Kelly will probably call you too.'

Ted looked concerned. It was a while since he'd been on call on days like this.

Johnny went to Josie to kiss the top of her head, and tucked his phone under his chin, calling Kelly. She confirmed the find.

'Jesus,' he said.

'I know. We don't know if it's her yet, but it's a female adolescent, and as far as I'm aware, I've got no others missing at the moment.'

'Fuck, Kelly, I'm so sorry.'

'I'm going up there now. What are you up to?'

'I've got to go up Skiddaw. All the others are busy guarding the area around Whinlatter.'

'Don't worry, the coppers will have plenty of backup soon, and they'll be able to relieve you.'

Johnny looked at Josie before he left, thankful that as far as he could tell she was clean from substances. She didn't seem to get agitated, apart from the obvious teenage triggers; her skin was clear, and she showed no signs of elevated organ stress. Before Johnny joined mountain rescue, he'd worked in rehab centres around London, counselling and intervening, trying to get as many addicts as possible onto a decent sober programme. Eighty-five per cent relapsed, and plenty of them died. Lots of them were old army buddies, unable to cope with the pedestrian pace of civilian life and the demons in their heads.

He grabbed his keys and went to the door, glancing back one last time.

And stopped.

Wendy wasn't the right colour. Ted saw the panic in his face and looked down at her, then sat up, holding onto her so she wouldn't fall. Johnny rushed to them and held his fingers against her neck.

'Josie, call 999!' he shouted.

'I didn't feel anything…' Ted stopped abruptly.

Johnny listened to Wendy's airway and heard a slight passage of air, but her pulse was way too low.

'What?' Josie turned around and took her earphones out.

'Hold her!' Johnny told Ted, and dialled the emergency services himself.

'Oh my God, what's wrong with her?' Josie had begun to realise that all was not well.

Johnny and Ted laid Wendy gently on the ground, getting her into position so they could administer mouth-to-mouth resuscitation. Both knew they couldn't do it if she was breathing; they'd kill her. Their eyes met over her limp body, and Ted shook his head.

'Ted?' Johnny took his arm. He needed him for support, but also for his expert medical knowledge.

'Wendy? Wendy?' Ted repeated over and over.

'Dad?' Josie sounded panicked.

'Get a cold flannel,' Johnny said, just for something for her to do.

'Wendy!' Ted shouted. Johnny knew they were losing her.

The ambulance was with them in under seven minutes. Wendy was loaded into it and Ted accompanied her. As Johnny watched it go, he called Kelly but she didn't answer. He ran to his car. He had to go to the Skiddaw job.

Chapter 53

Kelly drove with a heavy heart. It was what she'd dreaded, but expected at the same time. She'd authorised for the family to be told that a body had been found, but that it hadn't yet been formally identified. She prayed it wasn't her.

A crowd had gathered in Braithwaite, and Kelly found it difficult to get through. News had travelled fast, and it looked as though the journos were there already. She saw a van from Sky and realised that Christmas Day was just another day for other bearers of bad news too. A few uniforms struggled to keep a route open and rolled their eyes at her in sympathy as they waved her through.

The start of the Whinlatter Pass was running with water, and it poured down the road like a river. Kelly wondered if the poor girl had been up here since Sunday, hidden under the snow, ready to reveal her secrets when the weather turned. It made her shudder.

She parked at the Revelin Moss car park and walked up to the police tape. Stan MacIntyre was on duty; he raised his eyebrows at her, indicating that he'd rather keep his desk job than be in her shoes. A forensic officer was already at the scene. He nodded and gave her some covers for her shoes. Kelly heard flies and shook her head; they were never far away, even if their meal was frozen.

The thing she saw first was the short top that Colin Shaw had forbidden Faith to wear. The long green jumper that had been found with her backpack, three miles away in the centre of town, had been swapped. It was the kind of detail that was likely to stay with the father beyond all the others. She forced herself to look at the face, and then looked away again.

She made a quick call to Emma to confirm that it was Faith, then bent down to study the girl, who looked like a doll. Tears sprang to her eyes and she had to turn away for a few seconds to control herself. Faith's skin was white and her eyes were open. Her gorgeous long brown hair was straggled around her young, sweet face. She was in the foetal position and her trousers and pants were pulled down.

Kelly bit her lip and anger welled up in her chest. Bastards.

She mustn't jump to conclusions until the coroner had had a chance to perform the post-mortem, and she willed herself to be as objective as she possibly could. She had come across frozen bodies before, and she knew that often, before they succumbed to the cold, people in the late stages of hypothermia clawed at their clothes, desperate to take them off. It was called paradoxical undressing, and scientists reckoned that it was to do with the muscles trying urgently to contract to warm the core up, eventually causing fatigue and a surge of hot blood. But she couldn't get sexual assault out of her head either.

She knew that the temperature in Whinlatter Forest last Sunday evening had been around minus four degrees: easily cold enough to freeze someone to death. But she wanted to know why Faith had been here. The obvious answer was that her tormentors were still up to their old game of leaving her somewhere alone after tricking her to come with them. She imagined Luke enticing her into his car, and Sadie encouraging her. Kelly felt hot anger flood her gut. Again she willed herself to calm down.

Faith was only wearing one shoe, a light grey Adidas Cloudfoam: an early Christmas present from her parents. Kelly walked towards a uniform, asking him to help search for the other one. They soon found it. She beckoned the forensic officer, who took photos. Faith would have to be bagged carefully to collect the detritus around her. The likelihood of vital evidence in the immediate vicinity was immense.

'She's still pretty rock solid,' the forensic officer said. Kelly knew that this meant Faith would have to be thawed out in a carefully controlled environment at a specific temperature of thirty-eight degrees, to make sure that her extremities didn't begin to decompose before her internal organs were defrosted. It could take a few days before she was ready to autopsy. She'd have to call Ted, though he'd know soon enough anyway.

She looked around. The body lay in a shallow ditch not far from the road. Faith could have burrowed there to keep warm once hypothermia was advanced and she'd begun to experience hallucinations and amnesia; if she was still alive at that stage. Kelly's biggest question was how the girl had died: exposure or murder. She wouldn't know until Ted got her on his slab.

Another forensic officer arrived and Kelly agreed that it was time to get the body bagged up. They didn't want it out here warming up; a process that could allow vital evidence to slip away. She called Ted, but there was no answer. He and Wendy must be asleep, she thought. She envied them, full of Christmas dinner in front of the fire in her lounge.

She walked back to her car and called Emma again. The Miles family lawyer had been in with his client for over an hour, and had a statement prepared. That was, until the discovery of Faith's body: they were now in renewed intense negotiations as far as Emma could tell, and the exchange was heated.

'The most important thing is that he won't want to take the rap for this on his own,' Kelly said. 'We need to get him to start giving us some names. Has the CCTV footage come back yet?'

'That's another thing, guv. It came through to the office email, and I only checked it an hour ago.

'Please give me some good news,' Kelly said.

'There was a Highways Agency CCTV camera at the A66 roundabout, where traffic turns into Whinlatter. It was disconnected for replacement by a newer model, and sent to be recycled by the DVLA in Swansea.'

'Shit,' Kelly swore.

'But the images were downloaded onto the Highways Agency computer before it was decommissioned.'

Kelly held her breath.

'They found it.'

She closed her eyes, and fist-pumped the air subtly, walking away from the forensic officers as they began to carefully wrap Faith's hands, feet and head in plastic before lifting her into a black body bag. Moving a frozen corpse was a tricky operation, and Kelly didn't really want to witness it. Not after getting to know Faith as a living, breathing, beautiful and intelligent young woman with a full life to lead. She still hadn't accepted her death as real; it would probably take a few days, like it always did. They'd ploughed so much energy into finding her alive. She just wasn't ready to let that go yet.

'Go on, Emma.'

'We've got a positive for Luke's Hyundai travelling west at 9.17 p.m.'

A wave of emotion caught in Kelly's throat and she looked away into the forest. Faith had got into that car willingly, she knew that, perhaps for drugs, perhaps because she was in love with Luke Miles, or perhaps because her friends had said she'd be safe.

'It drives back east at 10 p.m.'

This was unexpected. It wasn't a long time to have a party, and it didn't make sense.

'Can you see the occupants?'

'It's not clear enough, guv. Seventy-six other vehicles passed through the roundabout between 9 p.m. and midnight. When I checked them through the ANPR, Danny Stanton's Ford Ka came up too.'

'Say again?'

'It drives west from the A66 at 9.55 p.m. but doesn't come back again. There's a motorbike that goes in and out around similar timings too. It travels west towards Whinlatter at 9.52 p.m. and east again at 10.21 p.m. It's registered to Maria Volantyne.'

'The woman who owns the lease on the fair,' Kelly said. 'Emma, can you run a national check on the ANPR for all three vehicles. Get someone to isolate all their hits and find a link. I want to know what ties them together.'

'Of course, guv.'

Craig Lockwood had told Kelly that Bobby Bailey had been taken in by Maria Volantyne as a teenager when his mother died, and she'd covered for him ever since. And that before his violent murder, Bobby had driven a motorbike.

Chapter 54

Danny Stanton sat on a train speeding towards Folkestone. It wasn't so much his car that he was concerned about. It contained a few packs of gear and that was about it: nothing to worry about. It wasn't even that he knew that Bobby Bailey was dead; news travelled fast at the fair if you knew who to ask. The loser meant nothing to him. It was more his own involvement as a courier that concerned him, and what had happened to that girl who'd turned up where he'd last seen Bobby.

His plan was simple: run away.

He'd made the journey several times, only this time he didn't have a return ticket. He'd take the Eurotunnel to Paris and then a bus to Athens, where he'd board a boat to Kos. He'd been left the villa in a will years ago; some old auntie with no other kin had named him as sole heir. It was about the best place he could think of to hide. He could stay there, away from the internet, away from the UK Border Force, and away from his Manchester source, for a few weeks, perhaps even more, then he could move on again.

He'd only gone up there to pass on some pills, but the young dumb kid had brought a carload of partygoers, to show off. He wouldn't have believed it had he not seen it with his own eyes. He'd told Bobby to get the hell out of there and leave them to it, but Bobby couldn't take his eyes off the girls: girls young enough to be illegal, with flesh hanging out all over the joint, willing and open to hard drug use. Danny had rolled his eyes; it was a recipe for disaster.

That was when he'd called Bella. He was too fucked to drive, especially over Whinlatter Pass, so he'd walked, and met her somewhere below the treeline. They'd smoked for a good hour or so, as well as drinking the beer she'd brought with her. Bella was old school: she liked a serious-grade joint, a good pint and a hard shag. She was Danny's kind of girl, and he hooked up with her whenever he could.

The last thing he'd expected was to be the centre of a manhunt when he woke up in her bed three days later. He'd screwed up, and he knew he'd have to pay; he just wasn't ready yet. His three mobile phones had been broken into pieces and distributed between bins across London as he made his way from Euston to St Pancras. He kept the drugs he had left; he wasn't that paranoid, and there were fewer border controls between Britain and Greece than Christmases he'd spent with his mother.

He'd told Bella he'd take her to the States, and she'd believed him, ready to go anywhere with him. He felt a bit of a bastard, but it was the only way to plant any sort of disinformation for the police. It would buy him time. It would take them ages to get Bella to talk.

He'd changed gigs before, and he was growing bored of the Lake District anyway; it was full of small-timers like Bobby Bailey, too keen to inject the stuff themselves to bother to keep half an eye open. He should have stayed in Manchester, but that was another closed door, for much the same reason, though none of it had been his fault. He'd chosen the wrong friends, and he knew he was better off on his own. He'd toyed with the idea of getting clean before: not clean as in obeying the law, but as in sober. He'd known a few guys who'd done it and swore by it. Some of them had turned into born-again hippies and that wasn't his bag, but the idea of not needing it when he woke up was appealing, and he predicted that he'd have to abstain for the foreseeable future anyway, so it was a good opportunity to try. They said it was tough, giving up, but how hard could it be?

As the train emerged from the tunnel in France, Danny felt like a new man: he was embarking on the adventure of a lifetime, and he should have done it years ago.

–

Danny Stanton's only problem was that he'd underestimated the power of digital surveillance and international cooperation. CCTV footage of him buying his train ticket from Oxenholme to Euston was passed to Kelly within a matter of hours; from there, she knew he'd either go to ground in London or abroad. When they found him purchasing a ticket from St Pancras to Paris with the same card he'd used in Oxenholme, their task became even easier.

Europe wasn't that far away, and his details were passed as a matter of course to all borders, as far as Britain's diplomatic relations allowed, including France, Italy and Greece: the exact route of his bus trip. He was apprehended in Lyons before he even had the chance to browse his Greek guidebook. Before the sun set on Boxing Day, he would be on his way back to the UK.

Chapter 55

It took Kelly half an hour to reach the Penrith and Lakes Hospital. Her mother had been taken to the cardiac ward, and she ran from the car park to the lift. The hospital was quiet, and it intensified her need to reach Wendy as soon as she could.

Nikki was already there, and Johnny walked towards Kelly, moving her backwards, out of the way, before the two women could exchange unpleasantries. Kelly's chest heaved from the exertion of running, and she pushed against Johnny, but he was way stronger than she was.

'What are you doing?' she whispered. She was mindful of her location, but she didn't understand what was going on. Nikki glared at her from the other side of the hallway. She saw Matt, Nikki's husband, who acknowledged her presence and then looked down at his feet again.

'Kelly, stop. I need to talk to you first. Don't give her the satisfaction of seeing you lose control.'

'What? Why would I?'

'Come in here.' He drew her into an empty side room.

'Where's Mum?'

'She's stable, but you need to prepare yourself. She's really ill. She stopped taking her last round of medication three weeks ago; at least that's what they told Nikki. They'll only talk to you and her, and you weren't here.'

'You know where I was!'

'Of course I do.' Johnny closed the door.

'It was Faith,' was all she said.

'I know. I tried to call, but when you didn't answer, I knew you were busy. Ted and I agreed that we'd let you get on with whatever you were doing and just keep trying your phone. We got hold of Nikki straight away.'

'And she thinks I've put my job first again?'

'Pretty much. Look, don't let it rile you. It's predictable behaviour, rise above it. The important thing is your mum.'

'What happened?'

'She collapsed. We thought she was asleep, but she changed colour. I—'

'Oh Johnny, I'm sorry,' she said.

'Don't be sorry, how could you have known?'

'What do you mean, she stopped her medication?'

'The course she was taking came to an end and the result wasn't positive enough to start another one straight away. She's losing her resilience.'

Wendy had been ill for over a year now, and she'd had close scrapes from time to time when they'd thought they might lose her and had prepared for the worst, as well as periods of relative health. She was willing to try anything, and chemical substances had kept her alive for longer than was predicted.

Kelly sniffed at the irony: here she was investigating the fact that illegal substances had snuffed out too many kids' lives, at the same time hoping that legal ones would keep her mother alive. Who got to choose which ones were passed for human consumption? There was a fine line between the ones that killed and the ones that prolonged life. It was just that the lines were being smudged. Prescription drugs a hundred times more powerful than heroin were flooding the market, and no one warned the kids they were there.

Her theory was that Faith had been forced to take something and had fought back. From what she'd found out about the girl, she was a fighter, just like Wendy, and she'd have no doubt resisted to the end. On a summer evening, the traffic would have been busier and she would probably have been spotted and picked up, maybe still alive. But it was winter, brutal and unforgiving.

Kelly had her characters lined up on stage and ready to perform; now she just needed to finalise the order in which they appeared. She was left with a sinking feeling that she might not be able to tell her mother that she'd closed another case. She always told her. It wasn't some kind of trophy-gathering, like the top shelf in her old room where she'd displayed her hockey and netball medals; it was more an excuse to connect with Wendy.

'I want to see her,' she said.

'Of course. I just wanted to prepare you, and for you to calm down. I knew you'd be wired when you came in. I just wish I'd been able to speak to you earlier.'

'I know.'

'You find out what happened?'

'Not yet. I need the autopsy to be done.'

'I'm not sure Ted's up to it.'

'He will be when I ask him,' she said.

'He's pretty shaken up.'

'It's all right, it'll take the body a day or so to thaw out properly.'

Johnny looked sideways at her.

'God, I'm sorry.' She realised how cold she must sound. The job did that: made her hard at times.

He went to her and put his arms around her. She allowed herself to be held. She felt the ring on her finger and caressed it, trying not to let tears drop out of her eyes, because the moment they did, they wouldn't stop. It wasn't just for her mother; it was for Faith, and Jenna, and the other kids who were so fucking unhappy and unlucky that they wound up dead too young.

The moment passed, and she straightened and looked at Johnny.

'How is she?'

'She's out of it. She's had an MRI scan and her heart is occluded. The tumour has begun to grow again and it's threatening to obstruct a major artery. Surgery has never been performed for this type of complication; it's not done.'

'Why not?' Kelly's voice was a whisper.

'They explained to Nikki that it's not an option. They can fix lots of things, but the removal of the tumour would leave too much tissue to be replaced from other arteries, and she's not got many of those intact.'

'Her legs? They said they'd use tissue from there, and her back.'

Johnny shook his head. Kelly remembered a conversation she'd had months ago with the surgeon, Mr Yanni, who'd laid out Wendy's options before the new drugs had begun to shrink the latest tumour. Why had she run so spectacularly out of options?

'I don't understand,' she said. Her voice broke.

'Why don't you speak to the oncologist?'

'They got an oncologist to come in to work on Christmas Day?'

'Come on, let's go and find Ted. I think he could do with some support. Your sister has been giving him her "you're not part of the firm" look, and he's a bit bewildered.'

They found Ted by the coffee machine, and before Kelly could resist, he had her in a bear hug. She stiffened, but he didn't let go, and after a few seconds she allowed him to remain there, just holding her and breathing. She looked at Johnny over Ted's shoulder and caught Nikki's eye. Her sister looked baffled but intrigued; but most of all, left out.

'Ted?' Kelly whispered softly.

He backed away and she looked at him. His face had lost all the charm and sprightliness she'd seen this morning. Wendy had been wearing a mauve suit and her hair had been curled. She'd smelled of new perfume, and Kelly had figured right away that Ted was spoiling her. Of all the bastard unfairness that she'd seen this week, she reckoned this was the worst of it, but admonished herself for such childish thoughts. Life wasn't fair for anyone, and it wasn't supposed to be.

'I'm going in to see her,' she said.

Ted nodded. Johnny took her hand and they went into the room, passing Nikki without a word.

Kelly was unaccustomed to treading so carefully. Her days were full of movement: arranging to go somewhere, getting there, leaving again. This was despondent stillness. A lack of motion that she didn't trust because she didn't know her place in it.

Wendy lay on her back beneath a sheet. Her eyes were closed and she breathed rhythmically, thanks to a mask. Kelly stood at the foot of the bed, not knowing what to do. She didn't understand the bleeps and lines on the monitors, and she looked to Johnny for support, but he could give her none, apart from being there.

An hour later, when her phone vibrated, she knew that she had a decision to make.

Chapter 56

DC Emma Hide dealt with Tony Blackman.

She had several jobs to take care of: the first was to inform him that the CPS had dropped all charges against him; the second was to try and talk him out of suing the force for an apology and compensation; and the third was to try and figure out why one of his pupils would accuse him of sharing drugs with students. She was no diplomat, and she was much better at dealing with numbers and stats, but her boss was at the hospital with her mother, and no one else was around to take on the unfortunate task. It was Boxing Day and the office was empty. They'd finally managed to locate Blackman by phone, and he'd explained that he'd visited a friend in Manchester for Christmas.

Tony Blackman was a changed man, and that was no surprise. He couldn't get his life back to how it was before the charges, but at least he wasn't going to prison. Emma didn't like the anonymity laws any more than the next person, but she wasn't a lawyer or a judge. Some people seemed to assume that the police could change the law as and when they chose to, but in reality they had no role in judicial matters whatsoever. But it didn't really change public opinion of them.

Sarah Peaks was with him. Emma greeted them both with a handshake, and invited them to follow her to a seating area. She couldn't help feeling liberated on Blackman's behalf. It was great when you got to catch a criminal who thought they could break the law with impunity, and boast about it, but it was equally satisfying when somebody was exonerated. She would have happily informed him at his home address, but he'd insisted on coming in. She guessed he wanted to celebrate his freedom, and it was symbolic that he could walk into a police station and not be a suspect.

'Can I speak freely?' she asked him.

He looked at Sarah and nodded. 'Of course. Sarah knows everything, she's been there from the beginning.'

Tony Blackman was a small man with piercing eyes. He was quietly spoken and Emma got the impression that he was used to being in charge, though that contradicted his size and presence in the room. Sarah was the opposite; she was thickset, and covered her sizeable waistline with cardigans and scarves. She fidgeted, but he was as calm as the surface of Rydal Water before a storm.

The news from the CPS had come through on Christmas Eve. There was no evidence to support Tony Blackman's ownership of the images, there was no evidence to support assault, and there was no evidence to support Sadie Rawlinson's accusation that she was lured to his flat, or groomed in the preceding weeks. In other words, there was no case. It was a waste of everybody's time, and processes were now in motion to charge Sadie Rawlinson with perjury and obstruction of justice.

'It must have been a horrendous experience, Mr Blackman.'

'What will happen to Sadie?' he asked.

Sarah nodded. 'She's only a child after all. She needs help.'

'That's something for the CPS to decide. We gather evidence and identify suspects; the law courts decide if someone is guilty.'

'Will she go to prison?'

'It's difficult to say. At her age, rehabilitation is key. Courts don't like incarcerating juveniles. She could get hefty community service or a suspended sentence. I really can't say. It's a separate case to be investigated.'

'She'll probably get away with it. You know she's a drug addict? So is Luke Miles, her boyfriend. They were the ones who got Faith hooked on the stuff,' he said.

'Tony—' Sarah began. He put his hand up to shush her, and carried on.

'You name it, they do it. No wonder Faith was found so far away from the fair. Has Luke confessed to giving her the drugs that killed her? So sad, another innocent life.' He looked away and shook his head. Sarah put her hand on his. But he wasn't finished.

'As soon as I saw that the colour of some of my icons had changed, I knew they were up to something. You see, protection firewalls that are set to very specific personal criteria are so sensitive that even a slight blip can cause a real meltdown. I knew what they'd been up to, but it was too late.'

Sarah looked at Tony, and Emma looked from one to the other.

'They?' she asked.

'Sorry?' Tony Blackman replied.

'You said "they". It was just Sadie at your flat, yes?'

'Oh, of course. I simply refer to them as a unit; they're inseparable. Whatever you find out about Sadie, it'll be true of Luke, and vice versa. I hope that helps.'

'Right. Mr Blackman, there is one more thing. As part of our wider school inquiries, we did have one pupil tell us that you have used illegal substances with some of your students.'

'That's ludicrous!' he laughed.

'More lies,' Sarah added.

'So you deny ever taking illegal substances?'

'Absolutely. Categorically.'

Emma stood up. 'Well, the matter is closed, Mr Blackman. I hope you will accept our formal apology.' She'd been told to say that, but it didn't sound right.

'Well, I'm seeking legal advice.'

'Right, OK, enjoy the rest of your Christmas.'

Emma watched the pair walk to the front entrance, and cast her mind back to when Sarah Peaks had come to them, bereft and desperate to prove her boyfriend was an incompetent buffoon when it came to computers.

But it wasn't just his technical language that made Emma go to her computer. It was the fact that Faith Shaw was still in the mortuary fridge awaiting autopsy. No one yet knew if she had drugs in her system, or whether it was drugs that had killed her. Not even the police. And how the hell would Blackman know that the most likely scenario was that she'd been taken to the forest and left there?

She'd given the registration details of the three vehicles to the ANPR data centre. So far they were on upwards of fifty hits, and Emma had told them to keep going. Scouring camera images took police hours, but most of the initial work was done by a computer, and they were after something very specific: all three vehicles in the same time frame and the same location. So far, nothing had been found, except what they already had on the Whinlatter roundabout.

Emma looked to see if they had any registration details for a vehicle owned by Tony Blackman. They did, as part of their initial charging process. She called the data centre and asked them to add his details to the list. After ten minutes, she had a call back.

All four vehicles had been tracked travelling south on the M6 two weeks ago. They had all pulled into the same service station within ten minutes of one another, and left within five minutes of each other. Emma called the service station and told them she was on her way to examine their CCTV.

Chapter 57

Kelly ordered a crime-scene reconstruction where Faith had been found. The thaw had revealed vehicle tracks that an expert said were fresh before the snowfall. He could absolutely prove this beyond doubt, because they were frozen to perfection. Once the surface ice had thawed, the soil underneath was virgin, unsullied by the common detritus of the forest such as twigs, leaves, animal droppings and spider's webs. An estimate was made that several of the tracks – two sets of car tyres and one set of motorbike tyres – were made only hours before the first snowfall. The only other tracks in the vicinity had been soiled with fragments of foliage and weathering, indicating that they were much older. The three fresh sets were filled with plaster and sent away to be made into prints. The process of identifying the types of tyres, and then linking them to vehicles, would take weeks normally. Kelly reckoned that in a case like this she could speed it up to a week.

The re-creation of any crime scene involved, first and foremost, sterility. The area had been preserved as it had been found, minus the body, and Kelly watched as the crime-scene specialist walked this way and that, pulling tape, planting poles, asking questions and looking up to the sky. She was a local and knew the area well, which was always a bonus. Kelly had once witnessed a reconstruction in London where the investigator had stopped thirty minutes in, looked up to a block of flats and announced, 'It came from number 32, my cousin lives downstairs.' He'd then proceeded to inform the team of all the exits from the block, which one was likely used and even which petrol station the suspects could have stopped at on the way out of the city. He'd been correct, and CCTV footage from the garage had caught them.

Kelly didn't need to be here, but it beat sitting beside her mother's bed in hospital; she allowed Nikki that honour. It was extraordinary that since she'd found out about Ted being her father, her guilt towards Nikki and her own behaviour had disappeared. She owed her sister nothing, and didn't even feel any compulsion to explain. She could tell that Nikki was puzzled, wondering where her arch-nemesis had gone, but Kelly didn't care anymore.

She'd checked on her mother twice already this morning, and her condition had neither worsened nor improved. Sitting in a waiting room drinking copious amounts of tea made by staff hovering like funeral directors didn't help anybody, and Kelly wasn't about to indulge anyone's need to weep. She'd forced Ted to leave and go back to his hotel, to shower and sleep, and had given Matt a hand finding something to entertain the kids while Nikki kept vigil. Everybody had different needs when faced with sadness, and no one had the right to judge what others chose. She toyed with the idea of offering Ted her spare room. His flat in Carlisle was an hour's drive away, and the intimacy of sharing her home was intimidating. He was comfortable in a small guest-house near the castle, and that's how she left it.

At work, she could focus, and she was never far away from Penrith. Each time she'd been to the hospital, she'd been aware of Nikki's glare, scrutinising her for her blatant callousness. Kelly wasn't interested. She was liberated. Nikki wore her fatigue and the dark circles under her eyes like badges of honour, as if saying to anyone passing by: 'Look how dedicated I am in my grief.' Fine.

Fucking fine.

'The car parked here and turned here,' the CSI said, indicating. 'The footprints down here evidence a struggle; either that or they were dancing or jogging on the spot. See how the footprint is incomplete, and the sharp, narrow trail away from the full print, here? Then over here, where the body was found, there are crawl marks and drag marks, here and here.'

Kelly followed her, and nodded with every point.

'But they could all be explained away by a group of teenagers having fun, or play-fighting,' she pointed out.

'Of course, but you've got a deceased person, so it wouldn't really convince anyone.'

The forensic officer nodded towards the dog handler, who'd been waiting patiently with a spaniel called Maisie. She was a drug dog. Police sniffers were bred for generations from trusty workers with illustrious histories, and Maisie's ancestors were fourth-generation police workers. The bond between canine and handler was awe-inspiring, and Kelly and the CSI watched as Maisie was let off the lead. Her nose never left the ground and her tail pointed upright in the air, the excitement of pleasing her handler almost too much. It didn't take long for her to begin howling and barking from under a bush, and the handler joined her and spoke to her as though to a toddler.

'What is it, girl? What have you got?'

Kelly watched with admiration as the handler bent down and retrieved a small plastic bag. Maisie sat obediently and the handler rewarded her with her favourite ball and some treats. Kelly took the bag with a gloved hand: it contained a dust-like substance. The chances of it being the sugar portion for someone's school food technology class was remote. It was bagged and tagged.

The forest was eerily isolated, and Kelly thought it an odd place to choose to score a drugs deal. There were plenty of places around Keswick that could offer the privacy needed for such an activity; they really didn't need to come so far, unless the intent to cause harm was already there. There was always the possibility that things had spiralled out of control, and Faith was the unfortunate victim. Kelly had yet to work out who the real ringleader was, but she suspected it wasn't who'd she initially thought.

Her phone buzzed: it was Emma.

'Guv, I've just had the strangest conversation with Tony Blackman.'

'I'm listening. What did he have to say for himself?'

'Two things bother me. One is that he told me that Sadie Rawlinson and Luke Miles are both drug addicts and it was probably their drugs that killed Faith Shaw.'

'But we haven't got any toxicology results yet.'

'Exactly. He also on two occasions said that "they" – plural – were in his flat, rather than just "she", as in Sadie.'

'What about what the caretaker's son said about him?'

'Flatly denied it. The second thing is that he talked about his computer like an expert when I told him of our findings. At one point he mentioned firewall settings.'

'I thought he was supposed to be a technology dummy.'

'Exactly.'

'It sounds all wrong.'

'That's what I thought, boss. That's why I ran his car through the ANPR with the others. I got an instant hit, but that's not all. There's a fifth vehicle and they've got an image for me. Have you got your Toughpad on you?'

'It's in my car, why?'

'I'm emailing you the image of the car and its driver. I swear it's your Nedzad Galic.'

Chapter 58

Back at Eden House, Sadie had been brought in. Her mother had not accompanied her. Kelly was in no mood for games and she wanted some straight answers.

She'd been to see Faith's parents. She hadn't stayed long; just enough time to make a vow to nail whoever had done this to their beautiful daughter and to find out exactly what had happened in the last few moments of her life. Looking into Michael's eyes had been the hardest moment of her career so far, and she'd found it tough keeping her voice steady. It had made her want to kick something, so she had to be careful with Sadie, who was, after all, a minor.

The girl looked terrible.

'I'm struggling here, Sadie. It seems to me like everyone is lying, including you. Why don't you do yourself a favour and tell me what you know? You're fifteen, aren't you?'

Sadie nodded.

'Too young for this shit. What's going on?'

Sadie put her head in her hands and started sobbing.

'It was just a joke.'

Kelly passed her a tissue and Sadie blew her nose hard. Kelly waited, not wanting to ruin the moment, but inside, her blood boiled.

'We left her in the forest. It was a joke, I swear. She never wanted the gear. She was amazing like that. I always told her I didn't know how she did it. I wish I could.'

Kelly's phone buzzed and she glanced down at it: Johnny.

'We forced her out of the car. She pretended to play along but I know she was scared.' Sadie wiped the snot from her nose.

'Did you keep her bag?'

Sadie nodded. For just a moment, Kelly wished she wasn't a police officer. She could easily have reached over the table and punched the girl.

'That's nice.' Her teeth were gritted.

'We went back, but we couldn't find her.'

'Let me get this straight. You all went to the forest. Drugs were taken, you partied. You played a joke on Faith, forcing her out of the car, then you drove away.'

Sadie nodded.

'Where did you go after that?'

'Up the pass, until I said we should go back.'

'It was your idea to go back?'

She nodded again.

'You went back at what time?'

'I dunno. I don't have a watch.'

'Your phone?'

Sadie shrugged her shoulders.

'Goddamn it!' Kelly stood up. 'Your friend is dead. *Dead*. What time did you go back?'

'I think it was before ten.'

'It *was* before ten, because at ten o'clock we have CCTV footage of Luke's car leaving the forest.'

Sadie's eyes widened.

'I've also got Bobby Bailey's motorbike and Danny Stanton's Ford entering the forest at the same time.'

'He called them.' Sadie began to shake.

'What?'

'Luke. He called Bobby in a panic. Faith was saying she'd go to the coppers. He was bragging about what he'd done to Jenna and said he was going to do it to her too. She was so scared.'

Kelly took a breath and tried to process the information in her head. She spoke very quietly, forcing herself to remain in control. The uniform who was in the room to chaperone the girl had glanced at her a few times and she knew she had to be careful.

'And what did Bobby say?'

'Not to worry, that he'd fix it.'

Kelly left the room, slamming the door, and called Johnny.

'I know I was only supposed to call you if it was about your mum, but I just wanted to let you know that Ted came over to yours and we got talking.'

Kelly closed her eyes and tried to be understanding. It wasn't a good moment.

'What about?'

'Everything. You. The girl. He'll do the autopsy. He's gone into the hospital this afternoon to make a start.'

'It's too early.'

'He knows that, but he'll at least be able to give you an indication of when it will be. He needs something to do, Kelly. The guy's crushed.'

'Thanks, Johnny. I really appreciate that. I'm going to ask him if he wants to stay at mine for a while.'

'I think he'd like that. Any joy?'

'Ah, the usual crap. These kids can't tell the truth to save their lives. Literally. I'll get there. I'm sorry I've screwed up the holiday.'

'Don't be stupid. I'll see you later.'

They hung up, and Kelly felt a tenderness towards Ted that she'd only experienced before she'd found out about her parentage. They used to share so much time together, just the two of them, chewing over facts and figures, crime scenes and scenarios, and she'd missed him.

She called him.

He was breezy as always, and she realised that she loved that about him: he was indomitable. No matter what the rest of the world was up to, Ted Wallis's ability to stop the madness and reset time was utterly indestructible. She felt safe with him just on the other end of a phone. He sounded as though he was thankful to be busy and the work would do him good. They were so similar.

'I've examined her, and I reckon another few hours.' It was quicker than expected and no-one could really predict with frozen bodies.

'You have no idea how happy that makes me, Ted.'

'I think I do.'

She looked at her watch: it was gone two o'clock. That meant that Faith wouldn't be ready until this evening, and the operation could take hours. She had to figure out how best to fill that time and use it to her best advantage. If she could go for a pint with Ted and mull it over, he'd come up with a few solutions – they both would – but she didn't have that luxury available at the moment.

She called Craig.

'Anything significant found at the scene?' She referred to Bobby's trailer.

'Merry Christmas.'

'Sorry.'

'No worries. We're looking through his phone. There are some interesting photos on it.'

'What sort of photos?'

'Of Faith Shaw on Sunday night.' He let the news sink in. 'He was watching her.'

'Christ, Craig. I feel sick to my stomach. I've got Bailey placed at the scene by a witness this end, plus I've got motorbike tracks. I think Faith threatened to squeal, and Bobby was called in as the hard man. It's pathetic. I can't even begin to imagine her alone in the forest with him, and what he might have done to her. The autopsy will start tonight.'

'I've got some other news too,' Craig said.

'Go on.'

'I gave my pal in the Manchester drug squad the details of the bike, and he came back with a positive in the vicinity of an active surveillance they've got going on. They've been watching an illegal from Sarajevo for eight months now and they're close to making arrests.'

'Oh Jesus. It looks like your friends and I have a lot in common. We've got the same man meeting a couple of weeks ago with two other suspects. Do they know our angle?'

'They didn't know about Bobby until I flagged him up. They reckon he was a courier. They've tracked the bike back and forth to Cumbria seven times in as many weeks.'

'Do they have a name for the foreign national?' Kelly's gut twisted. She thought of Dale Prentice's details being found on Tony Blackman's computer. It was no coincidence. She knew now that Blackman had been told to find the boy.

'Nedzad Galic.'

Kelly closed her eyes. So, Galic had come back for his son.

After she'd finished speaking to Craig, she went to find Emma and told her to arrest Blackman.

'Yes, guv. I've got Luke Miles' mobile phone records back,' Emma said.

'Tell me there's one to Bobby Bailey's number.'

'Yes, but there's also one to Tony Blackman's just before it.'

'What?'

'Look, at 9.39 p.m., then a minute later, the call to Bailey.'

'Bailey's motorbike was seen travelling into the forest at 9.52 p.m. So whatever Luke said to him, he got there fast.'

Kelly sat down on a chair and stared into space.

'I wonder how long Tony Blackman has been dealing drugs to his students.'

'And shutting them up,' Emma said. Kelly looked at her. 'Why else would Sadie try to frame him, unless she was terrified of him?'

'They wanted him out of their lives,' Kelly said.

'That's why Luke and Sadie were both at his flat that evening.'

'Sadie would have been too scared to go on her own. So Luke was with her. They played on his computer while he organised a quantity of drugs for them to take with them: to sell, no doubt.'

'That's when they downloaded the images,' Emma said.

'And he figured it out, but too late. He must have been ripping.'

'And they've been terrified ever since.'

'It's plenty to get an arrest,' Kelly said. 'Have you got Jenna Fraser's mobile records to hand?'

Emma nodded and brought them up on her computer. Previously, Blackman had only skipped about on the perimeter of their inquiries, but now they scoured the records for his phone number. It was there.

'That's the week before she died.'

'He's calling her three times a day.'

They looked at each other.

'Why didn't we find anything in his flat when he was arrested for the indecent charge?'

'Sarah Peaks?'

'Surely not. She doesn't look the sort at all.'

'They never do.'

Chapter 59

Ted tried to concentrate on scrubbing up. He knew that as soon as he placed his mask over his face, switched his mic on and unzipped the body bag, he'd be fine: his nerves would melt away and he'd be able to focus on what was in front of him. But at the moment, all he could think about was Wendy. He was doing this because he needed something to distract him; he was also doing it for the poor girl who lay under the plastic, but most of all he was doing it for his daughter.

Kelly was like him: she needed something to keep her busy. He knew she was desperate for these results to complete her investigation into the disappearance and death of the girl on his slab. As a coroner, he was independent of the government, but equally, he was held to their guidelines, and they didn't much care for the verdict of suicide: it didn't help keep the figures down, and the number of suicides amongst kids was frankly shameful. It was the biggest killer of ten to twenty-five-year-olds. She hadn't told him her theory about the girl's death lest it cloud his judgement, and that was admirable. He approached the cadaver with an open mind. All he knew was what the forensic reports from the crime scene said: that she'd been found frozen in a ditch.

He approached the bag and unzipped it while his assistant busied himself with making sure Ted had everything to hand: sharp scalpels, his striker saw, a hand saw and various other instruments. It was a sterile environment, though not for the protection of the patient, like in a normal working theatre; rather for the safety of the staff. Corpses carried a multitude of dangerous pathology, and Ted's gloves and mask were to reduce the risk to himself. The zip made a loud buzz that echoed around the mortuary room, and Ted caught his first glimpse of Faith Shaw in death.

They hadn't rearranged her body during her defrosting, and she was just as she was when she'd been placed in the bag. He knew that establishing the time of death from tissue damage would be virtually impossible, and he'd have to use the contents of her stomach. The reports said that she'd eaten a hotdog at around 8 p.m. Digestion took three to four hours, and so the remnants of her last meal would tell him much about whether her body had fully digested it, and at what stage she'd frozen.

The freeze-thaw cycle wreaked havoc on cells. When the ice crystals formed during the freezing process thawed, they caused cell membranes to rupture, and also created changes in proteins and enzymes, leaving behind organs that didn't look like they would normally. It was a pathologist's nightmare. Ted hoped that the slow defrosting process would have minimised any molecular and DNA damage, but he wouldn't know until he cut her open and examined her internal organs. First, though, he had to conduct his external inquiry.

It was quite clear that the body had not started to decay, and so the girl must have frozen soon after death.

She was known from a phone call to have been alive at 8.47 p.m., and the snow had started to fall around nine o'clock. The beginning of the decomposition process was called the 'fresh' stage; Ted couldn't see any evidence of it, though the more minutes that ticked by, the more the corpse would deteriorate, as the cycle of decomposition after thawing was greatly sped up. Faith's lips were black and her eyes were staring; though they'd collapsed a little, he imagined them full of life. He picked detritus out of her hair with tweezers and searched carefully for foreign bodies. He examined her ears and eyes, and inside her nasal cavity. Then he turned to her mouth. As he opened her jaw and pulled her lips back to peer down her throat, his attention was caught by red marks on her gums. They were accompanied by tiny cuts and abrasions on the inside of her lips. He pulled her top lip back and forth a few times, and nodded his head: it had been forced so power-fully against her teeth that it had broken the skin, and the marks were preserved beautifully; he could even tell which tooth had made them.

He considered the markings and concluded that they were consistent with something being held over the mouth for an extended period of time. But that wasn't all; it was quite clear that something had been shoved into the mouth cavity. The damage to the gums was consistent with violent rubbing, and her maxillary frenum was torn. It reminded Ted of his girls, and how much blood the damn flap of skin joining the top lip to the gum produced when they bashed themselves on a bike handle or a door. He looked closer, and spotted what he thought was residue of frozen spittle, or perhaps congealed powder or food. He scraped a sample off and placed it in a tube.

His assistant photographed the wounds and he moved on to her neck, clavicle and chest, cutting away her upper garments to continue his analysis. There were slight bruises on her chest, indicating again that she'd been held down, and he had them photographed.

Picking up one of her hands, he noticed that the girl had extensive damage to her fingers. Several were broken and bloodied: classic defence wounds. He scraped underneath her nails and gathered a significant amount of matter, including several fibres. He continued downwards and had her trousers cut away, though they were halfway down her legs to begin with. He'd already ordered a rape kit and now set about swabbing her.

The body was turned over and he spent another twenty minutes gathering fibres and residues, as well as photographing her from different angles. It was the girl's last chance to speak, and he desperately wanted to allow her to shout out from the highest rooftops: *This is what happened to me, now you know!*

Finally, it was time to eviscerate her body. He cut from clavicle to belly button and opened the precious cavity designed so astoundingly well to protect her vital organs. He used a striker saw to get through her sternum and set about the task of breaking her ribs. It was gone ten o'clock at night, but he was unconcerned with time. He'd see the whole operation through tonight, no matter how long it took; Kelly would be awake until he finished, he had no doubt about that. He was to call her with any news. Sometimes during an autopsy it became abundantly clear what had caused the demise of a human being, but at other times it was a puzzle that could only be pieced together when all the histology, toxicology and pathology was collected and brought together. He was hoping that this body would yield some answers for him so he could at least give Kelly something to work with.

It was almost midnight when he finished and left his assistant to wash down the slab. Slices of organs had been placed on slides, whole organs had been weighed and photographed, and he'd done about as much as he possibly could. He'd even examined those areas of the body that weren't usually bothered with, such as her spleen and bowel. An investigation of her stomach had revealed it to be full: a soupy mass of pre-digested bread and sausage sat there waiting for her digestive juices and enzymes from her pancreas to attack it in preparation for moving on to the intestine. It meant that she had died sometime between 9 p.m. and midnight.

As for cause of death, it was unclear; they'd have to wait. He called Kelly.

Chapter 60

Kelly couldn't sleep. Too many things whirred around her head. She guessed it to be still night-time but was surprised when she looked at her phone that it was 4.30 in the morning. Her mother always called it the witching hour, when demons and ghouls roamed the world.

She sighed and sat up in bed; there was nothing else for it, she might as well get up. She thought about Luke and Sadie spending the night in the cells, and what they'd done to their friend. Blackman had gone AWOL again, and she had entered his details on the PNC nationwide for immediate arrest with caution.

She went downstairs. There was no one else in the house. Johnny had taken Josie to see a movie and had gone home afterwards, guilty that he wasn't spending enough time with her. Most parents in north Cumbria had suddenly become paranoid about the welfare of their children. Kelly experienced the same acute desire to protect those around her, and it manifested itself in visiting her mother. She'd gone to see her late last night and found her comfortable, but weak, and hooked up to a drip. She was also receiving regular doses of morphine from a syringe driver in her wrist.

She refilled the coffee machine (a Christmas present from Ted) and popped a pod into it. When she switched it on, it made percolating noses reminiscent of a Parisian bakery. Kelly figured that she would've been good at night-shift work, as the small hours seemed to suit her: they were quiet and private, giving her the head space she needed to tackle her job.

Her mind went back to her conversation with Ted. Faith had given up some of her last secrets, and now it was up to Kelly to find out what had happened to her after her so-called friends left her alone in the forest. Her suspects were varied. It could have been Bailey, Luke or Danny Stanton, though she was unclear how he was involved yet; he was awaiting interview in Dover. They already had Bailey's DNA, and she was hoping that some of it had been found on Faith, but with freezing, one could never be sure. She wanted as many answers for the family as possible.

She decided that if she finished her coffee and had a long shower, by the time she'd dressed and stopped off in Penrith for another coffee, it wouldn't be too early to pay a visit to Sadie Rawlinson in her cell. She knew from speaking to social services that teenage mental health was at breaking point, and children with mothers like Belinda Rawlinson, who were whacked on drugs for most of their existence, stood little chance of breaking the chains of learned behaviours. But she refused to dwell on it. Sadie was key. The girl had cracked halfway yesterday and then clammed up in the middle of a full-blown comedown.

When Kelly left the house, the dark sky hadn't yet shown any sign of changing colour, and the street was empty and black. Pooley Bridge was deserted and the road to Penrith the same. The castle shone red in the emerging dawn and she parked behind Eden House. She wondered what sort of a night the kids had had. The cells were quiet, and she went to Sadie's and swung the grate across. The girl sat on the small cot bed, rocking back and forth.

'What do you want?' she asked.

'I want to talk to you, Sadie.'

'Why?'

'Because I don't believe that what happened to your friend doesn't hurt you. You've been pretty much blamed for everything, haven't you? I want to hear your side. If you really want Mr Blackman out of your life, you need to tell me everything you know.'

There was a pause.

'He'll kill me.' It was a whisper. Kelly got the uniform on duty to open the door.

'Not if you tell me what he did. Sadie, listen to me. We can help you get clean, we can keep you away from all of them, but you have to tell me the truth.'

The girl had dark circles under her eyes and her hair was matted and greasy. Getting her clean would be a struggle. They had drug squad briefings every month and the tide was turning in favour of the addict. Money was being poured into detox and recovery, but altruistic as it was, there simply weren't the incentives to keep the sobriety going: relapse ran at eighty-eight per cent. It was endemic.

'Come on, I'll make you a hot drink and get you something to eat.'

Sadie looked up, and Kelly thought she looked ten years older than her true age, and exhausted. She stood up and let the blanket fall away from her. Kelly hadn't noticed how skinny she was. She led her upstairs and got some food from the small kitchen. The interview rooms were warm and there was a sofa for Sadie to curl up on. She visibly relaxed and accepted a hot chocolate as well as a prawn sandwich, which she devoured. The munchies were always strong in the absence of poison. Her hands shook.

'Withdrawal?' Kelly asked. Sadie nodded. 'How much do you do?'

'Enough. Faith could take it or leave it.' The girl's face crumpled and the tears came. Kelly waited.

Once Sadie had calmed a little, and the tears had subsided, Kelly began.

'I'm going to record you, Sadie.'

The girl nodded.

Preliminaries out of the way, Kelly started with the forest.

'You went to Whinlatter for a joyride and a party?'

Sadie nodded again.

'Tell me for the tape; I need you to describe exactly what you remember.'

'I never used to be addicted. He gave me more and more until I was.' Sadie put her head in her hands and Kelly thought she might lose her again. The despair was palpable.

'Who?'

'Mr Blackman.'

'Where? We found nothing in his flat.'

'He was always careful. He has another place too, but I never went.'

'Did Faith cause a problem? Did she threaten to snitch?'

'We used to play this game where we'd take Faith to places and leave her there. We were animals.'

'You regret the way you treated her?'

'Yes! She was so sweet. I was jealous of her.' It was a heartfelt admission, but it didn't take away the fact that Faith's death had indeed been caused by animals, and Kelly held that thought.

'Luke said we should do the same that night. Faith begged us not to. She knew we were in the middle of nowhere. Danny came to do a deal with Luke. Faith had been drinking, but she was saying she wanted to go home and she was crying. I don't think they knew what to do. When she started screaming and trying to leave the car, Luke pushed her out and phoned Bobby. Just to scare her.'

'What about Justin?'

'He's terrified of Luke, he said nothing.'

'And you?'

'I tried to get between them. I tried to get out of the car, but I was so spiced.'

Sadie looked at her fingers and picked the skin around them; they were already red and sore. Then she put her hands to her face and began to sob, rocking back and forth on the sofa. Kelly couldn't decipher her words and tried to be gently persuasive, but she was losing her.

'Did you see Bobby arrive?' The picture unfolding of Faith's last moments was causing Kelly's gut to turn over. She switched off the recording equipment. 'Tell me, Sadie, or I will make sure you never get out of juvenile correction. You think you have it rough now; you haven't lived. And don't even think about whether I have the power to do it or not; believe me, I'll make it my mission.' She switched the equipment back on.

'Bobby was on the phone to Mr Blackman when he arrived. I watched from the car, but then Luke took off and left her.'

'With Bobby?'

Sadie nodded.

'You need to be very careful what you tell me, Sadie, because you've already had one case against Mr Blackman dropped by the CPS. They now think that was a miscarriage of justice, but you're telling me that he's behind all of this? You planted those images, didn't you?'

Sadie nodded.

'You wanted him out of your lives?'

She nodded again.

'What did he do?'

'You won't believe me. No one will. He's so clever and he'll never get caught. No one will ever believe us! Mr Clean, Mr Popular, Mr Friendly. Mr Fucking Devil!' Sadie screamed.

It was the classic mantra of an abused child, and Kelly had heard it a thousand times before. Don't tell: no one will believe your word against mine.

'Tell me from the beginning,' she said. 'I believe you.'

Chapter 61

Kelly secured warrants for both Blackman's flat and Sarah Peaks' cottage. She hated being double-crossed, and she'd been duped, outdone, sewn up, and whatever other phrase her furious brain came up with to spit out the rage that she was trying to divert into the investigation.

It wasn't working.

During the period of his suspension from work, Tony Blackman had spent most of his time at the home of Sarah Peaks, his alleged friend-cum-lover. Kelly arranged for both places to be searched at the same time to avoid either of them getting a heads-up and being able to hide anything. It was still unclear if Sarah was involved; Kelly kept an open mind. Meanwhile, she went back to Luke Miles and delivered the news that Sadie had come clean.

By 8.30, her team was assembled and she briefed them on what had come together overnight. Faced with Sadie's testimony, Luke had changed his statement again. He was informed that due to Mr Blackman's coercion and manipulation, a plea bargain would be accepted in principle by the CPS. It was two weeks before his eighteenth birthday, and he'd be charged as a minor.

Ted called with the toxicology results: Bobby Bailey's DNA matched the DNA from the rape swab.

'The residue inside her gums was ketamine, and the injuries inside her mouth prove that it was rubbed into her skin forcefully enough to cause tearing and trauma. It would have entered her bloodstream very quickly.'

Ketamine was fast becoming known as a date-rape drug. It could be snorted, injected or smoked. It was also marketed to kids as 'Special K' to make it sound cool.

'How long would she have been out of it?' she asked.

'Enough time to be raped. Cause of death was freezing, though. I'm sorry.'

'I need to prove that the drugs were a fundamental part of her death.'

'What difference would that make? Bailey is dead.'

'If the victim of drug misuse is a minor, the dealer can be convicted of murder. I told you before, Ted, I'm nailing these bastards for the deaths of Jenna Fraser and Jake Trent.'

'Faith didn't die of an overdose, though.'

'No, but the drug rendered her unconscious in sub-zero conditions, and she was left for dead.'

'Is that sufficient intent?'

'Yes, because she died as a direct result of being administered that drug.'

'Difficult to prove.'

'If I can prove that the teacher, Tony Blackman, was the kids' main dealer, I could get him for gross negligence manslaughter, because he was in a public position of power, and murder, because Faith was fifteen. There's also oblique intent for indirect murder because her death was as a direct consequence of his actions. If – and that's the kicker – I can get the others to testify.'

'I'm proud of you, Kelly.'

She hung up before either of them said more.

There was still no sign of Mr Blackman as they worked on his culpability and the escalation of his involvement. There had never been any evidence that the suicide of Laura Briggs was connected to Blackman, but Jenna Fraser was another story. Emma had been doing her homework and had traced a web of texts and secret WhatsApps between Jenna and Luke Miles. She'd also found three texts from a number they now knew very well: Tony Blackman's. He'd threatened to tell Jenna's parents of the secret addiction that was destroying her Olympic dream.

–

After twenty-one hours in a cell in Dover, Danny Stanton, accompanied by a legal aid lawyer, admitted that he was a regular conduit between Manchester and Barrow for Tony Blackman. The Revelin Moss car park was a frequent rendezvous point, and the night of Faith's death, he said, he was merely there to drop off a load of drugs to Luke Miles, but that they'd partied and ended up taking a quantity of cocaine. The last thing he'd seen after he'd dropped off the packages and decided to leave his car in the carpark, was Luke and a bunch of kids driving away, and Bobby cornering the girl.

He was asked why he hadn't intervened, given his knowledge of Bobby's character, as well as Faith's vulnerability. His reply was that it was none of his business, and that news broke Kelly's heart. She'd seen enough pictures of Bobby Bailey to know that he'd been physically wasting away. Danny Stanton, on the other hand, was a healthy, strapping young man who could easily have stopped the attack. But as usual in these cases, he was saving his own skin. Still, she knew that Stanton would have a hard time convincing a jury that he'd merely walked away and not participated in the attack. His DNA was taken and sent to the lab.

He was also asked about his contact in Manchester. He was only able to tell them that it was some guy who didn't speak very good English, but he positively ID'd Nedzad Galic. It was enough to go after him, and Kelly informed the Manchester drug squad.

—

The atmosphere at Eden House was tense, and Kelly had to remind herself to be patient. Several moving parts were in action at once, and it felt like they were nearly there. The incident room was hushed, the only noises those of furiously tapping keyboards, ringing phones, and the odd word. Her team wheeled their chairs between desks to swap and compare information. Out on the streets, Blackman was being hunted, the trap was closing around Nedzad, and Bobby Bailey was cremated at public expense because no one claimed his body.

Kelly took a call from the reception desk downstairs and was puzzled by what she heard. She left her seat and jogged into the incident room.

'Kate, come with me. Sarah Peaks has just walked into the station.'

Kate grabbed her phone and radio and they both went to the stairs. It was quicker than waiting for the lift, and their adrenalin was pumping, urging them to move. When they saw Sarah, they both loosely framed a likely picture in their minds of what might have gone on. Sarah held a bundle of tissues to her eye. Her hands were shaking and she was having trouble getting her words to come out correctly. Seeing Kelly only made her worse, and she began babbling. Blackman's name was mentioned, and she kept saying that he'd tried to kill her. Their priority was to calm her down.

'Come on, Sarah, let's go and sit down,' Kelly soothed. She nodded at the officer at the front desk, and they were buzzed through into the corridor where the interview rooms were situated. Sarah was still breathless and desperately scared. As they escorted her, Kelly saw that she was missing two fingernails, her ear was bloody and an angry dark red bruise was swelling around her eye.

They went into the room and Sarah sat down. She appeared to be more composed and took a few deep breaths.

'You're safe now,' Kelly said.

Sarah nodded and accepted water from Kate.

'What happened?' Kelly asked.

Sarah's face crumpled and she held the tissues to her eyes again, wincing as she touched the bruised one.

'I saw him with… a woman. She used to teach at the school. She's called Amanda. I knew they'd had a thing, but he was *with* her.' Sarah peered between Kelly and Kate. 'He was kissing her.'

This event was evidently hugely important and hurtful to Sarah, and Kelly quickly surmised that she and Tony Blackman were more than likely lovers. She glanced at Kate, who opened a pad on the table and began to take notes. Sarah gave them the details of the woman.

'Where did you see them together?'

'I didn't know where he'd gone and I was worried. He'd told me about his other flat, where he went to relax. He kept it quiet because of the trial; it was an old rental property that he bought years ago. I never went there but he told me where it was and I thought I might try it. I thought he might be waiting for me to go there, scared of leaving or something like that.'

'Do you have the address?' Kelly asked.

Sarah nodded and gave it to them.

'Do you think he might still be there?'

'I don't know.'

Kelly spoke into her radio and called for a patrol car to proceed to the address, with caution. Sarah's eyes widened.

'How did you sustain your injuries?' Kelly asked her.

'He was going into the flat with this woman, and I shouted. He looked at me as if...' Her face crumpled again. She had been truly betrayed, and her pain was real. 'As if he hated me.'

'Carry on. Tell us what happened next.'

'I confronted him about his interview with the police – the one where he was cleared of all the charges – and told him that he knew too much about the computer, and that he was mixing his facts up. His face changed then, and I was scared for the first time. He turned away from me and I screamed at him. I wanted to know what he was doing. I...'

She blew her nose and dabbed her eyes again. Kate pushed a box of tissues towards her.

'He unlocked his door to go in and then he just grabbed me. It came from nowhere and my head smashed against the door. The pain was so terrible. I don't know what happened, but I knew that if I didn't get out of there he was going to really hurt me. I kicked him between the legs and he howled. I ran and ran and ran until I didn't even know where I was, but I knew he wasn't behind me.' Her face softened for the first time, unburdened.

'He didn't see that coming, did he?' Kate said. Sarah managed to smile.

'Well done. You did an amazing job. The officer at the front desk has called a medic and they're coming to check you out. Kate and I have to go now, to see if we can find Tony. I'll call someone in to sit with you, and then we'll take you home if you don't need treatment. Those nails look sore.'

Sarah looked down and winced; it was obvious that she hadn't noticed them before. It often happened in cases of abuse and domestic violence, when adrenaline ran so high that the victim had no idea of the extent of their injuries. 'You're safe now,' Kelly told her.

Chapter 62

Nedzad glanced once more around the flat, then picked up his son and locked the door with the other hand. The boy had been spoiled, and was used to some kind of routine whereby he received regular meals and playtime. It was a disgrace; they had made a girl of him. The child sucked his dummy rhythmically and stared at his father with large sad eyes. Nedzad tutted.

He headed for the car across the street, but checked both ways first. A few vehicles dotted the road, and one in particular caught his attention: it had lingered there too often. He hurried to bundle the boy into his child seat, then leapt in and pulled away, checking frantically in the rear-view mirror until he was clear of the junction. He'd become jumpy. His photograph had re-emerged on social media, as it had done two years ago. He had several methods of disguise, but not for the boy. He'd heard on the radio that police in Cumbria were working on the presumed kidnap of a two-year-old, and that he was wanted for questioning in connection with it. It irked him. He thought that two years with no profile had allowed him to morph into somebody different. He quickly realised that they must have other stuff, and this was confirmed when he heard an update on the case of the missing girl.

They'd found her body in the forest and had a couple of kids in custody; meanwhile, they were actively looking for the teacher. It was enough for Nedzad to calculate that he had less than twenty-four hours to leave the country. But first he was meeting Blackman. There was no longer a job offer, or a promise of a better life, and the friendship had ceased to be of value to Nedzad. But there was a huge problem: Tony Blackman owed him money, and a lot of it.

He'd been lenient; he'd spoiled Blackman and he'd turned a blind eye to the girl in the forest, thinking that Bobby's mistake could easily be covered by his timely death. Not so. He'd toyed with going to Scotland, or simply lying low for a while, but now he had his son to think of, and it wouldn't be so easy to stay unrecognised. He decided that his best option was to use a courier who regularly ran gear over to the Isle of Man from Workington Port. It was a much longer journey and he wasn't sure if he could persuade his contact to take him all the way to Ireland: his best, and only, bet at the moment. But with the money Blackman owed him, he might be able to talk him into it.

He noticed that a car had stuck with him all the way to the M6, and his guts began to churn. He headed north and kept checking in his rear-view mirror.

He was heading for the heart of the Lakes. It was a place he'd first come to as a slave, in the back of a lorry, double-crossed and penniless. That had been two years ago, and since then he'd been a busy boy. Guns and knives meant that there were always employment vacancies in the Manchester drug scene. Gone were the days of well-established gangs maintaining top position for decades;

now it was transitory, unpredictable and brutal. Nedzad Galic had walked into a vacancy and turned it into a thriving business. Under the noses of the Manchester squad he'd infiltrated Cumbria, and until now, they hadn't pinned down who he dealt with inside the county. Now, though, that looked to be unravelling. In crime, there was no word of honour when it came to the law. If you were caught, you were alone.

He thought he'd lost the car and smiled to himself. It had probably just been a neighbour heading to the motorway for business, like thousands of others. Nedzad was anonymous, and he'd worked hard to keep it that way. His nerves stilled and he settled into the drive. He was already halfway to the turn-off for the Lakes. His son murmured in the back of the car, waking from his nap. Nedzad had decided to name him Daris, which in Persian meant 'the valuable one'.

The winter sky was clear and blue, and the sun shone into his eyes as he drove. He listened to the radio to quieten the doubts in his head. It had been so much easier on his own; he could disappear and reappear whenever he wanted. This new responsibility was surprisingly hard work, and it meant changing the way he operated. Eventually he'd have to find himself a woman to look after the boy, but right now there was no time for romancing; too much was at stake.

He tried Blackman's numbers again, and one of them worked.

'Where are you?' he barked into the phone.

Blackman told him. 'But not for long. I need to leave.'

'You and me both, brother. I have an idea,' Nedzad lied. 'Wait until I get there. I'm twenty minutes away.'

'I can't hold on longer than that. I'm out of here.'

'Wait a minute, my friend. Where is my money?'

'I have it safely stored. It's not here.'

'We will go together. Wait for me.' He hung up. Daris had begun to sing, and Nedzad smiled warmly at him in the mirror. As he turned off the motorway, his heart raced and he had to concentrate to negotiate the traffic on the outskirts of Penrith before heading to the address Tony had given him, in Keswick.

–

There was no way on earth that Tony Blackman was hanging around for Nedzad Galic. The guy was a liability, and besides, he needed the cash. He had to admit that technically it belonged to Nedzad, but in this game, accounts weren't kept. There had once been genuine trust between the two of them, but in a world of risk, trust was an ephemeral thing. It was a commodity, like everything else, only binding if it brought value, and it had ceased to do that. The ties had to be cut. There was no other path. He had twenty minutes.

He'd got rid of Amanda by sending her home to pack, believing they were eloping together. Now he had to make sure that there was no clue in the flat to where he might be going. He rushed to fill a holdall and selected clothes that made him look casual and ordinary. He shoved toiletries in there and kept listening out for signs of sirens.

He had no doubt that Sarah would go to the police, and he kicked himself again for his stupid mistake. The incident had made up his mind. If only he'd been able to get her in the flat, he'd have been able to shut her up. He hadn't seen the kick coming; he'd thought her meek and mild, which was why she'd been the perfect companion. He couldn't believe his stupidity at letting her go.

He had to keep a cool head and think. His picture had been released to the press, and he was already a pariah in the area because of Sadie Rawlinson's accusations. That little bitch: maybe he should pay her a visit and finish her off. Or he could try and maintain self-control and focus on what was important: his own safety. Sadie would die from an overdose sometime soon anyway. But the need to hurt someone overwhelmed him, and he couldn't help himself.

He checked outside again. Perhaps Sarah hadn't gone to the police after all; perhaps she was too scared. It was a possibility, otherwise surely they'd have been here by now. He looked at his watch. Sadie Rawlinson's flat was only two streets away, and he smiled at the serendipity.

He pulled on a hoody and a woolly hat, and wrapped a huge knitted scarf around his face. Then he threw the bag over his shoulder and left the flat. In the distance, carried on the wind, he heard sirens; he thrust his head down, and began to jog, making his way through the rabbit warren of streets.

He'd supplied Belinda Rawlinson for years. When he reached her flat, he banged on the door and was welcomed like an old friend. She told him that a message had been left on her phone about Sadie being held in custody, but she'd forgotten to check on her. Tony looked at her with disgust: she was all skin and bone, sunken eyes and flaky skin. Her nose was bulbous and red and her teeth were rotten. Anger welled up inside him and he felt an overwhelming sense of self-pity and frustration. He couldn't understand how it had all unravelled.

The rage built. His heart rate elevated and blood rushed to his cheeks. The woman in front of him swayed slightly from side to side, and he was filled with the red-hot desire to make somebody pay for fucking everything up. He heard her voice asking him if he had any gear. He looked at her and noticed that her face was changing, as if in slow motion. She looked scared.

Then he was chasing her, and in no time at all, he was on her. All he could see was Sadie Rawlinson, the bitch who had started every ball rolling against him until he had nothing left. He knocked her over and pinned her down, straddling her like a beast. His hands tightened round her throat and her eyes bulged in terror. He pinned her struggling legs with his knees. She clawed at his hands, but she was turning purple and he heard, and felt, something snap in her neck.

It was a few minutes before he realised that his rage was subsiding and she'd stopped moving. He looked down at her and began to shake. He refused to believe what he'd just done. He released his grip around her neck and stared at the scratches covering his hands. He couldn't bear to look at her face, and he got up to fetch something to cover it with. He threw a tea towel over her head and stood back.

Holy shit. Adrenalin hit his gut and he rushed to the sink in the kitchen and threw up. Then he grabbed his bag and left, pulling the door tightly shut behind him.

Chapter 63

Radio contact with Eden House was constant. The operation was overseen by the strike force chief from the Manchester drugs squad, who had been looking for a way to get to Galic for eight months. He spoke to DCI Porter every half-hour. She sat in the incident room and bit the skin around her nails. She looked at her watch and wondered why it was taking so long to arrest Tony Blackman. With Stanton in custody and Bobby dead, Galic was the final missing link. But they couldn't risk any harm coming to the boy, so they had to be patient.

The strike force chief had called in that they'd located Galic and had him under active surveillance. They'd also confirmed the presence of a small boy in his care. He was heading to Cumbria, but they couldn't decide how to proceed: the strike chief had his remit and so did Kelly. They finally agreed to tail him into the county and have several vehicles on standby.

It didn't take long to work out that Galic's vehicle was heading in the direction of Tony Blackman's second flat. Which was empty. Kelly had arranged for a thorough search of the property; meanwhile, their absolute priority was apprehending the man himself. The charges against him were stacking up, and she prayed that he hurt no one else. When suspects fled, it meant they'd reached a stage of fear and desperation so intense it made them incredibly volatile, and no one really knew what Tony Blackman was capable of.

Kelly beckoned Rob. 'Come on. I want to be on the scene for this one,' she said.

Rob was only too willing to accompany her. They'd have to hang back, behind the patrol cars already heading to the address. The man had been wanted for two years over an area comprising four jurisdictions; and internationally, much longer than that.

Once in the car, they used a police light and fired up the sirens. Even with the warnings, the general public was lethargic as always and parted for them only stubbornly. Regardless of this, the anticipation was raw and they felt the familiar satisfying joy of an impending arrest.

Nothing had prepared them for what they found when they arrived.

The address was surrounded by patrol vehicles, and a number of uniforms were standing underneath a fourth-floor walkway, trying to negotiate with a man. Hanging by his hands over the edge, kicking and screaming in fear, was a male toddler. Kelly instantly knew that it was Dale.

She and Rob made their way to a group of officers who were frantically trying to cobble together stuff from their cars to make a landing for the boy, should he fall or be dropped. From that height, it was unlikely that he'd survive. Kelly spoke to a uniform, who confirmed that a female negotiator was on her way.

'Not a woman!' she exclaimed. 'Nedzad won't listen to a woman. His culture is masculine; women are supposed to be mothers and wives, not police negotiators.'

It was a blunder, and she radioed Eden House to see if they could get a man. Meanwhile, they'd have to do the best they could.

'You!'

Kelly looked up to the walkway. Nedzad was staring at her, his face a picture of rage and hatred.

'Yes it's me, Nedzad,' was all she said. She stepped forward.

'You took my baby!' he shouted, and the child wailed.

Kelly looked at the little boy's face. It was a moment that made her heart fly into her mouth. From her position four floors below, she could just make out the terror etched into his little face. He'd gone quiet again, as if resigned to his fate, but the pain carved into his expression told of the horror of being exposed to such danger. She raised her hand, as if to try to reach him.

'Dale,' she said. The boy's eyes opened and flickered towards her. She smiled, and his mouth closed. His gaze held hers, but then Nedzad started to shake him.

'He's called Daris!' he roared. The toddler began to scream again.

The situation was rapidly getting out of control. And they still didn't know where Blackman was. Their efforts were completely concentrated on saving this little boy.

'Nedzad, what do you want?'

'I only wanted my son.' His voice had lowered and Kelly noted the use of the past tense. It was a worrying development.

She saw spittle spray from Nedzad's mouth. It fell like a mist. It was clear to all of the officers present that the man was desperate and inches away from doing something stupid.

She'd never seen Nedzad Galic up close, but she realised now what he was capable of. She swallowed and looked up again. Out of the corner of her eye, she could see that six or seven uniforms had joined together several high-vis police jackets and moved into position under the walkway.

'My boy!' Galic wailed. It was a guttural, primeval noise, and Kelly knew that he was preparing to throw his boy away; figuratively as well as literally.

She took to the stairs and sprinted up them. Two officers followed. They had to get to the man. His cry had been one of resignation as well as hatred and pain: if he jumped with his son, it was doubtful that they'd be able to catch either of them. Her lungs screamed, but she managed to sprint up the final set of stairs and emerge onto the walkway, panting.

'Don't!' she screamed, running full pelt towards him. He didn't expect her, and tucked the toddler under his arm and tried clumsily to climb up onto the wall. Kelly reached him and grabbed on to the boy with every ounce of strength she had. It unbalanced Nedzad, and he let go of his son as he tried to steady himself. He looked at Kelly as he began to fall backwards. She heard shouts from the ground below, and then the sickening thud of flesh and bone hitting concrete.

In the silence that followed, she looked down at the child in her arms. Dale was staring at her. He blinked, and Kelly smiled at him. She hoped with all her heart that he was young enough to forget this trauma. Holding him tightly, she walked towards the stairs. Nedzad Galic had ended up like one of his victims, twisted and broken like Jenna Fraser, in a pile of torn organs and cracked bones. Her radio crackled: the fall had been fatal. Nedzad hadn't killed his victims with his bare hands; he'd done it with his poison. But Kelly still wanted a conviction. Galic was dead. Bobby was dead. She knew too that there were always new thugs waiting to step into vacuums left by the law, but this was one that she would pursue.

She listened to her radio as she walked slowly down the steps. She heard that Tony Blackman had been apprehended and arrested not far from where they were now.

She closed her eyes. If she wasn't holding the child, she'd have fist-pumped the air. They had an adult to hold accountable, and the beginnings of a case for justice for the kids who, one way or another, had perished at his behest.

Chapter 64

'You look tired,' Johnny said to her. She knew that he spoke from the heart, and it was an expression of concern.

The investigation into Faith Shaw's death had drawn to a close and left the team at Eden House with a sense of weird, unfulfilled cynicism. It wasn't healthy. Kelly had tried to spin a sugar coating by emphasising the fact that they'd exposed the largest drugs gang in the north-west for many years, an achievement that was hailed by the drugs squad as damn fine police work. Her officers had provided the final pieces of the puzzle that the Manchester teams had so painstakingly pieced together. But that paled into insignificance every time Kelly thought about Faith's brother Michael, or Jake Trent's best friend, or Jenna Fraser's mother. It was like one huge, deflating let-down. An anticlimax like no other.

The snow had returned and coated the Lake District with a blanket of secrecy, hiding events that you might not believe possible should you peruse the scene from the top of a mountain. The main roads were clogged for hours every day as the gritters tried to clear routes across the National Park.

The hospital was warm at least.

Kelly held her mother's hand. She knew what was coming because the ward sister had suggested another pot of tea, and brought biscuits into the room. They only did that when they were about to lose one of their patients. Nikki and Matt were there with their three children, as well as Johnny and Josie. And Ted. The little room was cramped and stifling, even though the temperature outside was minus seven. The hospital heating banged out waves of arid, lifeless air that suffocated them and made them regret each item of clothing they wore; whether it be a T-shirt or a jumper, nothing was right. Nothing would be right for a long time.

Nikki sniffled. Matt fidgeted. Josie held onto her dad. Kelly was touched that the teenager wanted to be here. Josie reminded her a lot of Faith. Both girls were independent and fearless. And she had genuine affection for Wendy. Kelly imagined Faith fighting for her life, and hoped Josie never had to.

Kelly avoided her sister's gaze and leant against Ted. Nikki had stared at first, but even she didn't have the audacity to start an argument now. Wendy's chest moved slowly up and down; occasionally she'd mutter incomprehensibly and look unsettled and agitated. She wasn't to be resuscitated; when the moment came, she'd be allowed to slip away.

Beside her, Kelly felt Ted catch his breath. He pulled away and held her hands, nodding towards the bed. He was the only person in the room who knew death intimately; he knew exactly how long it took, and what was happening to Wendy's insides as she held on to the last breath.

'It's time,' he whispered in Kelly's ear.

He went to Wendy's syringe driver and checked the level. Then he checked her cannula, calling for the nurse to come into the room. He mentioned Haloperidol. The drug was administered to terminal patients at the very end of their palliative care plan, when they grew anxious and distressed. No one really understood why this happened, not even the top neurologists. It was thought that as the body prepared to shut down, the brain displayed last-minute signs of fretting.

The nurse smiled sympathetically at the gathered loved ones. Kelly watched as she checked Wendy's pupils. She knew that they dilated in the moment before death. This would be the second time she had seen a parent expire agonisingly in the face of the disease that slowly strangulated its human host. She glanced at Ted, who watched as the nurse carefully drew up the drug and squeezed it into the cannula. Then he turned to Kelly and nodded. Johnny knew what it meant, and reached out to her, placing his hand on her arm. She touched it, her ring catching a shaft of light from the window and sparkling.

The nurse left, and the only movement in the tiny room was the slow heaving of Wendy's chest and the sniffles of her family. Nikki watched Kelly and followed her lead by approaching the bed. They each took one of Wendy's hands.

Momentarily, Kelly thought she saw her mother open her eyes and look at her. She bent and whispered into her ear, saying her final goodbyes. Ted stood behind her and covered his mouth. Kelly turned and allowed him to squeeze in next to her. She took his hand and placed it on her mother's chest.

'Goodbye, Wendy,' he said.

Kelly closed her eyes and felt for Johnny's hand.

Another coughing fit took hold of Wendy and everybody froze, apart from Ted, who held her torso gently so as to soften the impact of the violent coughs. It was the kindest thing Kelly had ever seen. When he finally let her go, Wendy took a large intake of breath... and then nothing.

They waited. They watched.

Ted bent his head.

Kelly took her mother's hand, but it was limp.

Nikki sat on the edge of the bed, her sobs coming in shaking waves. Kelly turned away and sank into Johnny's arms, where she held onto Josie as well.

It was the thirteenth of January.

Chapter 65

Johnny bought a pre-owned thirty-four-foot 2004 Sealine S34 from a dealer in Windermere, and she was a beauty. He'd chosen luxury and performance and Kelly had been surprised that he'd gone for something so glamorous. She was thankful for the interior, which consisted of wooden decking and full wraparound covers. It had a tiny kitchen, shower and toilet, and bed. They'd been aboard for a week.

They stopped when they needed food or a restaurant meal, but the only other reason to shore up was for a swim. Otherwise, they powered gently up and down the lake at ten knots, which was the limit on Ullswater. They saw few vessels, and when they did, the captains were usually known personally to either Johnny or Kelly, and they waved and shouted greetings. Occasionally they'd go ashore for a pint, but more often, they'd stock up on wine for the boat. They were barely eight miles from their houses, but it didn't matter; they could have been in Alaska and it wouldn't have made a difference.

It was a peace they hadn't known for months, not since a weekend away in a hotel in Windermere. Josie had finally relented and gone to see her mother.

'How you doing?' Johnny asked Kelly regularly. It was a question without answer and he knew it, but it was his way of checking in and telling her that he cared.

Every day was different. Sometimes she remembered all the positive and joyful things about her mother, and she'd smile to herself, recalling a joke they'd shared or something they'd agreed on. Other days were hell, and she was consumed with regret and grief. Johnny counselled her on the process of mourning; it was, he told her, a journey.

'No it's not, it's a fucking cliché,' Kelly raged and Johnny let her. Anger was all part of the journey.

Occasionally, Kelly behaved like a child and used her fingers to denote speech marks as she analysed herself and regurgitated long words used by shrinks who dealt with loss. She'd learned to throw them out in answer to probing questions from concerned friends and relatives. 'Self-preservative numbness' was one of her favourites, and she laboured over the words with exaggeration if she was feeling particularly frustrated: a signal to Johnny that something intense was on its way. Usually an outburst – a kick, a slammed door or an expletive in response to a well-meaning question – was all that was needed to move on, but now and again Kelly went quiet, and Johnny knew that was a bad sign. It was easier when she shouted or told him to go fuck himself. He could argue, challenge her, refuse to leave, and all the other things you did for the person you loved. It drove Kelly nuts, but he persevered.

It was worth it.

Her moods wouldn't level out for perhaps a year, possibly two; that was what all the experts said. Kelly said she didn't give a flying fuck what the experts said, and Johnny said he knew she didn't.

A few psychos whom Kelly had put away over the years wrote sympathy cards, and it caused her to fly into thunderous strops. Johnny encouraged it. He gave her stuff to punch, he let her push him overboard, and he even wrestled her. Most of the time, it ended in laughter or tears, and that was the whole point.

'How the hell do they get my address?' she screamed at him.

'It's not difficult if you want it badly enough. People leave digital footprints everywhere.'

She hoped that she never heard from Tony Blackman. No one had ever prosecuted a single individual for the drug-related indirect murder of three separate minors, and it had been tried at the Old Bailey as a ground-breaking case. Every day of the seven-week trial, the courtroom and public gallery were full to bursting as lawyers, barristers and QCs alike listened to how the case was tried. Kelly knew they had him on gross negligence manslaughter if it fell through, but she needn't have worried.

They won. He got life, with a minimum of thirty-three years, for causing the deaths of Jenna Fraser, Jake Trent and Faith Shaw. Kelly had given evidence and she was the only witness Blackman had looked at. On the drugs charges, he'd received four sentences totalling seventy-three years. On top of his stretch for the murder of Belinda Rawlinson, he'd never see freedom again. Sadie and Luke both got suspended sentences, but their nightmares would be punishment enough. The screams of a terrified girl alone in the forest, knowing that her friends had left her there at the mercy of her attacker, would haunt them for the rest of their lives.

Kelly sat on the bow of the yacht. The lake was utterly calm and disarming. She peered into the depths below. As far as she could see, it could have gone down for thousands of metres, hiding secrets no one would ever find. It mesmerised her. Johnny handled the controls and watched her. The early spring sun caught the fire in her hair and it shone orange and red, reflecting her fire. They were sailing to the Peak's Bay Hotel to meet Ted. Kelly had taken her mother there for dinner on the night that she first suspected her parentage. It was almost a year ago now.

The plan had been to scatter Mum's ashes near Dad's in the hotel garden, under a rhododendron bush. But Kelly couldn't bring herself to do it. She also couldn't face telling Nikki why. The urn sat in a case in her bedroom, and she'd avoided Nikki's questions and demands to hold a ceremony and choose a resting place.

They approached the wooden jetty that led to the prestigious hotel and spotted Ted waiting for them on the shoreline with a member of staff. He smiled. Kelly waved, and Johnny manoeuvred the boat expertly towards the landing. He switched off the engine and tethered his new pride and joy, and they both jumped off. Ted approached and embraced his daughter, then shook hands with Johnny.

'I like the name,' he said.

They all looked towards the boat and admired the newly sprayed title, in blue, on the stern.

Wendy, it read.

Acknowledgements

I would firstly like to thank my agent, Peter Buckman, for his neverending encouragement and faith; also Laura McCallen and the team at Canelo for their passion and Jane Selley for her meticulous attention to detail. For their fascinating insight, Harry Chapfield, Cumbria Constabulary (ret'd), Inspector Paul Redfearn, London Met Police, and DI Rob Burns, Beds Police. I want to thank the Lemons: you know who you are, I love you.

And finally, Mike, Tilly and Freddie for being neglected at odd times of the day; I couldn't have done this without you.

About the Author

Rachel Lynch grew up in Cumbria and the lakes and fells are never far away from her. London pulled her away to teach History and marry an Army Officer, whom she followed around the globe for thirteen years. A change of career after children led to personal training and sports therapy, but writing was always the overwhelming force driving the future. The human capacity for compassion as well as its descent into the brutal and murky world of crime are fundamental to her work.

DI Kelly Porter